A Secret Rose

Kirsty Ferry

Where heroes are like chocolate – irresistible!

Published 2020 by Choc Lit Limited
Penrose House, Crawley Drive, Camberley, Surrey GU15 2AB, UK
www.choc-lit.com

A CIP catalogue record for this book is available
from the British Library

ISBN 978-1-78189-390-6

Printed and bound in Great Britain by Clays Ltd, Elcograf S.p.A.

A Secret Rose

*For my Grandma and Grandad Simpson, Fred and Maisie
– or, to give my grandma her full name, May Blanche;
fondly known within the family as 'The Duchess'.*

Acknowledgements

I started writing this book – or a version of it, at
least – in 1997. At the time, I was (and still am) a
huge fan of Victoria Holt and her Gothic romances
and thought I could write like her. I couldn't. Which
is why I printed the story up, stapled it together,
made a pretend book out of it with a graphic of a girl
leaning out of a window entitled *The Dreamer*, and
then let it linger for several years in a plastic pouch
in a ringbinder. Last year, after many failed attempts
to resurrect the book, I finally started to rewrite it
properly. As you can imagine, it doesn't really reflect
much of what was in the original manuscript, especially
considering the original one was set in Scotland, but
I'm happy I've made it readable – and into a 'proper'
book at last! The original story was very short, and
simply a version of the historical thread in this one;
then I discovered the poem 'My Last Duchess' by
Robert Browning and suddenly had a way to frame
the entire story. And it 'grewed and grewed', as they
say. I hope you enjoy reading this revamped version,
and that it was worth the decades-long wait!

Thanks must go to, of course, my lovely publishers
Choc Lit, who encouraged me to continue with *A
Secret Rose* and helped me unravel it, swooping in
like guardian angels at a point when I was totally
stuck with the idea and wanted to bin the lot. It's
just so good to be able to say I've finished another
full-length novel. Also, huge thanks must go to the

Panel who turned this one around in super-quick time with a resounding 'yes': Elena B, Dimi E, Donna M, Jenny M, Karen M, Wendy S, Jo O, Gill L, Carol F, Joy S, Sharon W, Vanessa W, Sharon D and Lucie W. And of course equally huge thanks to my wonderful editor and fabulous cover designer, without whom this would still be printed out and stapled together, with a random graphic on the front.

Finally, as always, thank you to my family who let me get cracking with it once the idea went 'click' and fed me chocolate, wine and coffee in various quantities as and when the occasion demanded it! Thank you xxx

... She had
A heart – how shall I say? – too soon made glad,
Too easily impressed; she liked whate'er
She looked on, and her looks went everywhere...
...Oh, sir, she smiled, no doubt,
Whene'er I passed her; but who passed without
Much the same smile? This grew; I gave commands;
Then all smiles stopped together. There she stands
As if alive.

Extract from 'My Last Duchess'
by Robert Browning

Chapter One

As soon as Merryn Burton pulled up to the gatehouse of Pencradoc and looked through the rain-spattered window at the driveway leading up towards the grey stone mansion, she wondered if she'd done the right thing.

It wasn't because the building was all creepy and Gothic looking (which it was). It was more because the idea of the project she was involved in was suddenly quite terrifying, and definitely the biggest thing she'd ever done in her career so far.

The logical part of her said there was no reason to panic – and the art dealers she worked for wouldn't be too enamoured if she turned around and drove the four and a half hours back to London; she'd left home at 6 a.m. as it was, and she knew that her friend Cordelia who was flat-sitting her little one-bedroom place in Kentish Town would be well-ensconced by now, despite the fact it was only mid-morning.

It was as she was sitting there, talking some sense into herself yet seemingly unable to make herself drive forwards, that she saw a dark figure appear at the doorway of the gatehouse and stare at her with a little frown on his face. It was, she saw, a tall, slightly untidy, yet very good-looking, dark-haired man.

She caught his eye and, her trepidation momentarily forgotten, stared back at him. The frown was, quite possibly, she considered, reflected in her expression. She knew him – she was almost certain. And he seemingly knew her. But for the life of her she couldn't remember how or where she knew him from. Perhaps he was part of the art world, which was a distinct possibility considering they were both here at Pencradoc today. That circle was fairly small in some ways, she thought, and it was quite possible they'd bumped into each other before.

She stared at him a moment longer, watching his face crease, watching him take one or two steps towards her.

Slowly, she wound the window down. 'Hello.' She was surprised how upbeat and cheerful her voice sounded – privately, she congratulated herself on that one. 'Am I at the right place? Pencradoc? For the exhibition. I'm here to catalogue the work. From Heptinstall Studios. In London.' She stopped before she lost the upbeat-ness and cheerfulness and descended into burbling.

The man nodded. 'Yes. That's right. You probably need to be speaking to Coren. He's up at the house and he's kind of put himself in charge. Just follow the driveway. Sorry—' He frowned, then grinned, then laughed, shaking his head. He looked even more divine than he had at first glance. 'I thought I knew you for a minute. If we *have* met, you'll be massively insulted that I can't remember when, so perhaps we'd best forget I sort of mentioned that.' Despite the strangely irrelevant conversation, Merryn found herself relaxing and grinning back at him. 'Anyway. I'm Kit Penhaligon,' he continued. 'I'm here to sort of stalk Ruan Teague. He was a famous artist and I'm more than a little interested in his work and the connection he has to this place. You'll more than likely have heard of him?'

'Ruan Teague? Of *course* I know him! Well – I'm familiar with his work. I don't know much about him as a person. He's the one I've come to discover. Okay – not him, exactly, but his paintings.'

'You'll possibly know then that there's only the one Teague painting we recognise in there, but you might be lucky and discover some more for us.' The man, Kit, glanced over at the house at the end of the driveway. 'Anyway. I'll not keep you any longer. I'll maybe see you later?' It was a rhetorical question, and Merryn simply nodded.

'Thanks. Maybe.'

She put the car into gear and drove off, towards Pencradoc. She could *do* this, she really could. And Coren Penhaligon was, she remembered now, the man she had been told to look out for. He'd apparently inherited the place with his brother; but Coren's name had floated out of her head as soon as she had seen Kit standing there. Kit Penhaligon was, most probably, the brother. It would be interesting to find out if she was right.

Kit watched the car move away and studied the woman in the driving seat as she grew smaller along the distance of the wide, grey drive. Her long, fair hair was unruly, falling in waves halfway down her back; her eyes had been dark green and curious. And extraordinarily familiar. He frowned, and wondered afresh where he had encountered her before.

Heptinstall Studios, she had said. Maybe that was it – perhaps he'd seen her at an auction or a sale, or some sort of event. Maybe a gallery opening. It wasn't unknown for him to travel to London and haunt these places – usually in the hope of a previously unknown

Teague appearing – so that could have been where he had met her before.

A little shiver crept down his spine. In the depths of his heart, he knew he hadn't met her in London. He had met her here. In Cornwall. Once upon a time.

Bodmin Moor, 1886

'It's haunted, you know.' Alys Trelawney turned, startled, as she heard the man's voice. He sounded amused, and towered above her, silhouetted on a chestnut-brown horse. Her own little white mare, Meg, grazed peacefully at the shore of the lake and barely twitched her ear as Alys got hurriedly to her feet, dusting her skirts down and trying to kick her notebook and pencil out of sight. She had been gazing at Dozmary Pool and dreaming about King Arthur, scribbling a story down in her notebook as the words came to her in the sunshine.

'I'm not sure I believe in ghosts.' She smiled at the man and he laughed. Dismounting, he patted the horse and it wandered off to graze beside Meg.

'Don't let Jan Tregeagle hear you say that. He howls and wails around these parts like there's no tomorrow.'

'Some may say it's simply the wind. And not a man who sold his soul to the devil.'

'Then *some* people have no soul.' The man bowed. 'I'm terribly sorry. My name is Jago Pencradoc.'

Alys bobbed a small curtsey. 'It's very good to meet you. I'm Alys Trelawney. *Miss* Alys Trelawney.'

'Ah. A gentle reminder that you perhaps should not be consorting with a man you just met on the moor. Terribly improper.'

'They say that, but—' she shrugged her shoulders. 'It may be more improper for me to ask whether you are simply Mr Jago Pencradoc ... or you perhaps hold another title?' Her heart started pounding – she half-knew what the answer would be.

The man scowled. 'Improper? I'm sure I couldn't say either way, but I suppose if I was to use my *correct* title, I'd have to say I was the Earl of Pencradoc.' His scowl darkened. 'But it's usually a name I keep in reserve. I tend not to use it very much.'

Alys' heart somersaulted. She was right. 'I don't know how improper it can be to pass the time of day with a kind of relative.' She suddenly laughed, enjoying the look of surprise that passed across his face.

'Relative? But I would have thought I would have known if I was related to you, Miss Trelawney.'

'You would have done, had I shared a surname with my cousin Zennor. Now surely you know her?'

'Zennor!' He laughed. 'My brother's wife. Well now. I *have* been away too long.' He bowed, a low, sweeping bow. 'Then you will know, from my brother Ellory perhaps, that I have been in India for quite some time. I'm afraid I even missed the wedding.' He frowned. 'Which means, of course, that I missed seeing you.'

'And I missed seeing you. I had heard all about you and was a little disappointed that this legendary gentleman was missing.'

'Legendary?' He smiled and Alys couldn't look away from his sun-tanned face and the dimple in his left cheek. He rode without a hat, and his dark hair was blown awry by the Bodmin winds, the very winds that Jan Tregeagle's demon soul lived on in. 'I don't know if I'm very legendary.'

'To the rest of the family you seem to be.' She

leaned down and picked up her notebook and pencil. Knowing who this was, there was no point in hiding her amusements. If they were to be under the same roof for a while, then he would find out soon enough. 'Zennor said she was quite jealous of the fact that you had managed to go off and do something so exciting.'

'A privilege afforded to me and not her husband – unfortunately for him. Or perhaps fortunately. I am quite confident, however, that Ellory would prefer to look after the estate. Yet I, on the other hand, managed to escape, and was happy to do so.'

'But why would you want to escape from Pencradoc?' Alys was genuinely surprised. There was nothing she didn't love about the mansion, which had been, so she had been informed, rebuilt on the site of the old Manor House around the year 1700, the best part of two hundred years ago.

Pencradoc was all grey stone and glass windows and turrets, set on an estate which bordered the hauntingly beautiful Bodmin Moor. Ellory was the Duke of Trecarrow, and Zennor had married into the family six months ago, not long after the death of Ellory's first wife. Alys, alone and without the commitments of close family, yet happy with her own company in Berkshire, had been invited to stay with Zennor for a little while.

'I wanted to see the world. Make an independent income.' Jago smiled. 'And it is, quite frankly, my first day back. I know I should have headed straight there, but I wanted to ride on the moors and enjoy my freedom while I still had it.' He nodded to the horse. 'I bought him in Launceston and sent my luggage ahead on the coach. I have taken the liberty of including a note for my brother with a raft of excuses on it.'

Alys laughed. 'Then I would not like to be in your shoes when you return late. He has been, as Zennor says, prowling. Certain you're due home, but unsure when, and becoming quite cross about it.'

Jago shook his head. 'Ellory was always a fretful child. He and I were never close. He favoured the Duke, I favoured our mother. I always wanted to be out in the estate riding or climbing trees, and he preferred to stay indoors. But that is not your concern and I probably should not even be telling you that. Instead, how about you tell me what I've been missing?'

'That's rather difficult as I can't comment on how things were when you left. But I can say that Zennor is happy to welcome me into her home and I am very happy to be there.' Alys really wanted to tell Jago Pencradoc that Zennor was not settling particularly well into the confines of married life. She mourned her freedom and had discovered that being the chatelaine of Pencradoc was not all pretty dresses and hosting balls. In fact, they'd never even hosted a ball, which was a great pity to Zennor; but her greatest horror at the minute was the fact that she felt obliged to produce a son and heir, and as she had told Alys on more than one occasion, she found the actual act of lovemaking dull and boring with her milk-and-water husband.

'He has no *life* about him,' she had complained once, as the girls walked arm in arm to the rose garden along the banks of the stream that flowed through Pencradoc's grounds. 'I had supposed he would have more of a *spark*.'

'But surely you knew his character when you married him?' Alys was curious. To be fair the mysteries of lovemaking were so far from her experience that she couldn't understand Zennor's disgust at sharing the marital bed.

'I did, but I thought he may have had hidden depths. I fear he is as shallow as this little brook. Some men *do* have hidden depths, you see.' Zennor had stopped and faced Alys. 'When one reads romantic novels, one grasps the fact that some men understand what they need to do to pleasure a woman. Ellory just ... doesn't.'

'Zennor!' Alys felt her cheeks flush. 'You shouldn't say that!'

'Why not?' Zennor bent down and picked up a stone. She tossed it into the stream and watched as it sank into the crystal waters. 'It's true. God, I don't know if I can tolerate it much longer.' Her eyes took on a faraway look. 'I always hoped that it would be magical. That the first time wouldn't be so awful and so quick.'

Alys felt deeply uncomfortable. 'I don't know if you should be talking like this with me.' She looked around, worried in case somebody might be listening.

Zennor saw her nervous little glances and laughed. 'Ignore me. I'm just disillusioned. And bored. That, my darling, is why I asked you to come and keep me company.' She flushed. 'I told Ellory that if I was to have a child, I'd need you by my side to help me through the experience.'

'Are you ...?' Alys hardly dared breathe. A baby at last! How wonderful.

'Good God, no.' Zennor glared at Alys. 'And not likely to be if he continues the way he's going. I hardly know how he managed the deed with the Sainted Rose.' She referred to Ellory's first wife, who had tragically died from complications in early pregnancy. Nobody was ever allowed to speak of Rose and the woman had taken on, it seemed, a kind of mystical quality that placed her somewhere between the Virgin Mary and a tragic romantic heroine, beloved in the books which Zennor seemed to devour. 'But the truth of the matter is,' Zennor continued, 'that I *do* want you here because I absolutely hate it on my own and I think I may be starting to hate Ellory.' Then she clamped her lips together and had refused to say another word.

As Alys looked at Ellory's brother, she thought that he was the very opposite of milk and water, and that the first time, second time and any subsequent time with him would be as exciting as the romance in any novel.

Hoping that he couldn't read that in her eyes, she looked down at her book and cleared her throat. 'I suppose I should be heading back. Ride with me, Mr Pencradoc?' She felt the heat surge into her cheeks again. She desperately hoped he would agree.

Jago couldn't believe it. He had, as he had told Alys, bought a horse with the sole intention of riding across Bodmin Moor and seeing all his old, familiar haunts before eventually returning to Pencradoc; and to ride out his temper, he admitted to himself, as he could already feel it rising with the thought of reacquainting himself with his brother.

He hadn't expected to see a girl by Dozmary Pool – or, more to the point, a beautiful girl silhouetted against the blue expanse of water, the hazy shapes of the hills behind the mythical pool framing her like a portrait.

Now, as her fair hair lifted in the wind and the ribbons on her hat fluttered, he smiled, despite the thoughts of the past that haunted his every moment. Perhaps returning to Pencradoc wouldn't be as bad as he had anticipated if Miss Alys Trelawney was there as well. Perhaps she might help erase some of the horror. He could hope for that, at least. So long as they were out here, on the moor, far away from that place and the memories it held for him, he could certainly hope for it.

It hadn't been a lie when he said he and Ellory didn't get on. He tolerated his elder brother because he had to, but he would find it impossible to say he loved him.

'I hope your visit to Pencradoc is an extended one, Miss Trelawney,' he said now, smiling down at the girl. 'I shall certainly ride with you. But in a few moments. I wish to linger here just a little longer and enjoy the view. I haven't seen anything quite so beautiful in very many a year.' He found he was still smiling, which was something in itself. In a strange sort of way he felt as if he knew her already – had already learned all there was to know about her. He felt more drawn to her, in fact, than he did to Ellory and Pencradoc.

Wherever you go, I will follow.

The thought took him by surprise.

'I shall stay as long as Zennor wants me to.' She raised her eyes to his, locking onto them. Those eyes were a curious shade of moss-green, a startling contrast to her corn-coloured hair.

'That's excellent news. You're very kind to agree that.'

'I don't really have a reason *not* to be here. I have no ties, no other commitments.' Alys shrugged. 'I can't think of anywhere better for me at this moment. And here! Here on the moor—' She looked around, her green eyes suddenly sparkling. 'It's so full of inspiration and it makes me so happy.'

'Inspiration?' Jago nodded to the book and pencil. 'Is that what you're scribbling down? Putting your inspiration into words?'

'Something like that.' She smiled. 'But this is my own little world and I have been told before now that it's a strange place to inhabit.' She glanced at her book. 'But it still doesn't put me off writing my stories.'

'So you have a vivid imagination?'

'As an author, one *must* have a vivid imagination. Although Mr Tregeagle and his ghostly howling is even one step beyond for me.'

Jago was entranced. 'I'm so pleased you're going to be at Pencradoc for a little while. But I think you're right. We need to head back now. I owe it to my sister-in-law at least.' He did not say that he owed it to his brother.

'Yes. Ellory is quite insistent that we are all on time for afternoon tea.'

'He hasn't changed then.' Jago's voice was wry, slightly bitter even. Ellory had always been precise and thought it a poor show if one deviated from the expected norm. 'Tell me,' he said, suddenly curious as he indicated that they should walk to the horses. 'Forgive me for asking, but what did Zennor Bryant hope to gain from a marriage to my brother? From what I gathered, she was rather a free spirit, and completely different to what my brother might have wanted in a bride.'

'My forgiveness isn't necessary. Zennor's father was wealthy, but he died recently. It was a good match, and one my uncle had hoped to see through. She married him out of respect for my uncle and a dislike of being alone.'

'She's bolstered the family fortunes, then.'

'She has.'

'I see.'

Jago was certain it had to be much more of a marriage of convenience than a love match. Ellory had been widowed a while now, and he would be desperate to marry and produce his heirs. Ah well, time would tell. Perhaps love would grow he thought, helping Alys mount the little white mare. But then again, perhaps it wouldn't.

'Race me, Jago Pencradoc,' she said, surprising him. Then, laughing, sped ahead on her little white mare.

Chapter Two

Present Day

Merryn pulled up at the front door of the house and gripped the steering wheel tightly. Seeing that man, Kit, had intrigued her more than she thought possible. Deep down she'd known this trip would be special. It wasn't every day you got an opportunity like this. She sat in the car for a moment, needing a little while to steady her nerves before she met Coren Penhaligon.

She had a job to do, and a professional position to maintain, so she needed to get over herself and just do it. She got out of the car and, dodging the rain, hurried to the grand, wooden entrance door. It was propped open with a box and she sidestepped that, then looked around the hallway.

'Oh – hey there!' A man carrying a box appeared in a doorway. He smiled. 'Can I help?'

'Hi. Hey. Yes, I'm Merryn Burton.' She put her hand out to shake his, then dropped it, realising he had no hands free. 'From Heptinstall Studios. Kit said I'd find you here. You're in charge?'

'Merryn ... ah! They said we should expect a lady called Merryn. Jeremy couldn't make it, I understand?'

'That's right.'

'Then it's good to meet you, Merryn.' The man had fair hair and grey eyes; colouring as far removed from the other man as possible, really, considering they were probably the Penhaligon brothers Heptinstall Studios had told her about. He put the box on the floor and held out a hand. He had a firm, confident handshake. 'I'm Coren Penhaligon. But I'm not really in charge. I'm Kit's brother, and I've got a vested interest in the building. I'm the one with the grand plans for the place. So ...' He grinned.

'Well, it's good to meet you too. Would you like me to make a start now, or are you still sorting things out?'

So they *were* brothers. Good. That made sense, then.

'I am – but can you just give me a second? I made some notes for you. Hold on.' Coren smiled and jogged off towards another corridor, then disappeared around a corner.

Merryn wondered what the notes might be. She hoped they'd be some guidance – something sadly lacking when she had been assigned the newly-named "Pencradoc Collection" to value. When the brothers had inherited the place and subsequently discovered that the house came with a raft of paintings and sculptures and pieces of art that may or may not be valuable, someone – Coren, she guessed now – had contacted the art dealers Merryn worked for, and within days she had found herself on her way here.

She hadn't been scheduled to come, but her colleague Jeremy had gone down with a nasty bug and she was enlisted at short notice. She had, however, followed the discussions at work closely. Some artists' names had been bandied around in the gallery, and she had recognised one of them as a man with quite a reputation. The Pencradoc Collection would, she knew, end up like some high-end garage sale, with nice expensive paintings awaiting little red dots in the corner of their frames. This was a way, Coren had suggested to Heptinstall Studios, of raising much-needed funds to renovate the house and secure its future as, quite possibly, an arts centre.

But she brought her thoughts back to the present day. The artist she was most interested in had garnered quite a name for himself in the late nineteenth century. Ruan Teague, renowned for his portraits, had been closely linked with the Pencradocs and many of his paintings depicted Pencradoc family members.

Merryn had often mourned the lack of her own artistic talent. She knew nobody would ever pay for her artwork, but they had loved her enthusiasm at the little dealers just off New Bond Street in London when she had decided to channel her love for art elsewhere. Plus, it was so maniacally busy, she had no time to fret about what she couldn't do. Heptinstall Studios were just starting out, and were happy to give her a chance.

Her career had indeed taken off. The little dealers had flourished and she had flourished with them – and so she found herself here today, amongst the Pencradoc Collection.

Kit stayed in the gatehouse for a little while, checking the cupboards and boxes, seeing if there was anything hidden amongst the detritus of discarded paint tins and plant pots and garden equipment that might be better placed in the house – Coren had some idea of creating a big event to showcase the artwork and get the place on the map, so to speak, and had tasked Kit with poking around the outbuildings to see if there was anything important lurking around.

Kit suspected that there wouldn't be anything of the sort in there. His Aunt Loveday hadn't been the sort to discard anything important in such a way. She had been an open and honest woman, and laughed unashamedly at the link between the family and Ruan Teague, which had, she said, apparently scandalised Society.

'Why should we hide who we are?' she had always said. 'If someone doesn't like me, it's their problem, not mine.'

Throwing a piece of wood down and wiping his hands together, Kit decided to call it a day in the gatehouse. It was a glorified shed. Nothing more. And if Coren wanted to poke around himself, he was welcome. Coren and Kit were very different. Kit was never happier than when he was painting, teaching and running his art business in Marazion, on the Cornish coast; whereas Coren had a career in investment banking and was always looking for the next challenge. Of all the plans Coren had drawn up for Pencradoc, the arts centre was the one Kit agreed with the most. Hence, he had said he would help him get it off the ground to the best of his ability.

It was a good time to head back to the house, anyway. Plus, if he was lucky, Merryn Burton might be there. Working. Or something. The idea of the 'or something' made him smile and, unbidden, the idea of Ruan Teague flitted into his mind.

There was at least one portrait by Teague in the house – an 1886 depiction of Zennor, Duchess of Trecarrow – and the hope was that more paintings would turn up as they went through the place. And when Kit saw Merryn Burton drive up to that gateway he knew, however he felt about the place that, deep down, he was meant to be there, right there, at Pencradoc, on that very day ...

Because of all the art dealers in London, Coren had to go to that one. And that chap, Jeremy, had to fall sick. And Merryn had to come.

Kit looked up and saw the shape of a woman moving around behind the glass of one of the upstairs windows and frowned. Coren hadn't wasted much time in putting Merryn to work had he? And he'd started her off upstairs, in the west wing? That seemed illogical for his brother. But, whatever worked for him, he guessed.

Dismissing the thought from his mind, he hurried up the steps to the front door and pushed it open. It was only as he stepped inside that he realised the woman's hair in the window had seemed quite dark – and as Merryn was fair, it was clearly something his brain had made up. He shivered, inexplicably, and shut the door behind him.

1886

They rode together, in the end. Alys reigned her horse in, and happily found Jago Pencradoc very easy company and, as it often did, her imagination took flight somewhere in the middle of Bodmin Moor. She found herself imagining what it would be like to spend more time in this man's company – a lot more time.

Her good mood and the light conversation, however, lasted until they had dismounted from their horses and stepped inside Pencradoc. Jago's good mood, unfortunately, lasted approximately less time than that – from the moment they rode through the ornate metal gates, a cloud seemed to descend over him, and he became quiet and brooding. This was a different man entirely to the one she had laughed with and raced with on Bodmin.

Almost immediately, Alys felt the atmosphere settle

heavily upon her as she stood, slightly awkwardly, in the entrance hall waiting for direction of some sort. Despite the fact she had lived here, quite happily, for some weeks, it felt different availing herself of the facilities when the heir to the title was standing next to her, taking off his gloves and his cloak and scowling at the room.

'I do appreciate the welcoming committee.' Jago's scowl became even darker as he looked into the dining room and saw afternoon tea already spread out. Sitting at the head of the table, was Ellory – tall, spare and seemingly carved out of immoveable granite. At the other end of the table, Zennor sat, her dark hair framing her oval face, her eyes – violet, not the moss-green of Alys' – downcast as she pushed a small cake around her plate, chopping it up into small crumbs before squashing them back together. 'I may be late, but really? Ten minutes, brother?'

'Ten minutes is ten minutes.' Ellory stared at Jago and Alys felt uncomfortable. She cast a glance at Zennor who bobbed her head up warily. Her expression softened as she saw Alys, and she beckoned to her. Alys, hot and dishevelled, still in her riding habit with her hair all awry, took her bonnet off, slunk into the seat next to her cousin, and accepted the teacup Zennor pushed towards her. A maid appeared out of nowhere and filled the cup as Jago still stood, awaiting his invitation to sit, commanding everyone's attention as he did so.

Eventually he gave up, and muttered something uncomplimentary as he stalked over to the chair next to Alys and roughly pulled it out. 'We clearly don't have time to change into more suitable clothing. I'm sure we wouldn't even dare to. Instead, I see, we are to join you as we are. Nicely done, brother. We haven't been in the damn house very long, and already you have attempted to wrong-foot us.'

'Yes. Please sit.' Ellory ignored the comment, remaining unmoved. Alys dipped her head, embarrassed. This was a different side to Jago Pencradoc entirely. She raised her eyes, half-dreading how Ellory would react.

Ellory, however, sipped at his tea. 'I was particularly anxious for you to be on time today, as I have another guest arriving at precisely five o'clock. Therefore, I had no time to waste.' He nodded, almost imperceptibly. 'But you are here now, so we must abide with that.'

'Then I shall hurry my afternoon tea, just to pacify you.' Jago raised his cup mockingly. Then he turned to Zennor and smiled. It was as if the sun had come out and Alys raised her head properly and found she couldn't look away from him, despite the atmosphere that was clearly building between the two brothers. 'My dear sister-in-law, I presume? Forgive me my tardiness.' He leaned across Alys and took Zennor's hand, raising it to his mouth and kissing it. He was very close to Alys, and part of her wished he would take her hand like that and kiss it. She could feel the warmth and energy crackling from his body and she bit her lip, looking away lest he see her blush at his proximity.

'I am indeed. It's very good to meet you at last, Jago. Please don't worry about being a little late. We aren't going anywhere.' Zennor smiled at him and he nodded, then released her hand. 'But, Ellory, who are we expecting?' She leaned forward and Alys knew her cousin was crackling with suppressed excitement herself.

Ellory took his time answering. He cut up a sandwich into tinier pieces, and finally deigned to reply. 'An artist.

As the Duchess of Trecarrow, it is expected that your portrait shall be painted—'

'A portrait to match the one I see you have had made of yourself in the hallway? And who painted that one? I suspect it was not de Amato. Which other poor sop did you invite here to satisfy your vanity? One who, I see, made a very good likeness of your good self. Excuse me.' Jago scraped his chair back and stood up. 'But I suddenly find I'm not very hungry at all. It's been a long day. I shall leave you to your ... discussions.'

The cake Alys had been nibbling suddenly lost its flavour as she watched Jago stride out of the room. 'Oh.' The syllable was out of her mouth before she could stop it.

'Oh indeed,' whispered Zennor. She paused a moment then addressed Ellory again. 'And who might the artist be? The one you have engaged for me?'

'Ruan Teague.' He clearly was not going to elaborate on the almost life-size portrait of himself on the grand staircase. Alys didn't particularly like it, but it wasn't her place to comment. Rather, she just dipped her head when she passed it and didn't look at it, if she could help it. 'Teague is of the Singer Sargent school, the James Jebusa Shannon school.' Ellory waved his hand dismissively. 'I've heard Teague's portraits are second to none. I would have commissioned Singer Sargent himself, but after the *Madame X* scandal, I just can't risk it.' And yes, even Alys had heard about that scandal – the artist in question had painted a very *risqué* portrait of a society beauty, Virginie Amélie Avegno Gautreau – and it hadn't even been commissioned. He had just done it, because he wanted to. Alys quite admired the man for his daring, and so, she knew, had Zennor.

Zennor flashed a glance at Alys which seemed to have a spark of excitement in it. 'How wonderful,' she said. 'Thank you, Ellory. I look forward to meeting him. I quite understand the need for urgency now, for having everyone finish tea by five.'

Ellory nodded, and turned his attention back to his food. Alys, however, turned her attention to the door. Exciting as it was, and delighted as she was for Zennor, all she really wanted to do was run after Jago Pencradoc and ask him why he had abandoned them all so swiftly after his return.

Jago managed to keep to his rooms for a reasonable length of time. He left the door ajar though, and, despite his better judgement, gravitated towards it when he heard voices in the hall below and hurried steps on the staircase as people made the visitor welcome. That life-size portrait of his brother, looking cold and unfeeling, would be watching everything.

The huge canvas was incongruous, somehow, and had clearly been commissioned when Jago had been abroad. It had not been there when he left – it was his brother, the Duke of Trecarrow, captured forever between duchesses.

The thought made a bitter little smile twist his mouth. His brother's self-importance knew no bounds.

Jago sat on the window seat, his legs pulled up in front of him, much as he had sat when he was a boy, and tried to distract himself by reading a book. But that just led to thoughts of Alys Trelawney and the words she was writing in her notebook. That thought led, most unwillingly, elsewhere and Jago eventually gave up, tossed the book aside and headed to the door.

He stood in the doorframe, one hand either side, and leaned out into the hallway, listening.

'Oh, for God's sake.' He punched the doorframe, and strode out of the room, then pounded down the stairs.

'Of course, I must insist my wife is constantly chaperoned during the sittings ...' Ellory's voice was droning pompously from the study and Jago raised his eyes heavenwards.

'Chaperoned. Of course,' Jago muttered, then he stood straight, tugged his lapels together and threw the door open. He strode into the study and nodded at the assembled company. Ellory was, of course, behind his desk. Alys and Zennor stood behind him, one each side flanking him, and – even though there was a chair opposite the desk – a tall man with fairly wild-looking dark brown hair stood in front of it. He didn't look subservient or in awe of the Duke of Trecarrow. Rather, he looked cool and collected, quite louche and slightly unkempt – not worried in the slightest about what impression he was giving.

'Good afternoon.' Jago smiled politely at everyone, and swept his gaze across the group. It lingered a little longer on Alys Trelawney, and for a moment his smile relaxed into something quite genuine; then it was gone again. 'I'm so sorry. I seem to be making a habit of being late today. Mr Teague. I'm delighted to meet you – I saw some of your work on the Continent.' He held his hand out and the man raised his eyebrows. His eyes were shrewd and brown, and Jago had the impression they could look into his subject's soul and bare it all on the canvas if you just knew how to read the art. He realised that he liked and respected the man on sight, and Ruan Teague shook his hand firmly.

'Thank you. I've had some success on the Continent, I must admit. The French *salons* in particular.' He grinned. 'Something about the subject matter, I think.'

'The current *beau monde* adore it, I think.' Jago grinned back.

Ellory cleared his throat. 'Excuse me, Jago. I was in the middle of discussing business with Mr Teague. And I certainly do not wish for anything *risqué*.'

'And you do not wish to drag Shannon from London, or Singer Sargent from Europe just to paint your wife. I understand.' Jago's words were pleasant enough, but the meaning was, Jago knew, not lost on Ellory. He continued, addressing the artist who now looked slightly amused. 'His last Duchess was painted by another artist. Giovanni de Amato? I'm sure you've heard of him. He wouldn't ask that gentleman again – it is a beautiful portrait, but my brother would not want to bring him out here a second time. I'm sure it would generate an awkward discussion.'

'Enough.' Ellory stood up. 'You are being deliberately obstructive. Mr Teague, I think we have covered everything we needed to. When can I expect you to begin?'

'I am free right this moment, your Grace.' Teague bowed to Ellory. 'But I fear the Duchess may not be quite ready. Shall we say a week today? That will give me time to gather my equipment and arrange accommodation.'

'Oh there's no question about it, you should stay here. But in one of the guest rooms in the west wing.' The family rooms were in the east wing. Jago hid a bitter smile. Chaperoned and separated? His Duchess was a very attractive woman. Ellory knew that much, at least.

Jago hoped for her sake that Zennor's pedestal wouldn't crumble the way Rose's had.

Chapter Three

Present Day

Merryn was in the grand hallway, admiring a marble bust of a young girl with long, wavy hair in a style that indicated the late nineteenth or very early twentieth century. She estimated the little girl to be about four years old, and thought she had the most delightfully mischievous expression she'd ever seen on a marble bust. There was a beautiful, dried red rose lying on the plinth, which to be fair looked as if it had seen better days. Merryn couldn't resist touching the little curls that fell onto the girl's forehead and smiled at the fact she almost wanted to brush them off her face and behind her ears.

The door behind her opened and she turned, her heart suddenly galloping with the idea that she might see that man again. Kit.

She was indeed rewarded by seeing him standing there, silhouetted in the doorway, and she felt her lips tilt upwards into a smile.

'Oh, hello ... Merryn.' But the man stopped dead and stared at her in some confusion.

It wasn't the most enthusiastic greeting she could have hoped for from Kit Penhaligon, and Merryn couldn't help but frown. Had she misconstrued the smiles and easy chatter back at the gatehouse?

'Ah. Yes.' She flapped her hand vaguely in no particular direction. 'Coren was just ...' She actually had no idea where Coren had gone.

Kit seemed to pull himself together and shook his

head. 'Sorry – sorry. That's my fault. I thought I'd seen you upstairs in one of the windows. And I've literally just realised it couldn't have been you at all, and it most likely wasn't *anybody* at all – just a shadow or something. Clearly I'm wrong. It was just a surprise seeing you – here. Not – there. You know?' He grinned shyly, obviously embarrassed, and Merryn relaxed. She smiled back. All was not lost then. 'And I see you've met Elsie,' Kit continued, smiling at the marble bust.

'Yes! She's adorable. Who is she? Did she live here?' Merryn looked at the image of the little girl again.

'Her parents were Ellory and Zennor Pencradoc.' He nodded to an imposing portrait above the hallway fireplace. A tall, fair-haired man stood looking down at them, his eyes hard and holding quite possibly the coldest gaze Merryn had ever seen on a human being. He made her skin crawl and she couldn't look away fast enough. Ugh. 'That was Ellory. Elsie was the only child from that marriage, so the inheritance passed to Ellory's brother Jago, but then somewhere along the line it reverted back. Coren and I are descended from Zennor and Ellory – from Elsie herself. Our Aunt Loveday was our grandmother's youngest sister, and we all trace back to little Elsie here. Aunt Loveday never married, and just lived here on her own while all of her siblings gradually got married off and moved away. She always had a soft spot for us two though. We're the only ones who ever showed much interest in her as a person, rather than someone who could present family members with a nice big house.' He frowned, remembering, perhaps, other relatives' views on Pencradoc. 'She used to love telling us family stories,' he continued. 'Said we were the only ones who ever listened. And Elsie herself was an exceptionally gifted artist.' Kit gazed around the hallway. 'But this place is too big for a normal family nowadays, though, and there's just me, I live alone ... so Coren and I have had some discussions and we came to a compromise.'

'Oh! Is that the arts centre my company mentioned you'd been considering?' The sheer size of Pencradoc would, she knew, take too much cash to upkeep without the general public having a stake in it.

'Coren was originally considering buying it and developing it into something else.' Kit pulled a face and reached out, touching the banister of the staircase. 'But then we decided that we both loved the idea of an artists' hub – like a gallery and an arts centre, and some studios that people can use. Rooms for retreats. That sort of thing. But there you go.' He shrugged. 'I'm an artist and it seems wonderful to me, but we just don't have that sort of capital at the minute, so we're hoping the sale and exhibition will help.'

Merryn nodded and looked at Elsie. 'I know what you mean. But it's such a shame to break up the collection. And Elsie here, I bet she's been here all her life.'

'She has. And she'll be staying, that's non-negotiable. However, unless a miracle happens, and we find a lost Rossetti or a hidden Picasso, I think we'll have to say goodbye to the old place as a house and sell some of the less beautiful pieces of art. That's where you come in.' He smiled. 'But it'll be nice to see the house being used for something that will give a lot of people pleasure.'

'I'll do my best to find something good for you.' Merryn meant it – oh and she hoped, she *desperately* hoped she could do that for him.

'Thanks – we can live in hope. In the meantime, I do

know where the original Teague is, so if you like, I can take you there. It's upstairs.'

There was a fizz in Merryn's stomach that owed as much to going up those stairs with Kit Penhaligon, as it did to the thought of the Teague at the end of it.

'If you wouldn't mind, that would be marvellous.' She put her hand on the banister and turned to speak to Kit again; but for a moment, reality blurred around the edges, and Kit seemed to look different. He was dressed differently – instead of his faded jeans and white T-shirt, he seemed to be wearing a grey coat, fastened just on the top button and a grey waistcoat. His trousers were black and he had a black ascot tie around the starched collar of his shirt. Merryn caught her breath and blinked, and the image was gone. The man who stood before her was as he had been when she first saw him.

First saw him? No – she had seen him way before then. When she first saw him at the gatehouse, today … that was not the very first time she had seen him …

It registered, somewhere in her mind, that Kit was speaking, and she brought her focus back to his words.

'My aunt was a little superstitious and locked up the rooms because she was convinced that area of the house was haunted,' he was saying, with a slight frown on his face. 'She thought Zennor was the one who drifted around. She said she'd seen a dark-haired girl in the room where the Teague is several times. Having said that, I don't think she grasped the concept that ghosts can walk through walls. Also, having said that, I'm sure that was the room I thought I'd seen you in.' There was a beat as they looked at one another and a little chill crept up Merryn's spine as she remembered the hazy image of a moment ago. Seeming to want to get off the subject of haunting, Kit barrelled on. 'My aunt was a lovely lady. She was so very proper and old-school. Made sure we had tea made from proper leaves and served in china cups—'

'Aunt Loveday?' Coren's voice interrupted them. 'She was amazing. Here you go, Merryn.'

Somehow, Coren inserted himself in between Kit and Merryn and turned his back on Kit. 'Notes. This is what I've found on my first sweep of the property. Now, it's not really my area, but I think the more commercial paintings are in the east wing, which is where the family rooms are—'

'Oh – oh, thanks. At least I've got somewhere to start ...' Merryn took the piece of paper almost automatically and stood looking awkward and embarrassed at the foot of the stairs, one hand still on the banister.

Kit felt a bubble of anger rise and burst inside him. He'd never been particularly angry at Coren in the past, and the feeling took him a little by surprise. But at that moment, he could have cheerfully punched his brother.

'Coren? We were talking?' He heard the warning note in his voice and quenched it quickly.

If he lost his temper here today, there would be bloodshed ... long overdue bloodshed ...

That thought made Kit freeze and instead, he pushed his hands into his pockets and forced a smile onto his face. 'Merryn and I. We were talking. Sorry, mate.'

'What? Oh! Oh – yeah. Sorry.' Coren stepped back, a look of surprise on his face. 'It's just I promised her these notes.'

Kit nodded. 'And I promised to show her the Teague.'

There was another beat. 'Do you want to come up as well, Coren?'

Kit caught Merryn's eye as she stood at the bottom of the stairs, and he watched her turn scarlet. She was the first to look away.

'I wouldn't mind, actually,' said Coren, shrugging his shoulders. 'She was pretty damn good-looking.' He cast a glance at Merryn and that cheeky grin flashed across his face – the one that had all the girls falling for him all the way through school and university. Kit wondered if Merryn would be taken in by it, but she didn't seem to be melting into a puddle of lust, so there was a hope that she hadn't registered the cheeky grin for what it usually indicated. There was an ache in Kit's face which was caused by him clenching his jaw and he made a conscious effort to relax his expression.

Was he jealous?

It was a weird thought. He'd known this girl less than half an hour, and, obviously, he'd known Coren forever. No girl had ever come between them in the past, not even Lowenna down in Marazion. Why should Merryn Burton be any different?

There was another pause, but Merryn eventually smiled, encompassing the two men with it as it lit up the hallway. Kit blinked. He had seen that smile before, he knew he had.

'I think the Teague might be a bit more interesting than the other portraits, if you'll both forgive me for saying so?' Merryn said with a laugh. 'I do appreciate your list, Mr Penhaligon, but I really, *really* want to see the Teague!'

Somehow, it defused the situation – if there had even been a "situation", which, now the moment had passed, seemed a rather silly and childish thought to contemplate.

As if to make amends, Kit reached out and slapped Coren on the back, who looked at him in surprise. Coren, then, hadn't been aware of a "situation".

'Ladies first, then.' Smiling, Kit stepped back and swept his hand out, inviting Merryn to proceed up the stairs before them.

'Well, if you're sure.' Merryn turned and headed up the stairs. Kit noticed that she was very carefully *not* holding the hand rail and instead clasped the notes Coren had given her very tightly between her hands.

And although Kit wanted to run up the stairs two at a time and burst into the room the painting was in, dragging her by the hand after him, he restrained himself and let Merryn get ahead.

Wherever you go, I shall follow.

Chapter Four

'It's left.' Coren had somehow managed to get ahead of her, and he led them through the corridors of the house, a suppressed sort of excitement almost visible in the energy that seemed to crackle around him. She turned, as he indicated, left into the west wing. The corridors were darker in here – less busy, somehow – and there was a strange atmosphere about the place.

'I'll just run ahead and get the keys – I know where they're kept. They're in the old linen press, ridiculously enough. Aunty wanted to be sure burglars wouldn't find them and it seemed disloyal to move them, so I left them there when I was doing my walkaround,' Coren explained. 'I'll not be long.' He dashed off, and disappeared down a side passage, leaving Merryn staring after him. She looked ahead and scanned the hallway. Her gaze drifted to the third room on the left. It just looked – *right*. She continued to walk, a sense of excitement she didn't quite understand building up from somewhere. To her left, there was a movement – just a shadow thrown onto the wall perhaps, as Kit walked behind her.

These had been, of course, the least used rooms at Pencradoc, and it was strange how that feeling permeated through the house. What a shame. They were probably beautiful rooms – as beautiful as the east wing, but Jago had always preferred this side of the house—

Merryn brought herself up short and stopped suddenly. Jago? The Duke of Trecarrow's brother? What had put *that* into her mind? But here she was, outside that strangely familiar room with her hand already on the door knob.

'Sorry. You might want to warn me when you decide to freeze.' Kit sounded amused. He was right behind her. So close that his breath was warm on her skin and tickled her neck.

She knew if she turned and tilted her head to this exact angle, her lips would meet his and—

No. This was ridiculous. She was fantasising, she had to be.

She steadied her breathing and was just about to reply when he spoke again: 'But good guess. This is it. You've stopped just outside the correct room.' Then Coren's voice carried along the corridor and Merryn was forced to turn around.

He was hurrying along the corridor, keys jangling. 'Thanks for waiting. I just need to unlock. There.' Coren smiled down at Merryn. 'I'm sure Zennor will welcome you with open arms. I—' He looked down at his phone and swore as it rang. 'Damn. I have to take this ... it's the office. Sorry. Forgive me. Just go ahead. I'll talk to them in the hallway.' Coren vanished up the corridor towards a long, leaded window, barking out a greeting which would have made Merryn quail if she'd been on the receiving end of it.

But once she was inside, there was no room for the outside world to intrude.

Kit came to a dead halt as he stepped into the room, as he always did when he was faced with the Duchess of Trecarrow. He didn't see the dustsheet-covered furniture. He didn't smell the old, faded scents of lavender and rose pot-pourri, or feel the edge of the rug beneath his feet. He saw, instead, the Teague portrait of Zennor.

Sitting in profile, almost, she was gazing at something outside the edge of the picture. Dressed in an ebony-coloured gown, her hair was black with hints of chestnut where the light caught it, worn loose, falling over her right shoulder. The woman's face, neck and arms were startling in contrast, almost alabaster against the dark background.

As a man, Kit could appreciate the beauty of his long-ago relation. As an artist, he could very much appreciate the desire that cried out from every stroke of the brush. Ruan Teague was in love with this woman and only a very dim-witted viewer could fail to see that.

'Wow. He really loved her, didn't he?' Merryn's voice by his shoulder was quiet and awestruck.

Kit chanced a glance down at her. 'Yes. It's a time bomb waiting to explode, isn't it?'

'It would have shocked Society.'

'I suspect so. But nowadays, nobody would consider it strange. Have you heard about the artist Patrick Allan Fraser?'

Merryn was silent for a split second, then nodded. 'Yes. Didn't he marry an heiress?'

'He did. Elizabeth Fraser. The last heiress to Hospitalfields, in Scotland.' He gestured to the portrait. 'So an artist falling for a wealthy lady could and did happen. And Teague made his feelings very clear on that canvas, to my mind.'

'Zennor is gorgeous.'

'And wild.' Kit grinned and felt another moment of connection. They both liked the portrait. They both saw the same things in it.

And yes. He did feel a sense of ownership towards it. Zennor was a grandmother so far back, that the young girl in the Teague portrait was as far removed from a granny as it was maybe possible to be. But he also felt a pride in the fact that she had been so beautiful and Ruan Teague had captured her so perfectly.

Merryn could see Kit in Zennor – there was something about the set of his eyes and the shape of his nose that hinted at the relationship. Diluted now, obviously, with multiple other genes throughout the generations, the nose and eyes still said they were related. The hair colour as well. There was more of Zennor in Kit than there was in Coren.

She forced her own eyes away from Kit. She didn't want to study him and invite a raised eyebrow or two as he wondered what she was staring at. To distract herself, she began to look around the room, her professional self mentally assessing the artwork, and her private self imagining what it might have been like when Zennor, Duchess of Trecarrow lived here.

Her gaze drifted to a display cabinet built into the wall. There were numerous carved woodland creatures in the design and she smiled – she had a particular fondness for the woodcarvers' art and those little mice that were the trademark of Robert Thompson's "Mouseman" furniture of the 1920s. She would need to take a closer look, but she wanted to see what the animals were like on this piece – although the style was a lot older. You could look at around ten thousand pounds for a Mouseman chair, so if this unit was one of his ... incredible.

Of course, this probably *wasn't* a Mouseman: but

still. She broke away from the magnet that was Kit, and walked over to the cabinet. Someone must have been in here at some point, as there was another faded rose lying on one of the shelves, but she didn't give that much more than a passing thought: the figurines were just so sweet – yes, there were mice. But also squirrels and birds and even a tortoise. A perfectly carved owl caught her eye on the right hand side, shiny and smooth. She frowned. Surely his feathers should be a little more ruffled? He had an awfully smooth head, and—

Before she was really aware of it, Merryn had taken hold of the owl's head and pulled him towards her. He gave with a *click* and a creak, and the cabinet seemed to jump out of the wall.

'Kit!' She stared at the shelf. 'Kit – look at this!' She peered around the corner of the unit, her heart thumping in her chest. It was dark and a breath of stuffy air burst out. She blinked and called him again. 'Kit!'

'What is it?' He was at her side, and she jumped, unaccountably on edge at the feelings that assailed her.

'This … this cabinet. And the owl. Look. I touched his head, and it's opened up a door!'

Kit leaned towards the gap, his body very close to hers, and, despite herself, despite the fact she didn't know him, let alone know if she could trust him, she edged closer to him.

'It's a room … definitely. Well I never!' He stared at it for a moment, then looked down at her, a question in his eyes. 'Shall we?'

Merryn nodded and, knowing instinctively what he was thinking, put her hands on the edge of the door. Kit took hold further up. 'On the count of three – one, two, *three.*'

As one, they tugged on the door and it creaked a little more, then, annoyingly, got wedged on a piece of carpet. Merryn ducked down to roll the edge of the rug back, as Kit pushed the door inwards a couple of centimetres, giving her some space. Then she stood up and helped him pull the door open properly.

A small room was revealed – a pair of tattered red velvet curtains faced them, a golden tassel hanging down on the left-hand side.

'I wonder if this was a priest's hole?' Kit was in awe. Merryn herself had always loved stories of secret rooms and passages and also loved anything that was based on folklore and fantasy.

'Maybe ... but look. What do you think is behind the curtain?' Merryn's attention was arrested and she stood frozen, looking at the curtains. Half of her wanted to tug at the tassel to open them, and half of her was panicking like a mad thing and wanted to run straight out of the place.

'Dorian Gray?' Kit's voice was wry. He nodded at the tassel. 'Go ahead. Open it. You found it.'

Merryn hesitated only for a split second, then tugged at the tassel. As the curtains pulled open, she felt herself sucked away, dragged back in time, back to the first time she had seen this portrait ...

1886

Later that evening, after everyone had retired to bed, Alys found it impossible to sleep. She lay on her back in the large, comfortable bed and stared at the golden silk canopy above her head. Her mind was filled with swirling, whirling images of the day: Dozmary Pool, and herself racing alongside Jago Pencradoc, and the dreadful afternoon tea, and the visit from Ruan Teague—

There was a rattle of her door handle as someone tried it, then a more desperate rattle. Alys shot upright and pulled the covers up to her chin. She found herself thinking how ridiculous that was, and if someone really was going to barge into her bedroom with the worst of intentions, what good would bedcovers do her? She let them drop, her cheeks heating up with the thought that if it was by any chance Jago Pencradoc rattling her door handle with the worst of intentions, it was probably easier just to go along with it and not resist very much at all ...

'Alys!' The voice that hissed at the door did not belong to Jago Pencradoc.

Alys sighed and threw her covers back, then slid out of the bed and padded across to the door, the floorboards where the carpet didn't reach cool beneath her feet.

'Zennor! What are you doing out there? It must be close to midnight.' She unlocked the door and ushered her cousin inside her bedroom.

'It's past midnight. It's almost one o'clock. It's the witching hour!' Zennor scurried over to Alys' bed and sat on it. 'Would you like to have a little adventure, Alys?' Her eyes shone in the lamplight. Alys had just left it burning low, finding it more comforting to be staring into a partially lit room than have her thoughts churning over in infinite blackness.

'An adventure?' Her cheeks burned again as she dismissed the thoughts of the adventure she had been idly contemplating with Jago Pencradoc.

'Yes. After our chat with Mr Teague earlier, I began to think of the Sainted Rose and that mythical de Amato portrait.' Her teeth glinted in the lamplight as she flashed a wicked smile at Alys. 'But it's not so mythical when one knows where it's hidden.'

'Truly?' Alys stared at Zennor, her eyes wide. The portrait of Rose had been hidden away when she died, and it was well known in the household that Ellory didn't want her face on display anywhere. Alys thought it was tragic and beyond romantic at the very same time. 'He must have loved her once upon a time. I can't understand why he would have hidden her away?'

'I don't know myself.' The lamplight threw Zennor's face into shadow as she frowned. 'I tried to ask him once, but he wasn't very forthcoming.'

'So how did you find it then?' Alys sat next to Zennor, wanting to hear the tale before she built her hopes up at seeing the portrait. She adored de Amato's work anyway, and the thought of seeing a real one – it was very exciting. De Amato's work was darker, more dangerous and more sensual even than his great contemporary, Boldini's.

'By accident. It's in the house. I found it when I had only been here a few weeks, I explored one day, and got a little lost.'

'Easily done.'

'Yes. It's probably easier to show you.' Zennor took Alys' hand in hers. 'Promise? A cross-your-heart promise that you won't tell him we know where it is?'

The girls had done cross-your-heart promises all the time when they had been growing up in order to share their very deepest, darkest secrets and plots and plans.

Alys knew that this indeed must be solemn and rather grave, and nodded. 'Yes. Cross my heart.' She did so, very seriously, as they held hands and then mirrored the motion of a cross over their chests.

'Good. Now, come with me.'

'Don't I need a robe or a cloak?'

'No – nobody will be around. Ellory is in his room, I heard the door lock and that's him tucked away for the night.' Ellory and Zennor had adjoining rooms. Ellory did not care to visit Zennor in the marital bed very frequently, it seemed. And if he did, he didn't stay there afterwards. 'The servants won't be in that area of the house, and really, can you imagine Jago creeping around the corridors late at night after a journey such as he has had today?'

Alys couldn't. 'No. I can't. Very well. If you think it will be safe enough, we shall go.' She shivered a little, and wasn't quite sure if it was excitement or fear or the cold.

'Come on then!'

She slid off the bed, and soon they were in the corridors, trying to be so very quiet and stifling nervous giggles as they passed the family rooms.

Alys followed Zennor, a white shape in the night as she fled through the house, her bare feet making no sound on the carpets. At one point, Zennor vanished around a corner and Alys hurried after her, the darkness seeming to press against her as she ran across the landing, at the top of some stairs. She shivered again, and looked quickly over her shoulder, convinced she had heard footsteps and imagining a dark shape melting out of the shadows. She ran after Zennor even faster, and determined not to look over her shoulder again.

'Here we are!' Zennor was breathless as she stopped outside a door. 'In here.'

'In here? Well, if it's in a room, it's not really very hidden away, is it?' Alys was indignant. She had expected something a little more exciting than it being merely in the other wing of the house.

'Come in. You'll see.' Zennor opened the door and they stepped inside what looked like a formal sitting room, with all the furniture covered over and a sad, neglected air to it. 'I think this was her room – isn't it sad? It was probably a very friendly room when she had it, but it's just all dust covers and things now.'

'Oh dear. How awful.' Alys looked around the room. 'It would be pretty, you're right. It's so cold in here though!'

'I suspect a fire has never been lit since she died. I'm going to ask if I can use it, but I'm not sure if he would allow it.'

They were speaking in whispers, even though the place was far enough away from anyone who might hear them.

'I suspect you're right,' replied Alys, still in awe.

'Sadly, I think I am. But look … look at this.' Zennor suddenly produced a candle in a holder and a box of matches from under a dust sheet.

'Zennor! Did you plan this?'

'Of course. We couldn't really light our way through the corridors, now could we? I hid this away after dinner, after Mr Teague left. It was the sensible thing to do.' She lit the candle, and walked over to a display cabinet built into the wall. The candlelight threw odd shapes and again Alys felt that sense of unease she had experienced in the corridors. Mentally, she wondered whether it would be easy enough to burrow beneath a dust sheet to hide away if need be. Her thoughts transported her to places that should only really exist within the pages of her stories, and so she pushed the notions to the furthermost area of her mind as she moved towards Zennor.

Zennor was holding the candle up to the side of the cabinet. 'Here we are. It's more difficult to see in the candlelight. It's a little more shiny than the others. Smoother and less dusty.' She touched a carved owl on the right hand side and Alys frowned.

'If it's less dusty, might that mean someone has been here more recently than perhaps you think?'

Zennor shrugged. '*He* probably comes here. But he won't be here tonight. Ah. Got it.' She pulled the owl towards her, and there was a click as the unit jumped slightly out of the wall.

'A secret room!' Alys peered over Zennor's shoulder, her heart pounding.

'It was probably the priest's hole, but I'm not sure. This family changed religious allegiance as often as they changed their boots.' Zennor stepped into the tiny room and put the candle carefully down on the floor. As Alys' eyes adjusted to the darkness, Zennor reached over and pulled at a gold tassel, which was attached to some red velvet curtains on the back wall. 'There she is. The Sainted Rose. She was extraordinarily pretty, wasn't she?'

Alys found herself face to face with Ellory's dead wife. 'Oh my God.' Her voice was no louder than a whisper as she stared at the girl in the picture.

Rose was extraordinarily beautiful, as Zennor had said. She looked, in fact, a little like Zennor. They both had the same dark hair, but where Zennor had a perfectly oval face and violet eyes, Rose had a heart-shaped face and eyes that Alys suspected were dark brown, but she couldn't be sure. The portrait was done in de Amato's classic, flowing style.

Rose was turned to her left, staring out at the side of the picture. There was a smile on her lips, which made one think that she was laughing with delight at something just out of sight of the viewer. Her gown merged into the background in feathered strokes of paint, her hair loose and curling around her shoulders. A single red rose was held delicately between her fingers.

It must have been painted in the very early days of their marriage, as she looked so terribly young. Rose had, Alys thought, hope in her eyes and in her heart. She was also particularly scantily clad – one shoulder was bare and this was, indeed, extraordinarily daring.

'I don't think one can accidentally stumble upon this!' Alys whispered, unable to tear her gaze away from the portrait.

'Ask me no questions, and I shall tell you no lies,' replied Zennor, amusement in her voice. 'It's enough to know she's here, is it not?'

'I don't need you to quote Mr Dickens at me.' But she didn't intend any malice. She was still staring at Rose.

'You're moonstruck by her, aren't you, darling?' Zennor moved closer and linked arms with Alys. The warmth of her body was welcome.

'Very much so. I—'

There was a creak and some hurried footsteps behind them, as if someone was running across the room to confront them. The candle snuffed in a blast of air and the girls were plunged into darkness.

Alys felt a scream bubble up in her throat, but just as quickly, a hand came over her mouth to quieten her.

'Shhh.' It was Zennor. Her voice was shaky, but she, at least, hadn't screamed either. She moved away from Alys and peered beyond the door. 'I think it's just the wind. It's nothing.'

'I think we should leave. It's a warning.'

'Don't be so fanciful. Nobody ever comes along here, I told you.'

'Nobody except Ellory.'

'Who's not going to be leaving his room.'

'But still ... we aren't really supposed to be in here. And I know it's your home, but Ellory is still in charge.'

It was a sad fact, but true and Alys sensed Zennor's shoulders slumping as the reality hit her as well.

'You've seen her at least.' Zennor's voice was flatter, more subdued now. 'You're right, we should go.'

'Oh, Zennor. I'm sorry.' Alys put her hand on her cousin's arm. 'I didn't mean to sound harsh.'

'No. It is very much his house. And hers. Rose's. I sometimes think she's never left. As if she has something still to say.'

'But ... it wasn't a *quick* death, was it?' Alys felt terribly disloyal, talking about Rose like this in her very own quarters.

'No. She must have known it was happening. I can't see how she would fail to realise.'

'What exactly happened to her?'

'I'm not entirely sure. From what I've gathered, she seemed to be miscarrying, and it just went on and on.' Zennor was silent for a moment. 'They said she was vomiting and then went on to have agonising stomach cramps. Eventually, she became unconscious, and died. Horrid.' Alys felt Zennor shudder. 'I think that if she had lucid moments, she would have perhaps known what was coming? They say she was found at the folly, you know. The tower. But I don't know who found her. They also said they suspected she had done it herself, as she was quite mad at the end, apparently. She had a terrible head injury. Perhaps if she hadn't fallen, it might have been different ...'

Alys felt for Zennor's hand and squeezed it. 'How hideous.' She shook her head and reached across Zennor to tug on the gold tassel. The curtains slid smoothly closed and hung there, gently swaying until they stopped. 'People miscarry every single day and they don't die from it. It must have been the injuries from her fall that caused it. I suppose it got to a point where she was no longer aware of anything. Maybe it was a blessing she died peacefully.'

'Maybe.' Zennor squeezed Alys' hand back. 'But now I'm thoroughly depressed and this wasn't at all as much fun as I had anticipated. We should leave.'

Alys wasn't going to argue and followed Zennor out, waiting in the room until she had closed the door to the priest's hole and hid the matches and candle back beneath the dust sheet.

Alys took one last look at Rose's domain as they stepped back into the hallway and then shut the door firmly. Just as it closed, she saw a dark shape waver around the fireplace, and what may or may not have been a bulky shadow spill out into the room. She shivered again and turned away, grabbing Zennor's hand and running with her back into the inhabited parts of Pencradoc.

He stood in Rose's room, a knife in his hand and watched the door shut on Zennor and Alys. He gripped the handle more firmly and went over to the cabinet. He touched the owl and the door slid open. He stepped into the room and tugged on the tassel. There she was, smiling out of the frame at the artist.

How little she knew of the future at that point. But perhaps it was best. He looked at the knife in his hand and back at the portrait. The anger that had fuelled him for so long bubbled up to the surface and his palms were slick on the knife handle.

'I'm sorry, Rose,' he murmured. Then he raised the knife and made the first cut.

Chapter Five

'It's Rose.' Merryn was staring at the portrait, not even reading from the gold plate on the bottom of the frame, fixing her eyes on the girl she saw there. 'His last Duchess. The one before Zennor. This was her. He hid her away in here! Why? Why do that? And dear God – it's a de Amato! Can you see? See the signature?'

Kit stared at Merryn, stunned at the expression on her face. For a moment, she had looked quite different. She'd looked less like herself, and more like ... *Alys*.

The voice whispered in his ear and he jumped, turning quickly in case Coren had crept up on them and seen the picture, seen them standing there, moonstruck.

Moonstruck? Where the hell had that come from? It was daylight, broad daylight—

'Rose.' Kit stared at the woman. 'She died before Ellory married Zennor. I don't think I've ever seen a picture of her – and I've looked back through the family history forever. And it's here.'

Merryn nodded. 'This was why. She's been discarded in this old room. You weren't far wrong with Dorian Gray.' She raised a fingertip, as if she was going to touch the paintwork, then dropped her hand. 'She's definitely not getting any older.'

'Twenty-two.' Kit's voice was almost a whisper. 'That's how old she was when she died.'

'Horrible.'

Kit remained staring at the picture; then, almost as if

he was drawn there, he tilted his head upwards. 'Look … up there. The top left.'

The canvas had been damaged, ever so slightly. There was a raised area beneath the black background, so close to the side of the frame that you wouldn't see it unless you were an art expert or knew exactly what you were looking for. Kit's own fingertips were centimetres away from the corner.

He had a sudden flash of memory: *a sharp knife in his hand, his fingers slick on the handle … the slight resistance as he cut into the canvas … Alys melting into the darkness beyond, him keeping to the shadows so she didn't see him. This was his secret. His and Rose's and nobody must find out—*

'I don't like that cut,' murmured Merryn.

'Me neither. But I wonder …' He took a deep breath and reached up, almost as if he knew exactly what to do.

You were the last one to touch it!

He blinked as the thought assailed him and he buried it in his subconscious where it had crawled from. This was not a conversation he was about to have with himself, now or indeed ever. Too much time had passed since then, and there was too much of an atmosphere here today. He glanced at Merryn. There was too much emotion.

Good God.

He took another deep breath and, ever so gently, his fingers sought the edge of the cut.

'What are you doing? Stop it!' Merryn reached up and grabbed his elbow. 'You can't do that!'

'Watch me.'

Merryn's hands flew to the side of her face. 'That's a *de Amato*. You cannot be destroying a de Amato!'

47

'I'm not destroying it. Someone else did that.'

'But it's a de Amato.' Merryn knew she sounded pathetic, which wasn't exactly professional. Her heart pounded, her mind flying through the possibilities.

'I don't care if it's a bloody Monet or a Rossetti or a Millais – there's something hidden in here and I damn well want it.' Kit's eyes were flinty, his voice dangerous. Merryn didn't argue further. She watched as he eased something out of the split in the canvas – a collection, it seemed, of paper, covered in small, neat handwriting.

'What the—' Kit looked at the papers he held in his hand, his eyes scanning the words, his brow furrowed. Then he looked at Merryn. 'It's a letter or something.' He turned the pages to the end and was silent. Then he passed the collection of papers to Merryn.

She took them, scared that she might damage them, and caught sight of the date. 1884.

Almost without thinking she spoke. 'When did Rose die?'

'1884. I think.' Kit's voice was more controlled than she thought it might be.

'The date of this letter.' She flipped the pages to the end. There, in faded ink, was a signature. *Rose, Duchess of Trecarrow*.

Merryn looked at Kit, and their eyes held for a moment. As Coren's footsteps came closer, two things happened at the same time: Merryn hid the papers in the pocket of her jeans, and Kit smoothed the split down so it was hidden within the dark background again.

'Good lord! What on earth have you found *there*?'

'I'm sorry, it was me ...' began Merryn.

Coren glanced at her, a curious frown creasing his face. 'What are you apologising for? Is this *her*, though? Is this *Rose*?'

'The Sainted Rose.' Merryn's voice was quiet. 'Oh! Sorry ... I'm so sorry. I don't know where on earth that came from.' Her face felt flushed, her cheeks red hot as she placed her palms against them. 'I must have read it somewhere.'

'I've never heard her called that before.' Coren moved closer to the picture, and, clearly not as reluctant as Kit and Merryn, touched it. He ran his fingers across the gold name plate and shook his head. 'I heard rumours there had been a portrait of Rose. I never knew where it was.'

If Coren noticed an atmosphere of guilt, excitement and mystery, he didn't say anything. He was apparently as stunned by Rose as Kit and Merryn had been.

'This is her, then? And who painted it – de Amato? Ah yes – there's his signature. Even I could tell it was his work. God, what a stunner.'

Merryn nodded, managing to put a professional veneer on. 'Yes. It's his classic styling.' She pointed at the dark background, then quickly moved her hand away from the top left corner. 'A de Amato they recently discovered in Paris went for about three million. So if you want to sell this you're looking at a lot of money.'

'We do need the cash, but it seems a bit of a sin to do that.' Kit stared at the painting again. 'I would love to know why she was stuffed in here though.' Then he turned away and shook his head. 'Perhaps it was as simple as the fact that he couldn't bear to see her after she died. You never know. But he married Zennor pretty quickly afterwards. Within a year, I think ...'

Coren found himself unable to look away from her; entrapped by Rose's portrait. He was vaguely aware of

Kit and Merryn's conversation fading away as he felt himself slipping into a different time, a different sense of place overtaking him.

It wasn't Kit and Merryn talking, not at all. It was Jago: his insolent, argumentative, arrogant half-brother, and that little blonde idiot who had latched herself onto his wife ...

Jago's voice was washing over him. He could hear the words, but they weren't really making much sense to him. Instead, all he could concentrate on was Rose. All Rose.

Her eyes held him in thrall, as they always had. She was mocking him, laughing at him through the paint of a lifetime.

He'd married again within a year. And within another year that woman had wrecked all their lives again. Within a year, she had—

'Coren? Coren, are you even listening to me?'

'Sorry.' The words startled him. Coren blinked and dragged his attention away from her, away from his last Duchess. His eyes locked on his brother's and he felt his fists clench.

He knew. He knew all about it.

And he had let it happen.

'Coren, exciting as this is, I'm sensing you want to be alone with Rose. So I'm going to leave you to it.' Kit waved his hand vaguely in the direction of the window. 'I'll continue outside. While it's still warm and sunny. I want to have a look in the old summerhouse, anyway, just in case Loveday put anything in there.' He doubted it, though. And the only thing he wanted to look at was the handwritten papers he had found hidden in the portrait. 'I'm going to head down through the Wilderness gardens.'

'Oh. Yes. Of course.' Coren seemed to be only half-concentrating, his mind elsewhere and his eyes blank. 'Perhaps head to the old rose garden. It was all part of a Gothic fantasy that Rose created.' His eyes seemed to harden. 'With the help of de Amato. She'd been inspired by their discussions about art, apparently.'

Coren's voice was cold and dismissive and Kit looked at him curiously. 'Yeah, of course I know all about the Duchess's rose garden.' He chose not to pursue the point. 'Merryn, it's worth a look if you get a chance. Anyway, I'll be down at the summerhouse for a while. Catch you guys later.' He nodded and smiled, casting a curious glance at Coren who had barely moved an inch, his attention now back with the Duchess of Trecarrow.

'Okay. I'll – um – look at these notes and see what else I can find. If that's all right?' Merryn was addressing Coren, who simply nodded, still staring at the portrait.

'Yes. But stay in the east wing. Don't come back here.'

'Oh. Of course.' Merryn hovered for a moment, then nodded, and hurried out of the room.

Kit glanced at his brother, ashamed of the curt way he'd spoken to Merryn Burton. 'I don't think you needed to be quite so sharp, Coren. She's here to do us a favour, after all.'

But Coren didn't answer. He remained focused on the painting.

Kit shook his head, then wasted no time in following Merryn out of the room and along the corridor to the staircase.

It was what he had to do, after all.

*

'Merryn.' Kit took hold of her shoulder briefly, just as they got to the top of the stairs. 'Do you *really* want to go to the east wing?'

Merryn turned and looked at him, aware of a burning, tingly sensation where his hand had touched her. 'No. Not really. I just thought he wanted me to go there ... I am being paid by you guys after all.'

Kit shook his head. 'Ignore him. Would you like to see the rose garden instead?'

'Well now. I think it would be shame *not* to see it. But I should probably do some work.' She gestured along the corridor.

'You should, I suppose. But, considering I'm paying as well, in a roundabout way, I think it would be good for you to see the scope of the place. There could be pictures anywhere. He's written notes – I'm more of a visual person; so I'm going to take you on a guided tour of the grounds. And again, please – let me apologise for my brother.' He frowned momentarily. 'He's not usually so ... heavy-handed. I mean, he doesn't tend to boss people around or tell them what to do; not too much, anyway, outside of the office. I'd hate working with him.'

'Oh – it's not a problem.' Merryn smiled and shrugged dismissively. 'Like I said, I'm here to do a job, at the end of the day. I've been spoken to a lot worse.'

'Then you had every right to walk out of wherever they spoke to you like that. However, I hope you don't see fit to walk out on me. Us. Pencradoc. You know.' He coloured slightly, and Merryn hid another smile.

It will take more than your brother's attitude to chase me away from here.

The thought flew into her mind, and she blinked; then it disappeared again.

'Of course. As I said, I'm here to do a job. It's a big property, and it'll take a while to do it. And to be honest, finding a de Amato has been a pretty good start to my first day here.'

'I bet. Now.' Kit patted his pocket, and Merryn felt a smile tug at the corner of her lips. She knew what was coming. 'The rose garden is a pretty quiet area. And as my brother thinks I am heading to the summerhouse, I think it's a pretty safe bet that he won't come looking for me.' He indicated for Merryn to begin walking down the stairs and she did. He kept pace with her. 'I don't know about you, but I think I want to have a look at these old papers. There was a reason they were put there.'

'Who do you think hid them?'

Kit paused, a shadow flitting across his face, and he spoke carefully – too carefully. 'I don't know.'

'Didn't your aunt ever mention anything about them? About any important papers going missing? Wills perhaps?'

'No. I doubt she even knew they were there.'

'Then it is a genuine Pencradoc family mystery.' They had reached the bust of Elsie again and Merryn smiled at her, quite automatically. 'That little girl is so gorgeous, I'm quite taken with her.'

'Little Elsie. Yes, even if I wasn't related to her, I'd feel the same about her, I think.' He patted her on the head as they passed. 'So – do you want to stay and do the east wing or explore the grounds to get an idea of scale?' There was a mischievous look in his eye, and she couldn't help but grin.

'I do need to get some things out of my car. I guess I could go the long way around.'

'I guess you could. Come on.' And together they went out of the big front door into the grounds.

Just then, another sense of mystery struck Merryn – because it felt like it was something she and Kit had done a million times before.

1886

Jago pressed the edges of the destroyed canvas together, then briefly leaned his forehead against the portrait – it was cold, impersonal in some ways. With his eyes closed, it could have been a painting of anyone there. Not Rose. It didn't *feel* like her at all.

He remembered how warm she had always been, so full of life. Her eyes had sparkled in reality, just like they did under de Amato's brushwork, and, before it all happened, she had an absolute *joie de vivre* that he couldn't put into words. He was no artist. He was no writer, no sculptor, he had no way to record how she was, how she had felt, how she had been. He just had his memories.

And sometimes they were the thing that hurt most.

The next day, Jago was up before dawn. Just as the sun was rising, he found himself walking through the dew-silvered grass and heading towards the folly. It was a tower, built to look tumbledown and romantic, with ivy and climbing roses creeping across the stonework, but it was a relatively modern creation, his grandfather having built it for his future wife.

His Scottish grandmother had been a devotee of Sir Walter Scott's work, and had adored the romantic poets such as Browning, Shelley, Keats and Byron. The tower had been her refuge from the world, somewhere she would indulge herself in their work, and soon she had a fairly comfortable sitting room in there, on the first floor, at the top of the stone staircase. It was somewhere all the women of the family had loved, and Rose was no exception.

However, the last memories he had of Rose here were not pleasant ones but it was, oddly, where he felt he needed to be today. It was where he felt closest to her, despite the portrait hidden away in the west wing. She had loved it here when they were children, and here they had pledged, innocently, to marry one another ...

'When we are married, shall we live here?' Rose had been ten years old and unspoiled, closing her book and rolling over onto her back, staring up at the ceiling. 'I think it would be delightful, don't you? Just big enough for the two of us, and nobody coming to bother us.'

'Like my brother?' Jago had poked at a cobweb with the tip of a sword he had smuggled out of Pencradoc to polish. At thirteen, he hadn't quite decided if he was going to become a smuggler or a highwayman, but both options, he had told Rose, would allow him some adventure and some travel abroad.

'Yes. I don't like your brother bothering us.'

'I'm very pleased he's away at school,' Jago said, glowering at the cobweb which refused to break away from the corner of the bookcase. 'I wish he'd stay away forever.' He turned to Rose. 'Then he'd stay away from *you* as well. I don't like the way he talks to you. I'll make him sorry, though, I will.'

'I'm not *scared* of Ellory,' she said thoughtfully. 'I just find him ... annoying.' She'd pulled a face, then rolled back onto her stomach. 'But when you are grown, you can send him away.'

Jago hadn't been very sure that was how it all worked, but he didn't correct Rose. Instead, he told her, quite seriously, 'Don't worry about Ellory. I swear to you, as a knight—' here, he had bowed quite elegantly, '—that I shall always protect you.'

Ellory had come and gone for several years after that, and Rose and Jago's resolve against him held strong.

It held strong until Rose came back from a Swiss finishing school, equipped with the necessary skills to become a loyal, suitable wife in Society, and the new and desirable curves of womanhood; and Ellory, having coolly considered his options, had eventually decided to make her his bride.

There had been no choice in the matter, no discussion. Rose's father had agreed to Ellory's terms, and thus the deed was done. They had married when she was twenty.

And she had died two years later.

Jago sat down in the middle of the ground floor tower room, which had used to be a pleasant foyer in the olden days, and looked at the staircase. He could still see her lying at the bottom, her body crumpled and blood pouring out of a gash on her forehead.

Then, behind him, the faint creak of the door as it opened and a footstep as someone entered.

'I knew you would come,' he said, without turning his head.

'Oh!' Alys halted, shocked and slightly embarrassed at having been caught out by Jago. 'I'm so sorry. I didn't think anyone would be here this early in the morning.'

'Did you not? I can't understand why – for example, *you're* here, aren't you?' He turned to her then, a smile on his face. His eyes, however, were haunted and she stood very still, a million excuses whirling around her head. She thought, eventually, it was perhaps easier to be honest. There was something about Jago that made her want to bare her soul and hold nothing back.

She bit her lip and looked down. 'I heard this was where – Rose – was found. Zennor and I were talking about her. I wanted to see the tower. I wanted to see if there was anything left of her. Do you understand? It's hard to explain.'

'You want to know if her ghost has been laid to rest. If Ellory still, perhaps, thinks of her.' Jago stood up and held his hand out to her. 'Come. I can guarantee her spirit is not here. She didn't die here, after all, you know. And why the fascination with her?'

The answer was simple. 'Because if she had lived, Zennor wouldn't be here today.'

'And neither would you. And that would be another sort of tragedy.' He was still holding his hand out. Alys understood it was his way of politely leading her out of the folly and away from the tower. She hesitated a moment, then took it. She felt that little tingle on her skin where their hands connected and shivered slightly.

'Are you cold?' Jago pulled her closer and tucked her arm into his side. 'It was nice here when we used to come and play. There was usually a fire to be lit. We—' he stopped, as if he didn't want to share any more, or even tell her who 'we' were. She assumed it was the two Pencradoc brothers.

'No. No, I'm not cold.' She didn't resist his proximity, but as they walked away from the folly, and back towards the house where he assured her there would be a substantial breakfast waiting for them, they talked of what they would do later in the day.

Yet even as she agreed with his plans, the draw of the tower was irresistible and she knew that she would return there; despite the clear hints that she should let Rose's ghost be, wherever it wandered.

Chapter Six

'I knew you'd come,' he said. 'I knew you'd prefer reading this old letter to looking at old paintings.'

'Am I so obvious? And I *love* looking at old paintings! It's what I get paid for, at the end of the day.' It was true. And that was why Merryn also loved her job so much.

'Yes, but there's no need for you to be bullied into it. I've truly never heard Coren like that before. I'm completely ashamed of him.'

'Forget it. Really. I know what it's like. I've got a younger sister and we don't always agree.'

'That's not the point. He shouldn't speak to people like that, and he doesn't usually. I'm hoping this inheritance thing hasn't gone to his head and he's going to start throwing his weight around. But, okay, I'll shut up about him. Right. Old paintings! Some of them must be so drearily boring.' Kit pulled a face. 'I prefer something with a bit of life in it. I mean, I know that bowls of fruit and stuffed pheasants appeal to some people, and I guess the symbolism in art is interesting if that's what you're after.'

'It is. But sometimes it's nice to get a painting you can just look at and appreciate. Like the de Amato. I could have stayed and looked at that for much longer.'

'Yes, it would have been so easy to stay there. Rose was pretty, wasn't she? She designed the old rose garden, like Coren said. I think she must have been a bit of a romantic, or just a typical Victorian in the fact she adored the Gothic and wanted spaces to reflect that on her estate. Can you see what I mean?' He paused and stood at the top of some steps which led down to a hidden section of the gardens, carefully designed to look wild and ethereal, all at the same time.

Old English roses in full bloom trailed amongst half-rotted stumps of trees and ferns, ivy twisting and turning here and there, entwining itself around rocks and Victorian affectations such as broken Grecian pillars and an artlessly designed half fallen-down wall. Merryn stared, entranced by it, all peaceful and, somehow, eerie. It gave her a little, pleasurable thrill. She could easily imagine sprites and faeries hiding from them, following them with whispered breaths as she and Kit wound their way down the steps and through the crazy paving into the secret area. There was the sound of water flowing just out of sight; but as they fully entered the garden, Merryn glimpsed the source of it – a waterfall, gushing down into a crystal-bright stream.

'Rose sort of combined the stumpery and the roses,' Kit was saying as he led her down to the hidden courtyard in the centre of it all. 'See how it all merges into the Wilderness garden? If you wander around the rose garden and follow one of those winding paths you sort of drift unnoticed into the wilderness. It's like a fairy garden. At least that's what I always thought when I was little. But it was more as if dragons and wizards inhabited it in my imagination.'

Merryn smiled at the thought. 'It's incredible. But I like dragons and wizards. I think Rose looked a little like Zennor, didn't she? I wonder if Ellory had a "type"?'

'Possibly.' He caught her eye and smiled back. 'He seemed to go for brunettes.'

'Looking at his two Duchesses, I think he did! His wives were beyond beautiful, weren't they? But he just looks so *cold*. So unfeeling. Maybe it's just the colours in that picture of him; the fact that he's got fair hair and there's not really any richness in the palette. Maybe it's just because I've never really been attracted to men with fair hair ...' Her cheeks burned as she realised what she had just admitted – she preferred dark-haired men. Dark-haired men with *feelings*. And oh my, Kit Penhaligon had dark hair, didn't he? Did he have "feelings" she wondered? Then she gave herself a little mental shake. She hoped he wouldn't think she was setting her sights on him – they'd only just met, and lo and behold, wasn't he the joint heir to this amazing place?

She had to stay professional. 'Oh – look. Is *that* real? I mean, a real ruin. Or not. Sorry. I know what I mean.'

A tumbledown tower was visible. It looked like something out of a fairytale – she wouldn't have been surprised to see Rapunzel hanging out of the topmost window.

'I know what you mean too. It's not a real ruin. It's a folly. The Victorians seemed to worship the Cult of the Ruin, and my family were no different. One of the earlier Duchesses used to enjoy reading her Byron in there, so they say. I used to play in there when I was a kid, but Coren wasn't that bothered about it. They say Rose loved it too, but unfortunately, that was where she fell down the steps. Don't look like that! She didn't die there – but Ellory would never go there again, apparently. He didn't much like anybody else going there either.'

'Oh. Perhaps I've misjudged him – maybe he's not as insensitive as I thought.'

Kit raised his eyebrows. 'Perhaps. Anyway – here we

are in the rose garden. So are you ready to look at the letter?'

Merryn glanced at the tower. For a brief moment she considered suggesting they went over there – then curiosity won the day, and besides there was just something about the tower that made her feel a little creeped out. Instead, she nodded decisively. 'Yes. Here seems a good place. Rose's Gothic fantasy is as decent an area as any.'

Merryn looked around her properly. Victorians had, indeed, been very fond of all things Gothic, and stumperies, created from wonderfully gnarled old tree roots and branches, were extremely popular. Rose's little fantasy was set in a wooded glade, and seeing it today sent a shiver down Merryn's spine. If the tower had been out of *Rapunzel*, this hidden space, now she was inside it, was truly out of a dark fairytale; and, actually, forget the sprites and faeries – she fully expected to see a witch or a vampire pounce out of a dark corner, never mind Kit's dragons and wizards. In fact, wasn't there something like a grotto hidden under the overhanging branches of a tree over there?

She turned to speak to Kit, and saw him staring at a point between two trees, at a flat rock overlooking the waterfall. The falls were perfectly positioned, it seemed, to be a focal point to the outside world. The shadows from the trees that overhung it made it look like there were two figures sitting there, heads bent together, half-turned so they were facing one another; then the wind blew and the branches wavered and changed shape, and the image was gone.

'Oh my,' she whispered, 'these shadows are playing tricks on me! I almost thought there were people there!'

'So did I.' Kit shook his head and turned to face her. 'But there isn't. Shall we sit?'

'It would be my pleasure,' she whispered, still looking at the rock in the shadows. The waterfall was dashing past the clearing as it had done for decades, centuries even, a constant rush of water that splashed and sparkled in the sunlight. It was mesmerising, and Merryn had to concentrate fully on the idea of the papers they had found – or she knew she would have fallen away somewhere with the water, and she had no idea of the destination.

1886

Jago's mind wandered back to that day, almost three years ago now.

'Why did you feel the need to bring me out here?' Rose had been curious, her smile questioning. Jago had noticed with a pang that her smile didn't reach her eyes any more. Those eyes flitted here and there, as if she was afraid of someone or something watching her, and her fingers plucked nervously at her skirt. Jago wondered when she had stopped being herself, when she had lost herself to Ellory's image of a perfect Duchess.

'Because I wanted to see you alone.' Jago glanced in the direction of Pencradoc, and satisfied himself that they hadn't been followed into the Wilderness garden. 'I've discovered something you should be aware of.'

'Oh? And what might that be?' She gazed at him, her smile wavering. 'Oh Jago. I am sorry, you know. I'm sorry that I married Ellory and not you—'

'Shhh.' He pressed his fingertips against her lips. 'It wasn't your fault, nobody could have stopped it.'

She removed his fingers gently. 'But it was always going to be *us*, wasn't it? We were always going to marry.'

'We were, but then we grew up. I could never compete with Ellory. Not in your father's eyes. Not in Ellory's eyes. And to be honest, what we had was a childhood dream.'

'It was a nice dream. Do you still love me, Jago? In a grown-up sort of way?' She smiled then, properly, and he laughed.

'In a grown-up *brotherly* sort of way. Those days in the tower were a long time ago. We've both changed – which is one of the perils of adulthood, I think. Anyway. I wanted to tell you that I have discovered something. I found a note Ellory made to himself and rather carelessly left lying around. He is arranging for an artist to come and visit. He wants your portrait painted.'

Rose's eyes widened. 'A portrait! He must ... love me then. In his own way.'

'He must. I'm sure he does.' Even as Jago said it, he felt the gall rise in his throat. Ellory loved nothing and nobody except for himself and his title; or if he did, he made a jolly good job of hiding it. Of hiding any emotion whatsoever. 'But I want to warn you, as a friend, or a brother, take your pick, that Ellory rarely does anything at face value. And he has not spoken of it to you, has he?' He worried, quite possibly unnecessarily, with a fear he couldn't put into words or even explain. 'I just wonder at his motives. It is something he has never expressed an interest in before.'

'I think I have ... one ... idea why he wants it done.' Rose looked down and blushed to the roots of her hair. 'But I feel disloyal telling you. And it's improper to discuss it with you.' She blushed again and the ground at Jago's feet suddenly seemed awfully interesting to her.

It was his turn to grip her hands more tightly. 'It's all right,' he whispered. 'You don't have to tell me. I don't need to know.'

Rose simply nodded. She didn't take her eyes off the ground, but she squeezed his hands even tighter. 'I think I do though. I think he is worried that it is taking so long to conceive I am starting to feel overwhelmed by it. I think that he wants to distract me with thoughts of something else. Perhaps if I stop ... worrying ... about what *isn't* happening and enjoy having my portrait painted, then I will relax a little and it will happen.'

'That could well be the reason then,' he said. But part of him still wasn't entirely convinced.

1883

The letter lay in front of Ellory, ready to post. It was written neatly, in his own hand, folded exactly into thirds and placed carefully in the envelope, then centred on his desk.

Ellory stared at it, absolutely certain that he had made the right choice of artist. Russo was elderly, well respected in Society and would paint a decorous portrait. His knuckles whitened as he gripped the edges of the desk, thinking of Rose and her vacant, meaningless smiles.

Her failings to produce an heir were rankling him. And he didn't find her as desirable as he had hoped. She was too sweet and too compliant. Too vague. And clearly barren.

He performed his marital duty perfunctorily, twice a week, when she lay obediently beneath him and he thought of the son he hoped he would create. Once or twice he had looked at her as she lay there and her eyes were closed, her mind obviously far away.

Then he had seen the way she looked at his younger brother. She never looked at him like that. Which made him very unhappy and rather angry.

The thoughts chewed him up inside – so far, he thought, he had stopped her attention straying to his brother. If there was another person in the house, and her attention was diverted, she would have to concentrate on something other than Jago.

His gaze drifted to another pile of paperwork in the corner of his desk: a business plan, for his interests on the Continent. Jago would be travelling to Spain and to France very soon anyway – not that he had shared that information with Jago yet.

He allowed himself a small, self-satisfied smile. It was perfect. Distract the Duchess with weeks, perhaps months of posing for a portrait and remove his greatest rival in the process.

What could go wrong?

Chapter Seven

Kit shook the strange images and thoughts away. This rock had the weirdest atmosphere, and it wasn't the first time he had come here and almost lost himself to daydreams. One that he'd had, ages ago, as he'd drifted off for a summer's afternoon nap, was knocking quietly on his memory – something about sitting on the rock while he talked about painting a portrait.

But he wasn't sure if he was painting it, or someone else was. He wasn't even sure who the girl was, but when he had seen that portrait of Rose, Duchess of Trecarrow, it had given him a jolt that may or may not have been related to that daydream.

Of course, that daydream may just simply have been related to a tale his Aunt Loveday had been telling them about the family who lived here so many years ago, and how there were some beautiful portraits around the house that had a lot of history to them. He had just been setting up his own studio in Marazion at the time and the work involved was preying on his mind more than was probably healthy.

Whatever.

He was here, now, with Merryn Burton, who was so far removed from that dark-haired beauty in the hidden portrait that he wanted to give her all his attention, and ignore any weird daydreams that threatened to demand more concern than they deserved.

So Kit and Merryn pushed through the few

overhanging branches to where the shadows had filtered through, and sat down on the rock. Kit pulled the papers he had found out of his pocket and he looked at Merryn.

'I feel a little disloyal,' he said. 'But I want to know what they say.'

'More than that – I think we have to know what they say.'

Carefully, Kit unfolded the paper, and smoothed it out in front of them. It was a letter, and as they had seen, it was definitely dated July 1884. And it was signed by Rose. The writing was spidery and untidy. Every so often, as if she had drifted off somewhere nobody could reach her before she pulled herself back, the ink changed colour slightly. It seemed as if she had started a fresh line at these points, and the gaps between each paragraph as they were laid out on the paper were unequal.

Kit scanned it with a dawning horror as he read and re-read the words in front of him ...

Dear Jago,

I know you risked so much for me, coming back from abroad after I wrote those letters and told you all my secrets. You were the only one, Jago. The only one. I can hardly believe any of it happened and often I think I am dreaming and none of it is real. Then something shifts and changes and I realise that it did happen and it was real and I can never be the Rose I was when we were young, because so many dreadful things have happened and I have done so much that is wrong.

My heart and my mind tell me that this will be the last letter I write to you or to anyone. Don't ask me how I know – I just know. It will take all of my courage to write it, and I truly don't know how much longer I have on this earth. My greatest regret is that, at some point very soon, I will be leaving you, my love.

And I don't want to Jago. I don't want to.

I think, had I married you, we would have been happy and filled Pencradoc with children. As it is, my child will never live here, and neither will I.

In another life perhaps it could have been thus that you sat by my bedside and we celebrated the birth of our child. As it is, I have the dawning fear that you will indeed be sitting by my bedside as I die.

I'm sorry. Was that unexpected? It isn't to me. To me, it is a case of when, and how he will do it. Not if. Not maybe.

He will be clever about it, I know he will.

All I can tell you – or anyone who reads this letter in the future, because that may happen, and I will be dead and gone and I will still hope that someone does read it and finds out the truth – is that Ellory will be responsible.

I don't know if I could say that he is a murderer – my murderer – because that sounds melodramatic, doesn't it? Perhaps he won't entirely mean to do it. But perhaps he will. He has always had a short temper and perhaps it would have been my fault, after all? And unlike Cathy and Heathcliff, I could never love my murderer. I love you, Jago, I always have, and I always will.

I wish our carefree days, where you and I loved each other, had lasted longer. I wish for so many things. More than anything, I wish that it had been us together at the end of my life, Jago, as lovers, as man and wife. For this is the end, I know it.

*Ellory knows Giovanni and I were lovers. He
said he'd found evidence that I had made love to
Giovanni, and the only way I think he could have
found out that I was close to Giovanni was by
reading my letters to you, Jago? It's too late now, but
I wish you had burned them, I really do. He then said
he suspected the child wasn't his, and he would have
to consider how to deal with it.*

Now what does that suggest to you, darling Jago?

*He only said that to me this evening, so I am
writing this to you so very quickly in the hope that you
can help me, that you can get us away from Pencradoc
as I asked you to, so many weeks ago when you were
still away from me. But now you are here, and I am
here, and I hope, I so very much hope, that you will
take me away from here as I wanted. I need your help,
Jago, I truly do. What will become of me otherwise?*

*And, if I am too late and I should die soon, then
you know the truth. You know what happened.
Whatever happens to me, know that I could not do it
to myself, no matter how it appears.*

You see, I could never leave you, Jago.

*I love you Jago. You're the only one I ever loved.
Hold me in your heart, I pray, as I was when we were
children and all was innocent – not as I am now. Not
what I have become.*

Yours, always,
Rose, Duchess of Trecarrow
July, 1884.

Merryn stared at the letter, unable to articulate what
emotions it inspired in her, but she could only guess that
Kit felt the same.

He had, after all, gone very quiet next to her, and he seemed to be miles away, lost in thoughts she couldn't read.

1886

The memories played out, unstoppable. It was 1884 now: July, to be precise.

He had jumped out of the coach almost as soon as the carriage pulled up at the house. The letters she had written to him while he was away were in his luggage, and the increasing urgency and fear in them, plus the secrets she had told him had spurred on his decision to return. He had told nobody his plans, and his head had been full of her confessions for the entire journey. He didn't know how he had made it back with his sanity intact.

Tired and travel-stained as he was, he wasn't going to wait until his belongings were safely stashed and unpacked. He was going to search for her now.

He had tried to put her desperate declarations out of his head, but the fact she had even written them gnawed at a small part of his mind that he didn't want to visit. The word "madness" clawed at that part of his mind, and he shook it away again. What on earth had happened to her over the time he had been away?

'Rose?' He called her name as he ran across the gardens, towards her new Gothic rose garden in the Wilderness garden she had been telling him about. He wasn't wrong. As he pushed through some overhanging branches, he saw her sitting on the rock by the waterfall, her knees drawn up in front of her, the stem of a rose in her hands as she tore the petals off frantically, adding them to a further pile of naked stems and shredded rose petals beside her.

'Rose!' He called again, and she turned.

'Jago! You came. Oh you came ...' She scrambled to her feet, tossing the stem away, scattering stray rose petals from her skirt and ran towards him, embracing him. 'Now we can be together, and you won't leave me any more, will you? I'll get my things – I'm already packed, ready for you coming.' She pressed into him, trying to find his lips with hers, and he felt himself drawing back. This wasn't what he had come back for, not at all.

'Jago? What's wrong?' She stopped as his arms came around her and he ducked away from her kiss, instead receiving it on his cheek. 'Didn't you come back for me? Jago – you have to take me away from here, you have to. I can't stay. I love you. It's *you*. Not Ellory, not Giovanni, it's *you*. Tell me you feel the same! Tell me that's why you came back?'

'Rose, sweetest Rose. I can't tell you that. You know I can't. We've talked about this ...'

'But you love me, don't you? You do love me?'

'I love you as a sister. As a very lovely, very special sister. But we were children Rose, when we said all those things. I can't – I *don't* – love you like that.'

'But you came back for me?' She dropped her arms by her sides, confused. 'You came back.'

'I came back, because you told me there was something dreadfully wrong. Your letter scared me, Rose. It was ...'

He didn't want to say irrational or terrifying, but it was both of those things. Instead, he just let the sentence hang, and she didn't respond. He wondered if she'd even heard. Because now, she was prowling around, wringing her hands, walking to the edge of the rock, pacing along the side of it, staring at the water, then pacing again.

'Well yes. Yes, there *is* something wrong. I'm with child, Jago, and quite frankly, I'm terrified.'

'Rose! I thought there was something wrong! I thought ...' He didn't know what he thought. He was utterly confused, thrown by the news and yes, angry. She'd brought him back for *this*? Demanded he returned because she was pregnant? He stepped away from her, almost instinctively. Really? There had to be more to it, more to the desperate pleas in her letter... She was *pregnant*? He couldn't see that it was anything but a cause for celebration. It was what Ellory had been striving for, and what she had yearned for as well.

Suddenly, she giggled and ran over to him, her hands outstretched again. 'Isn't that just the worst luck, Jago? The absolute worst luck? That I'm pregnant?'

He stared at her, not comprehending what she meant. 'What are you trying to say, Rose?' he asked carefully. 'Is there a reason why it *should* be bad luck?'

'No. No not at all.' She stared at him and he didn't recognise the eyes that looked out of her face. They were blank, shuttered – not the eyes of the girl he had once thought he loved. 'It's Ellory's. That's the truth. It has to be. Doesn't it?'

'Rose ...'

'*Doesn't it*?' she screamed at him, her fists suddenly clenched, red spots high on her cheeks. 'Doesn't it. Because it's *not yours*. And I wish it was. I truly do. Jago – are you sure you won't take me away with you? Are you sure we can't be together? And raise it as your baby? We could, you know. We could do that.' Her hands were now, unconsciously, it seemed, splayed out on her stomach.

Jago's temper evaporated as he slowly began to understand what she was saying.

Oh, Rose ... your lover was de Amato, was it not? The child, therefore ...

He reached out and gently clasped her hands in his own. Raising them to his lips, he kissed them and spoke to her slowly, his own heart thumping in fear as the pieces of the puzzle clicked together. 'We can't. You know that. That baby is the heir to Pencradoc. It's Ellory's child. It *is* his child. Your *husband's* child. But I will promise you this, Rose. I won't go away again. I'll stay and look after you and protect you as much as I can.' Protect her? She seemed, today, no more than a child herself. It wasn't going to be an easy pregnancy, for anyone, he thought. 'It'll be very strange for you, I completely understand that.' He was talking to her in a low voice, enunciating each word carefully as her eyes flitted hither and thither; terrified, guilty, occasionally fixing on him in desperation and hope before they slipped away again. 'A first baby is wonderful, but such a frightening time for the mother and for those who care for her.' He was cautious enough to say "care for" her. Not "love" her. He didn't want to mislead her at all. There was too much of a mess already.

'Thank you Jago.' It was astonishing; she was suddenly calm again. She nodded, assessing his last words. 'Yes. I think – you know I really do think – that I will need your protection. Once Ellory finds out. Because for now, it is our little secret.'

Jago's skin had crawled inexplicably again: *Once Ellory finds out. Our little secret.*

It did not bear thinking about.

Chapter Eight

Present Day

'Kit?' Merryn's voice must have brought him back to the rock and the waterfall and the twenty-first century from wherever he'd gone. 'What do you make of all that then?'

Kit just shook his head. 'There were so many rumours about Rose's death, that in one way, I'm not surprised. Poor woman.'

'Did they – did they think she was mad?' She had no idea where that had sprung from. But a voice seemed to be whispering words of a long-forgotten conversation: *They say she was found at the folly, you know. The tower. But I don't know who found her. They also said they suspected she had done it herself, as she was quite mad at the end, apparently ...*

'Mad?' Kit stared at her. 'I suppose that's one way of viewing it. She had ... changed ... quite a bit over the time she was married.' He frowned and looked out over the waterfall. A chilly little breeze whipped up from the water, lifting Merryn's hair gently and she shivered. 'A little harsh for her to go down in history as mad though, I think.' His eyes seemed to flash with suppressed anger. 'We should get back to work. Do you need me to walk you back to the house or can you find your own way?'

'Oh.' The sea-change in him was astonishing. He had, it seemed, just closed down, right in the middle of their conversation. Well. What did she expect? She'd just accused one of his relatives of being mad. And he didn't owe her anything, let alone a cosy chat by a waterfall on a work day. 'Yes.' She cleared her throat and stood up. 'I can find my own way, thanks. I had better get back and start my inventory properly.'

'I agree. Where are you staying tonight? It's going to take more than a day or two to sort the artwork out, I would imagine.' Kit stood up and brushed little bits of soil and leaves off his trousers. His fingers were stained with paint, though, she noticed. He was definitely an artist.

'I've got a room in The White Lady, the pub in the village. It'll be fine. I've stayed in a lot worse places, I guess.' The conversation felt too polite and too forced. It was rather uncomfortable, actually.

'Cool. Well, I'll maybe see you before you leave today.' Kit held up the letter. 'Is it okay if I keep this?'

'It's not mine. It was found in your family portrait. It's yours to do with as you wish. I won't tell your brother though.' She attempted a smile through the odd see-saw of emotions she was experiencing. She felt miffed. She really did feel miffed.

'Best not.' He smiled at her then, a flash of the man she'd felt – yes – a little attracted to earlier.

Oh hell. Who was she kidding? She still felt attracted to him – even though he was quite possibly a moody so-and-so.

'See you later, then—' He stopped abruptly and nodded. 'Bye for now.'

'Bye for now. Kit.' She nodded, briefly, then stalked off towards the house. Back to Pencradoc. And back, she hoped, to some more excitement artwise.

Because she was putting blokes on the back-burner as from now. She really bloody was. She'd thought Josh was bad enough, but at least she had found out where she stood with him; and that had turned out to be behind his ex-wife in the desirability stakes. Kit had seemed ... different. There had been a connection there, definitely. And now it had apparently gone, and she was being dismissed.

Or at least that was what it felt like.

Kit stared after Merryn, watching her retreating back as she stomped off. *Alys*. He'd been going to call her Alys. Where the hell had that come from?

'Goodbye ... Alys.' He whispered it. He had to, he had to say it.

Her name was drowned out by the rush of the water splashing over the rocks far below him.

If he'd looked more closely at where he stood, he would perhaps have seen a pile of rose petals lying on the rocks by his feet.

July, 1884

Jago remembered how he had found her in the tower.

He found her on the very day that he read her final letter.

He found her at the bottom of the stairs, with a gash in her head, unconscious. She lay, broken, in a pool of blood, and he gathered her up in his arms and ran back to the house with her.

It was a memory that would haunt him forever – and beyond.

Within three days, Rose, Duchess of Trecarrow would be dead: her last letter to him, where she spelled out her fears about Ellory and what he might do to her had been written in the dead of night and pushed beneath his bedroom door under cover of darkness. It had been a sad little prophecy, hand-delivered to him, hours before it happened.

But he hadn't found it. It had been placed on his dressing table at dawn by a well-meaning maid who crept in to make up the fire. By the time he saw it, it was too late.

He had read the letter with a growing sense of confusion and horror, and hadn't been able to find her, despite searching for her. Then, he had gone to the tower ...

If Rose's pathetic little letter wasn't the product of a deluded mind, Ellory had acted extraordinarily quickly. His half-brother was many things, but was he really capable of murder? He was cruel and selfish, certainly. And seemingly violent – Rose had implied as much to Jago in the past. But murder was pre-meditated, surely. Could Ellory be heartless enough to coolly plan his wife's death? Or was that Rose's fantasy life taking over her poor, broken mind?

He thought that he would never be able to forgive himself if it were true.

If only he had read it earlier. If *only*...

He had kept that letter separate from the others, in his breast pocket, close to his heart while he wondered what to do about it; but the others were no longer in his possession. He had his suspicions over that situation as well. He guessed that was another thing he would never find the answer to.

The sad fact was that he had failed her. If he had only seen it earlier, if he could have acted on her fears ... if only.

*

Jago spent the two days after Rose's death closeted in her rooms, staring at her portrait, drinking whisky like it was water.

On the third day, he finally cracked. '*Was it you?*' The ferocity of his voice broke the silence in the study as he clashed the doors open and stormed up to the desk. 'Was it *you*? Tell me! Be a man and *tell me.*'

He burst into the room, startling his brother into dropping a pen and blotting the letter he was writing. Two spots of colour appeared on Ellory's cheeks – the result of a filthy temper, Jago knew, not the result of anything else. Certainly not the result of grief or mourning. The man hadn't shed a tear. He had accepted the news calmly. Too calmly. 'Did you do it?'

'It occurs to me once again, that I did not give you permission to leave our Spanish interests and meddle in anything to do with affairs at home.' Ellory's voice was cold and bitter. 'Tell me again why you defied my orders? Why you came back here? I understand the woman was panicking ridiculously over her impending motherhood. Why did *you* feel this overwhelming need to defend someone who was clearly mad and blame an innocent party?'

'One of us had to be concerned for her welfare. She was unwell, could you not see it? Could you not help and protect her as you should have done out of duty? As you should have done as her *husband*?'

'You should return to Madrid. There is nothing to hold you here now. What happens at Pencradoc is not your concern, it— '

There was a crash as Jago launched himself across the desk at his brother and grabbed him by the collar. 'You tell me how you did it. You admit it, or I will beat it out

79

of you, I swear. There will be bloodshed. Long overdue bloodshed.'

'Pencradoc and the Duchess are not your concern! She ceased to be your concern when she married me.' Ellory was grappling at his brother's hands, trying to loosen them. 'Her suicide is none of your concern. All you can do is what I am going to do – say it was an accident. Try to protect her that way.'

'Protect her? You did not protect her when she was living. Rather, you hide the truth. I know what you did.' Disgusted, Jago threw him aside like a rag doll, and Ellory's chair overturned as he tried to stop himself following it onto the floor.

'You had no rights to her, despite your blatant interest in her and hers in you. Why do you think I sent you away? She was *my* wife.'

'And she was my sister-in-law. You had no right to treat her so appallingly. She was carrying your child, for God's sake! She needed help.'

'Who is to say it was my child? *Who*? She was always looking at you, always seeking you out. Who else do you think she was seeking out? Because you won't have been the first and you won't have been the last. I know she was with that fool of an artist. Anyone could have seen the way she acted with him. The smiles. The laughter. The … *intimacy* of that damn portrait!'

'She was only seeking me out because you did not have time for her! I showed interest in her as a person, as Rose Pencradoc. You only wanted an image of the perfect Duchess and that fool of artist, as you call him, gave you that. I gave her time, I talked to her. I did not simply try to impregnate her from the day I wed her.'

'How dare you. How dare you speak to me like that. That child, that bastard she carried—'

'Was yours. How many times do I have to tell you?' Jago laughed, mirthlessly. 'I wasn't here, was I?'

'No. But she had other opportunities. She *made* opportunities for herself. And anyway.' He picked up the chair and set it down on the floor with an angry crash. 'The Duchess is dead; dead by her own mad, unbalanced hand. I wasn't here. I could not have done it.'

'She did *not* kill herself. She did *not*.' Jago grabbed another chair and smashed it off the floor. 'If I ever find enough proof, you will hang for it, Duke or no Duke. And I will not be responsible for my actions. You were away on business. You left that morning. You covered your tracks well, created a decent alibi. But how long, I wonder, did she lie there before I found her? *How long?* And—' He paused, glaring at Ellory. May God forgive him, but he would lie for her, he would tell the Duke a lie: 'Don't forget that she lived. And she lived long enough to speak to me.'

With that, he had turned on his heel and stormed out of the study.

Chapter Nine

Merryn found her way back to the house with no problem at all – exactly as she had told Kit. It was as if her feet knew exactly where to go, as if each step had been part of her life for as long as she remembered. She determinedly did not think of Kit and his smiling eyes, or that weird sort of brush-off she was pretty certain she'd just experienced.

Just at the curve in the pathway, she looked up and saw the house standing over everything, all towers and windows and battlements. She was willing to bet there was a gargoyle or two there as well, somewhere high up.

Merryn shivered. Yes, that place could definitely be part of a nightmare. It just needed some creepy gravestones in the grounds, or a mausoleum or two and, on a stormy night you'd run for your life and never look back—

He would still catch you.

The voice came out of nowhere, whispered into Merryn's ear in the most sinister of fashions.

Merryn yelped and ran as fast as she could towards the house. Whether that was something unworldly or her imagination playing tricks, she wasn't going to hang around to find out.

Once she was back at Pencradoc and inside the entrance hall she felt a little more under control, and was ready to pass those strange words off as her imagination.

'Merryn! Have you found anything else exciting? A de Amato was a pretty good start.' Coren peeked his head around the corner, clutching a cup of coffee. His smile was wide and welcoming and for a moment, Merryn was thrown. It was like he was a different person to the unpleasant man who had been so brittle in front of Rose's portrait. She thought, ironically, that Kit and Coren had apparently swapped attitudes.

'I've just boiled the kettle. Do you want one?'

Coren raised the cup and Merryn shook her head. 'No thanks. I'm going to head back in there.' She pointed randomly at a doorway which she guessed would lead into the east wing.

'Sure.' Coren shrugged, good-naturedly. 'Wherever suits you.' He glanced up at the portrait of Ellory. 'You know, of all the many wonderful pieces of art my Aunt Loveday had, this one is the one that bothers me the most. He just looks ... soulless. Wouldn't you say?'

It was such a strange echo of the conversation she'd just had with Kit that Merryn could only nod in response.

'Okay.' Coren didn't seem to think it odd that she hadn't answered him. 'I'll let you get on. I'm just in the kitchen if you need anything. There's a pretty big collection of crockery. I'm going to see if I can make any sets up. Wish me luck. I'm hoping for at least some genuine Minton or a willow-pattern thing.' He grinned and turned away, the door shutting gently behind him.

Merryn stared after him, conscious of the Duke of Trecarrow's eyes burning into her, which of course was absolutely crazy.

She shuddered again and hurried towards the door she had indicated. Whatever was behind that door had to be better than spending any more time alone in the hallway with Ellory Pencradoc.

Merryn spent a productive few hours in the east wing, and by the end of it, she had a decent list of artwork and some very saleable pieces. It was an enormous job, cataloguing everything, but she was enjoying what she had discovered so far. She checked her watch and thought that she'd made a decent start, despite the fact she realised it would be a bigger job than Heptinstall Studios had originally anticipated.

That was quite a good thing though, and she couldn't help imagine the extent of Jeremy's exuberance, had he been the one to see that Teague. Merryn suppressed a smile, and gathered her notes together. It was maybe a little Luddite of her, but she preferred to work with a pencil and notebook, then log it all onto a computer when she had quite a few things to transfer across. It was just easier.

Kit hadn't appeared back at the house yet, which was also quite a good thing, perhaps, and so she went in search of Coren to tell him she was packing up and leaving for the day. He was sitting at the big kitchen table with piles of plates and bowls around him looking pretty organised, it had to be said.

'Hey. I'm heading off now. I'll be back tomorrow morning.' She smiled and Coren smiled back.

'No worries. Found any lost Teagues yet?'

'No such luck! And why has your family got such a liking for bowls of fruit?' She pulled a face. 'I've found so many iterations of bowls of fruit, I don't think I want to see an apple for quite some time.'

Coren pulled a face. 'I feel the same about side-plates.

Have you seen Kit on your travels? He's disappeared and I needed to see him about something.'

Merryn shook her head, hoping her ready blushes wouldn't give her away. 'Not since we left you with the de Amato earlier.'

Coren nodded, seemingly oblivious to the way he had behaved in front of that de Amato. 'He'll turn up. See you tomorrow then. And thanks again. Oh, where are you staying? Not too far I hope.'

'Just in the village. So I'll be in bright and early tomorrow.'

'Maybe we'll get a Teague then?'

'Maybe.'

Merryn smiled as she left. She didn't think the chances of that were very high, if she was honest. From what she understood, Ruan Teague's work had been well-catalogued over the years.

But, she could dream.

Later that evening, Kit pulled up outside The White Lady and sat in the car for a few minutes, staring at the sign. Like a lot of these old inns, the sign was hanging creakily from a chain, moving back and forth with the breeze. It was modern, however. There was nothing vintage about that sign at all.

The picture on it depicted the head and shoulders of a young woman, posed primly and not very imaginatively as if she was in an eighteenth-century portrait. She had dark hair and a simpering expression on her face. She was also quite chinless, in the style of those formal portraits. Kit didn't like the picture very much at all, and was conscious that he was pulling a face.

Rose Pencradoc – for that was who this poor,

unfortunate caricature of a lady was supposed to be – had definitely been much more attractive.

If he'd had the talent to paint her, he would have made a better job of it ...

He blinked and dragged his gaze away from the depiction. He, Kit, was a damn good artist. He knew that, so what the hell was he thinking that for? He shook his head. He'd spent too long in Pencradoc, too long looking for pictures that didn't exist and too long thinking about her ...

And there he was again, drifting off into some weird daydream. He hadn't thought of anyone much except Merryn Burton all afternoon. Regardless, sitting here glowering at the pub sign wasn't going to get him very far.

When she had left him to go back to Pencradoc after they read the letter, he had walked to the edge of the waterfall and looked over into it. A flicker caught his eye from up above, and he could have sworn he saw the vague shape of a woman up there, and he wondered briefly why Merryn had gone up that way – until part of his consciousness had registered that the figure he saw had dark hair, yet again, which was still a million miles away from Merryn's blonde.

He hadn't lingered for very long after that. And it seemed that the further away from the waterfall and the rose garden he got, the more the uneasy feeling he had experienced abated until he got to the point where he felt thoroughly ridiculous and more than a little guilty at brushing Merryn off so abruptly. But it had been the letter, the letter and the half-memories it seemed to stir within him that had made him shut her down and hide behind some barriers he didn't even know he possessed.

Ridiculous.

So here he was, ready to grovel and apologise and beg her forgiveness. It would be bloody awkward if they were to keep bumping into one another over the next couple of weeks or however long it would take, and to be ignoring each other.

Despite that, though, he still hated that inn-sign.

He glared at it as he got out of the car and walked into the pub. It was a typical country pub in a small village: log fires, snacks on the bar and a selection of unusual ales and local cider lined up behind the bartender. He scanned the room quickly and couldn't see Merryn anywhere – although to be honest, had he really expected her to be sitting in the middle of the locals, holding court and roistering with a pint of ale? Not Merryn. Not with her London gloss and professional manner.

Yet her name didn't reflect the fact that she was from London. It was as Cornish as his was. Strange. He should ask her about that one. If she was speaking to him, of course.

'Can I help, sir?' The bartender smiled at him and Kit nodded.

'Oh – yes. Please. I'm looking for Merryn Burton. She's working with us up at Pencradoc and staying here. Have you seen her? Fair hair, about so high...' He held his hand out at about shoulder height, then saw the bartender's face close up.

'I'm sorry, sir, but I'm not at liberty to say if a lady of that name is here or not. You could be a spousal stalker, or someone she doesn't want to see. I'm sure you'll understand, sir.'

Of course. How stupid he was. This may only be a small village, but people would still put security – and legality, he conceded – over telling a stranger where someone was; especially if that someone had said not to tell someone else where she was. He felt his cheeks grow hot with embarrassment. Maybe she had said nothing of the sort, the non-paranoid part of him said, but regardless, he wasn't going to get anything else from this gentleman.

'Fair enough. I understand. Look, I'm sorry to have bothered you. I'll catch her tomorrow. I—'

'Catch who tomorrow?'

'Merryn!' Kit spun around and saw her there, a laptop bag slung over her shoulder. 'Hey! You. I was going to catch *you* tomorrow. Sorry, I came out here to find you and apologise for earlier, and then I don't think I thought any further.' He pulled a face and hoped he looked apologetic enough. 'Sorry.'

Merryn stared at him for a moment, then shrugged. 'It's fine. I called your relative mad. You took umbrage. It happened.'

'It wasn't exactly like that.' Kit walked towards her. 'But I can't talk about it here.' He glanced over his shoulder. The bartender had suddenly found a stubborn spot of dirt on the bar and was rubbing at it, very thoroughly, very close to them. Kit felt his lips twitch into a smile. 'Can I tempt you into a little walk? In the village. Away from here?'

Merryn glanced at the bartender and finally smiled back. 'Sounds good. I'll just pop my laptop in my room first. I'll find you in the bar, shall I?'

'No. You can find me outside. I'll be by the car.'

This time Merryn's lips were twitching into a wider smile. 'See you there.'

Kit grinned as she headed through a door marked

'Residential Guests Only', then turned back and headed out of the front door.

He was leaning against the car, staring up at the inn sign when she came out. The evening was warm and he had just a T-shirt on. A different T-shirt to before, so he must have been back to Pencradoc and sneaked past her somehow. Either that or his home wasn't very far away.

'I hate this sign,' he said, by way of a greeting. He nodded up at it. 'There's something so very *off* about her.'

'The White Lady?' Merryn followed his gaze. 'You should know who she's supposed to be. It's named after Rose.'

'I know! It's sacrilege, really it is. That woman is *not* Rose. God, she's nothing like her. It's an awful, awful picture. I've never really studied it before. But seriously – look at it!'

'You've really taken against it, haven't you?' Merryn tried to hide a smile and failed. 'I suppose now we've seen the real thing—'

'Shhhh!' Kit grabbed her arm and his eyes sparkled mischievously. Merryn felt her own eyes widening. God. He really was gorgeous close up, away from the shadow of Pencradoc and whatever was lurking inside him up there. 'We can't tell them we've seen the real thing. We have to keep that one quiet a little longer. What if there's an unscrupulous art dealer around?'

'Or an unscrupulous artist who berates every depiction of the Sainted Rose that's not true to life.'

'Very true. There's definitely one of those here. God. That picture is *so* appalling. Come on. Let's get as far away from it as possible. I'm insulted on Jago's behalf.'

'On Jago's behalf?' Merryn looked at him curiously as they began walking towards a little lane that apparently led to a church, according to a sign that pointed that way.

'Did I say Jago's behalf?' He blinked and shook his head. 'I suppose I am. Yes. He was obviously very special to her, judging by that letter.'

'But was she as special to him? I'm not sure, you know. I do apologise for calling her mad. I'm wondering if deluded would be better.' She pulled a face. 'No. Actually that sounds worse.'

'Misguided? Confused?'

'That's better.' Merryn nodded. 'Yes. There was something wrong with the way she interpreted things, perhaps.' She sighed. 'Poor Rose.'

'Poor Rose indeed. Going down in history as that woman on the inn-sign. God, she's even from the wrong bloody era!'

'Of course she is! Yes, you're right. Dear me.' Merryn shook her head. 'I prefer the de Amato, don't you?'

'Absolutely. That was more like her, I think.' Kit stared off into the distance as they walked, a slight furrow on his brow. 'So you discovered that the pub is named after her, and I can't add to your local knowledge. That's a pity.'

'I asked the bartender. He was happy to tell me.' She grinned, seeing Kit roll his eyes heavenwards. 'Don't look like that. He was protecting me by not giving away my location.'

'I suppose he was.' He flicked another mischievous glance at her and she laughed. 'I suppose in the olden days one of the Pencradoc heirs would have had the whole village doing exactly as he said. How times have changed.'

'And for the better, I think.'

'Very true. Anyway, what else did he tell you? I need to know he's got his facts right.'

'He said Rose is supposed to haunt the gardens of Pencradoc, drifting around in a white dress and weeping for her lost love. Sometimes she's even seen as far down as the church. Look – this one here. It's where she's buried apparently, in the family vault. He didn't say, however, who her lost love was.'

'The bartender is right, more's the pity. I wonder who her lost love was? Interesting.'

'Well Ellory doesn't look very loveable at all.' She shuddered. 'There's just something about that painting in the hallway I dislike.'

'I understand completely. Hey. Shall we have a look inside the church? The bartender hasn't done that with you, I bet.'

The door was open, with a rack of leaflets just visible inside the building. The church was clearly happy to welcome visitors.

'He hasn't. So why not? I've spent the last hour or so in the local Costa, so it'll be quite nice to explore somewhere a little more traditional. Mind you, I did get a *lot* of work done in there. Yay for large Americanos.'

'Yay for caffeine? That, I can understand.' Kit gestured for her to walk in first. 'You couldn't be persuaded to do some work in the pub then?'

'No. I'm not programmed to work in pubs. Pubs are for relaxing in. I'm much happier working in coffee shops. And there's usually free WiFi.'

'Not to be sniffed at. There – that's the vault.'

They were standing in the nave now, confronted by a rather plain marble monument, surrounded by what could be likened to a wrought iron fence, gold-coloured arrowheads atop of each bar. Another faded red rose lay on the tomb, the sight of which did give Merryn a little, inexplicable shiver down her spine. Someone was happily laying roses around, wherever she went today; and she had a feeling it wasn't Kit or Coren.

There were some brass plaques dotted around, screwed onto the wall behind it, and Merryn was disappointed that there wasn't a figurine carved on the top of the vault. She had expected, somehow, that a Duchess of Pencradoc – and a Duke, as well, because surely Ellory was in here too – would have something a bit more exciting than what was in front of her.

'Oh. That's a let-down,' she said, frowning.

'It is, but if it had, for example, a carving of Rose on it, then that picture at The White Lady would have at least had a reference point.'

'You *really* dislike that don't you?'

'I really do.' Kit walked up to the monument and held onto the bars. He stared in at the tomb. 'It's perfectly flat on the top. I wonder if that was the intention, originally, to have a figure on it?'

'It's very sad. So the only image of Rose we have after all is the de Amato. And that was hidden away pretty well. It's like she's been erased from Pencradoc. You've got to feel sorry for the woman.'

'I do.' Kit was quiet, looking at the tomb. Then he grabbed the bars tighter, and, straightening his arms, pushed himself away quite roughly. Still staring at the monument, he folded his arms and a strange expression flitted across his face. 'I absolutely do.'

July, 1884

The workmen had done a good job. The priest hole had always bothered him; it had always seemed a waste of good space. If a person was contravening the authorities and the law, then they deserved a suitable punishment.

'So you are hiding things again. You are hiding her. What are you trying to hide, brother?' Jago had appeared next to him, as he, Ellory, watched the men put the portrait exactly in the centre of the wall. Jago's voice was cold, dangerous even, and he smelled of alcohol.

Ellory curled his lip in distaste. He knew his younger brother would be unkempt and unshaven. He had been since she had died. When he wasn't blaming Ellory, he blamed himself, apparently, for not reaching her sooner. The ridiculously sentimental idiot.

It would still have happened.

'It is no business of yours what I do in my house.' He stared at the painting and nodded, dismissing the workmen. He did not watch them leave. He did not take his attention away from the painting for one moment.

'I will ask you again. Why hide her away?' Jago came to stand between Ellory and the painting his hands curled into fists. As if he would strike him! Him – Ellory Pencradoc – The Duke of Trecarrow!

Ellory smiled. 'And I will tell you again. It is no business of yours.'

'Do you have a guilty conscience, brother?' Jago's voice was even more dangerous, and Ellory raised an eyebrow. This time, he did glance at him. The younger man's face was stone. And he had been right. He was very unkempt.

'I have no conscience, guilty or otherwise. She was my

Duchess. My wife. *My* wife. I shall remember her as I see fit. I see fit to put her in here. Away from Society. Away from prying eyes. She was mad. It's not something I want the world to remember.'

'If she was mad, you were the one that made her that way.'

'*If* she was mad? You speak it as if it was ever in question.'

Jago didn't comment on that, he noticed. Instead, he spoke thus: 'The truth will be told. I won't rest until it is.'

'The truth has been told. The truth is, it is tragic, but she is dead. This was my Duchess. She will smile no more, for any man, except me. That is how I shall remember her. I shall remember her as she truly was. Now. Please leave me to my grieving. I may be some time.'

'You have no heart. No soul. You will not grieve for her. You cannot.'

'Perhaps not. But it is simply more polite than telling you to go to hell and leave me in peace. But I find I am forced to do that. Leave me! Now!' Finally, he lost his temper and bellowed at Jago.

For a moment, they glared at each other, until Jago lashed out and punched the wall to the side of the portrait. 'Oh, I am leaving, Ellory. I am to go to India. I shall not return unless I have to. Goodbye, brother. As you told me, there is nothing to keep me here now. Nothing at all. And if I stay at Pencradoc, and breathe the same air as you do for any longer than I have to, as I told you, I shall not be responsible for my actions. It is safer for us both if I leave properly.'

Then he stormed out of the room, and slammed the door of the Duchess's quarters behind him.

Ellory made a mental note to ban all visitors to this room. If they wanted to pay their respects, they could do so at her grave.

If, that is, there was anyone who truly grieved for the woman – except, of course, for his delusional brother.

Good riddance.

To them both.

Chapter Ten

Present Day

Kit seemed to be lost a million miles away, and Merryn touched his shoulder gently. 'Are you okay? It's been quite a day, hasn't it?'

'You could say that.' He turned to face her and attempted a smile. 'This used to be on Pencradoc land, you know. This church. That's why Aunt Loveday said some of the family tombs were here. We didn't have our own church, despite the priest's hole. Religion was very much what was in fashion at the time.'

'Lots of big houses did that. I'm not surprised, really. They probably swapped sides during the Civil War as well.'

'Yeah, the Pencradocs have never really been faithful to anyone but themselves. I kind of hope that my ancestry leads back to Ruan Teague. I know – it's all wishful thinking, but come on – you've seen his portrait of her. What does that tell you? I don't want to have any of those errant Pencradoc genes in my system, thank you very much.'

'Those errant genes kept the family going, though.' Merryn smiled up at him. 'You can't argue with that.'

He grinned back. 'I guess not. Let's see what else there is in here. I doubt we'll find anything relating to anybody else directly linked to them. There's a plaque on the wall relating to a nursemaid that looked after Jago and Ellory's mother, I know that. Aunt Loveday told us that one as well. She kept the old lady on, to look after the boys, and even beyond that; when the boys were really far too old for nursemaids. But she swore she couldn't let the lady leave and try to fend for herself. Jago made sure she had a plaque – Ellory didn't bother, but Jago wanted to have a memorial for her. Look – there it is.' He nodded towards the wall, and sure enough, there was a memorial to *Miss Adeline Spencer, Faithful Nurse and Companion.*

Merryn smiled, thinking it was very sweet. 'It's not a very Cornish name is it?' she commented.

'No – Adeline came with Jago's mother from Bath. I bet she had a lovely retirement. But on the other hand, your name is quite Cornish and you're not from around here are you?'

He raised an eyebrow mock-accusingly and Merryn laughed. 'No. But my family have a long history of giving their children those sorts of names. My sister is called Tegan. I think generations ago we must have had a branch down here.'

'Then I can't understand why they left.' He shook his head sadly. 'There have been other Duchesses from up north – the Home Counties way, I think, the same as Zennor. Hey! Her family must have felt the same as yours. Fancy that.'

'Oh! Yes!' Merryn laughed. 'Zennor is a wonderful name. And now I've seen her, I think she suits it so well. And the home counties might be north to you, but it's still relatively south, if you think of a map of England.'

'Devon is north. Anywhere beyond Launceston is north.' He scowled, teasing her.

'You need to get out more!' She shook her head helplessly. 'Honestly, these southerners.'

'Hmm. Well, Jago liked the south. He isn't buried

here, in this church. I know that for sure. There was another house further south, just about twenty minutes away from my studio. He preferred that one.'

'Your studio?' Merryn was intrigued. 'So you have a proper studio – like an art studio?'

Kit nodded. 'Yes. It's even *further* south. I'd take you there if I thought you could handle it.'

'Anything relating to art and I will make an effort to handle it. Whereabouts are you based?'

Kit sat down on one of the pews, and stretched his legs out. 'I've got a gallery and studio in Marazion.' His eyes took on a soft, faraway look. 'I can see St Michael's Mount from the first-floor window. It's the best view ever.'

Merryn sat down on the opposite side of the aisle. The church was beautifully quiet, a little haven from the excitement of the day.

She watched some candles flickering and inhaled the comforting scent of wax and polish and old wood. 'I've never been there. It's a bit – *south*. You know.' She flicked a glance upwards and smiled to see him smiling at her comment, although he hadn't taken his eyes away from the altar in front of them.

'We should go. The house Jago had built down there, Wheal Mount, didn't stay within the family. It got taken over by the military in the war and it's been converted into an arts centre now. That's the sort of thing Coren has in mind for Pencradoc. There's no way either of us could afford to keep it on, and I said no way would I sign anything over to make it into a hotel. But, like I told you when you first came here, I can handle an arts centre. That way, I can stay involved with it where I can. Teach. That sort of thing.'

'I think with having the Teague link, it would do well.

And now we found a de Amato there – wow. Hey, that tower folly could be a tea room and exhibition centre, and the gardens could be opened to the public.'

Kit cast a sidelong glance at her, amused. 'We should employ you. You could do the marketing for us. Scout out talent for the exhibition.'

'It's a bit far from London though. And Heptinstall Studios.' She stood up, oddly deflated. It was a nice thought, actually. How lovely to be involved with a project like that! But, back to the job in hand. 'And you say Jago is down there? In a family vault, somewhere near his other home.'

'Yes. He didn't have any sons, which I suppose I should be grateful for, or Coren and I wouldn't be in this position now.' He stood up. 'Can I tempt you into a drink or not? I know you'll have had a long day, so I understand if you say no.'

Merryn wrestled with her better judgement for a moment or two. Her better judgement won, annoyingly. 'Actually, I think I'll pass, if that's okay. You're right – this morning I was in my flat in London, and now I'm in a church in a village near Bodmin Moor. In between times, I've discovered a de Amato and seen a Teague, and my mind is boggled with the potential of finding some more. And then I hammered away at a laptop and did some work before I gave myself a little bit of time off. I actually think I need to sleep.'

Kit laughed. 'I'm sorry. When you put it like that, I've dragged you out tonight and I shouldn't have done.'

'Oh no, you should have done, you really should have done. You were a bit grumpy and now you're not – now I know you're not *really* grumpy.'

'Not all the time, anyway. Come on, I'll walk you

back. I'll close my eyes when we approach that hideous inn sign.'

'Thanks. Before we go though, I just want to do something. I want to light a candle for Rose. And, I think, for Miss Adeline Spencer.'

'I think they'd appreciate that,' Kit said with a smile.

1886

Those thoughts of his last days at Pencradoc had been haunting Jago when Alys had walked in to the tower room in the dawn-light. He had known it was her; known if he had been left alone with his thoughts any longer, he would have descended into that dark place where, once upon a time, he had thought it would be impossible to ever climb out.

India had made him think beyond that. He had understood that what he felt for Rose in the end was plain and simple guilt. He had promised to protect her, promised to look after her; keep her safe from some unspecified demon. Sometimes, he wondered if the demon was indeed Ellory, or if it had, in fact, been something within Rose herself. He didn't suppose he would ever know. He only knew he had failed. He would always wonder if he could have stopped it, had he read her letter sooner.

He also knew that Rose had carried a huge amount of guilt with her to the grave, and only she knew if it was entirely justified or not.

He feared, however, that she had lost her innocence and her reasoning along the way. They all had, he supposed, in different ways.

*

The more Alys thought about it, the more annoyed she was. She was a little annoyed with Jago, but more annoyed at herself – why on earth had she meekly allowed herself to be taken away from that tower? They'd been having what she thought was a perfectly acceptable conversation, and then a shutter had come down in his eyes and he had led her away. Very politely, it had to be said; but he had definitely led her away. And it wasn't as if she was a child.

Rather, she was the cousin of the Duchess of Trecarrow, and he was – he was – well. He was her cousin-in-law? Wasn't he? Perhaps.

She wasn't sure of the relationship. But whatever he was to her, he was not her father, and he had no right to treat her as a child.

She was still bristling when she found Zennor in the drawing room with Mr Teague, the artist, and it brought her up short.

'Oh! I *am* sorry. I do apologise. I wasn't aware we were expecting guests today.' She smiled at Mr Teague, and he nodded politely at her.

'Please, think nothing of it,' he said. 'I find myself ready to start work today, as it happens. I was just trying to get to know the Duchess a little before we decided what to create in her portrait.'

'Good afternoon, Alys.' Zennor smiled at her. 'Yes, because Mr Teague didn't need to arrange accommodation, and because he was in the area, we decided that it would be a good use of everyone's time if he began work today. Well. I say "we". I mean, of course, the Duke.'

'The Duke. Of course. He wants to keep you out of mischief, I am sure.' Too late, Alys noticed Jago standing by the fireplace, a cup in his hand. 'May I interest you in a cup of tea, Miss Trelawney? The pot is still quite fresh.'

She was thrown. 'Oh – well. Yes. I suppose. Thank you.'

'Of course! Excuse my terrible manners, dearest cousin. Let me pour it for you!' Zennor made to stand up and head to the tea table, but Jago stopped her.

'No – please. You continue your conversation. I am sure Miss Trelawney and myself will manage perfectly well. Please – would you do me the honour of stepping over here? Alys.' His eyes met hers and she started. There was something in his expression she couldn't quite read, but she nodded and walked over to him almost mechanically.

'Let me do it,' he said to her as she reached for the pot. Then he half-smiled. 'As a way of apologising to you for my behaviour earlier. I didn't sit on ceremony too much in India, which I'm sure many people would object to. But I don't see why a man can't pour a cup of tea as well as a lady. Can you?'

'No. I suppose not.' She took the cup he offered her, but her eyes never left his. 'And really, there is no need to apologise.' The last few words came out a little stiffly, but he laughed and didn't take offence.

'Of course there is Alys. I treated you appallingly. I treated you as if you didn't have an ounce of sense and a mind of your own. Forgive me? Please?'

'If you put it like that. Mr Pencradoc—'

'Jago. Please. I think we are beyond formalities.'

'Jago.' His name on her lips gave her a thrill she couldn't quite explain. 'Then I suspect I must accept your apology. I do have a mind of my own, and I did feel perhaps a tiny bit offended that you ushered me out of the tower – even if you did it in a very polite way.'

'Ah, you tease me.' He laughed and she couldn't help smiling back. Her petulance over his actions seemed to dissipate like the steam from the teacup in her hand. 'I consider myself chided.' He bowed to her, still holding the dainty blue and white patterned teacup and she giggled; it looked so incongruous in his hand. 'Truthfully, though, I *am* sorry. That tower holds some very dark memories for the family, me in particular, and it's not somewhere a person should linger unless they want their own good mood to evaporate.'

'And has your good mood returned?'

'It has. Even more so, now I have seen you and apologised. I was searching for you earlier, you know.'

'You wouldn't have found me. The estate is quite large, and I find myself quite adept at losing myself in it.'

'I did wonder if you'd found your way back to the tower. It wouldn't have surprised me if you'd been in there again.'

'Defying you?' She raised an eyebrow, quizzical and only half-joking.

'Defying me? I don't know if I would have put it quite like that. I have no authority over you and I certainly wouldn't attempt to curtail your fun.'

'Apart from guiding me out of the tower.'

'*Touché*. But, as we have established, I am apologetic and in reality there is no reason why I would try to prevent your visits. Should you, however, find yourself back there, I would urge you to be very careful. The folly is old and the steps are worn—'

'Worn and dangerous.' Ellory's voice, clipped and authoritative, broke through the pleasant atmosphere of the drawing room as he strode over to Zennor and Teague. The door swung shut behind him with a bang.

'I would strongly advise you, Miss Trelawney, to avoid the place at all costs. I would not expect a young lady of your impressionable nature to wander over to the tower. One's mind can make up all sorts of stories, once one has seen the place. Do not go there again.'

Alys felt herself flush. He had a point, she supposed. Hadn't she already started fantasising and romanticising the folly and its original purpose? She opened her mouth to respond, to defend herself, perhaps, but saw that, as far as Ellory was concerned, the conversation was over, and his attention was now fixed on Zennor and Mr Teague.

'Ah. Mr Teague. You got my message.'

'Yes, Your Grace. I did indeed.' Ruan Teague looked slightly amused at Ellory's pompous blustering, and his mouth, Alys noticed, was tilted up in a slight curve: a half-smile which would normally be enough to make Ellory snap and scold in a churlish fashion. At least, that was what he did with Zennor when she had looked, as he probably deemed it, disrespectfully at him. 'I appreciate the early start on the commission.'

'Good.' Ellory took hold of Zennor's arm, quite possessively, Alys thought. 'My wife needs a distraction. Of the correct kind.'

There was a clatter to Alys' left and she looked around, startled, as Jago set his teacup back in its saucer.

'Distractions. Indeed.' Jago's voice was tight again, the thinly-disguised distaste in it directed, seemingly, at his brother's comments. 'I do apologise, but I have business to attend to, and must take my leave of you all. Zennor. Alys. Mr Teague.' He nodded at them, then stalked out of the room, his head held high.

It was only as she watched his retreating back, that

Alys realised he hadn't acknowledged Ellory in his farewells. Ellory, however, was ignoring that fact, and had begun a conversation with Mr Teague, moving closer to him, leaving Zennor standing, ever so slightly, behind him looking lost.

Alys watched for a moment, then made her way across to Zennor, a wide smile pasted on her face. Having seen the portrait of Rose with her exposed shoulder and all the distractions and undercurrents that suggested, she wondered if the fact that Ellory had deliberately positioned himself between Zennor and Mr Teague was not quite as inadvertent as he had made it seem. Did he suspect Mr Teague would depict Zennor in a compromising position as well, and therefore wanted to nip it in the bud before the idea settled in his head?

It was a definite possibility.

Chapter Eleven

Present Day

For a week or so, Merryn travelled back and forwards between The White Lady and Pencradoc. She had been right. The cataloguing job was taking much longer than they had originally anticipated.

'I don't think I'll be done for at least a week – maybe more.' She phoned Heptinstall Studios on the Friday morning, and spoke to Jeremy whose place she had taken on the trip.

'A week! Or more!' Jeremy was horrified. He was, it seemed, pleased that he hadn't trailed all the way to Cornwall. Jeremy much preferred jobs nearer home, but was a huge Teague fan, so had been the first choice for the Pencradoc work. Nobody had particularly realised that the collection was so big. 'Well forgive me, Merryn, but I'm glad it wasn't me there. I don't think I could have left the girls for that long.' Jeremy's wife had recently given birth to their second daughter, and that was a huge factor in him wanting to stay closer to home. As well as the fact his stomach had been dreadfully unpredictable when he was preparing to leave London.

'No, that's understandable. How are they?'

Jeremy launched into a dialogue about newborns and feeding schedules and Merryn made approving or concerned noises where she felt it was applicable.

'Jeremy,' she said, as soon as she could get a word in. 'I'm going to have to try and book myself a few more days down here.' She pulled a face at nothing in particular. The White Lady was nice enough, but the WiFi was rubbish and she was desperate to have a bath instead of a shower. And even more desperate to sleep in her own very comfortable double bed, rather than a rather hard single one. And the woman she'd spoken to about extending her stay had sucked in her already concave cheeks and went, 'Hmmmm – I'm not sure we have any vacancies next week.' So, she was a bit stuck, all things considered. She was hoping Heptinstall Studios could sort something out for her.

And she wanted clean clothes. More than anything, really. She'd only packed enough for the week and didn't feel confident enough to ask Coren and Kit whether she could wash her smalls in their aunt's washing machine.

'Oh dear. I'll have a word with the powers that be and see what we can do. Are you coming back home for the weekend though?'

'Yes. Definitely. I'm coming back to London. I'm missing my flat too much. I can't stay any longer.' She looked up as Kit walked into the library and waved at him. He stopped short and stared at her, then hovered around the door until she'd finished her conversation.

'Can I help?' she asked, once she'd disconnected the call.

'I was just wondering—'

'Hey!' Coren walked in, carrying a tray with three mugs on it. 'I figured we'd all be ready for morning coffee. Anyone fancy having it outside?' He nodded through the window to the walled gardens. 'It's a beautiful day. Summer is here, and a summer in Cornwall is the very best type of summer.'

'Sounds good to me.' Merryn cast a glance at the shelves. 'I was going to start on this room but it can wait.'

Merryn didn't miss the look Kit shot at Coren. For a moment, there seemed to be someone else behind his eyes and she blinked, taken aback. Then, as soon as the look had flashed across his face, he seemed to bring himself back to the moment and nodded, quite curtly. 'Yes. Outside would be good. Merryn, can I catch you about something before we head out?'

'Sure.' She stood up and Kit began to walk towards her, but Coren suddenly seemed to be in between them, gazing outside. 'We'll just go through the French doors. It's straight out onto the lawn. Kit, would you be so kind as to open them for me?'

'You'll have to watch the steps,' Kit murmured, but Merryn got the distinct impression that he was simply being polite, and didn't really care if his brother fell down them. She shivered. Suddenly, it was cold in that room, despite the sun streaming through the panes of glass. She would be awfully glad when she got outside.

Before she followed Coren, however, she cast a glance to the shelves in the library. She really had to make a start on them. They'd been bugging her; the whole room had, to be honest. She kept finding herself wandering in there when she had a spare few minutes and either sitting looking at all the old family photos and memorabilia around the room or using it as a makeshift office, spreading her notebooks and pencils everywhere she possibly could.

She felt dreadfully torn. When she had been speaking to Jeremy, she couldn't wait to get back home. But now, now she had practically decided what her next task would be, she was quite reluctant to leave Pencradoc.

Kit felt his hands curling into fists, then came to his senses. What the hell was he so angry about? His brother had simply suggested they take the coffee outside, and then – what? Oh. He glowered. That's right.

He had tried to deflect his attention from her, tried to keep them apart …

And she had mentioned leaving. And he didn't want her to leave – whatever it was that she was running from, it was within his power to stop.

'I can't stay any longer.'

The words had an unpleasant echo – he had heard them before. Sometime in the past, in the very grounds of Pencradoc. There was water – the waterfall, that was right, and she was running away, because—

'Kit? Please can you open the door?' Coren was scowling at him, the expression on his face incongruous with the fact he had three blue and white floral-patterned mugs on a tray.

'Sure. Yeah.' He took hold of the old handle and the door creaked and stuck slightly as he pushed it open, too many years of non-use making it stick to its frame like a seaside limpet.

He stepped aside and just stopped himself presenting a mocking little bow to his brother, as he waved him past. *Who did he think he was, lording it over them all?*

'There's truly nothing quite like a Cornish summer is there?' A soft voice startled him and he looked down at her, almost finding it difficult to place her.

He made an effort and forced a smile onto his lips. 'Oh! Merryn. Yes – it's even nicer on the coast.' He followed her out, and they sat down on the grass, Merryn stretching her bare legs out in front of her, facing the folly which was just visible behind the trees.

'The coast as in Marazion?'

'Yep. As I said, best view in the world.' He smiled at

her, properly now, the atmosphere seeming to lift and shift around them. He felt like himself again – like Kit Penhaligon. Not like ... someone else. Someone angry and bitter and holding some sort of huge grudge against his brother ...

God. He and Coren had always been fairly close. He didn't know exactly what it was about the last week or so, but he had been finding it increasingly difficult to hold his temper whenever the three of them were in the same room together. It was weird. Maybe it was good old-fashioned jealousy though – Merryn was a very attractive woman, he admitted to himself as he looked at her. Her hair was lifting gently in a warm breeze that had crept up on them from the moor, and she had a smattering of freckles across her nose that hadn't been there at the beginning of the week. Cornwall agreed with her.

He made a conscious effort to turn to his brother, intending to begin a conversation about something and nothing. Whatever was going on inside that house, he didn't want to think about. He much preferred to be out here, in the garden, with *her*.

But hold on: wasn't she planning to leave?

'Merryn. Sorry – just before, when we were in the library?'

'Yes? Gosh, I'm the one who should be sorry. You came in to see me about something, didn't you?'

'I did. It was only that – how can I put it ...' He smiled, embarrassed. 'I didn't mean to listen in to your phone call, but I heard you telling someone you needed to leave. I didn't think the cataloguing was quite finished?'

'Finished?' Coren interrupted. 'It's nowhere near finished! Sorry, Miss Burton, we can't let you leave quite yet!' He smiled, taking the edge off his words, and Kit wondered afresh as to why they had been so antagonistic with one another. Actually, that wasn't strictly true. He'd been gunning for a fight, over anything and nothing, but Coren had remained cool and aloof and treated him as if he didn't exist, half the time. It had been, if he was honest, a fairly unpleasant few days; only the fact that he'd had Merryn around had made it bearable. It was very unlike the brothers to act like that with each other.

'I'm not leaving properly!' Merryn was apparently horrified that he thought that. 'I'm still holding out hope for some more hidden Teagues. But I'm only booked in at The White Lady for this week. I need to leave, and go home, and pick up some more clothes. Then I need to come back, somehow.' She screwed up her face. 'But when I mentioned extending my stay, The White Lady wasn't too helpful. So I'm not too sure what I can do. I've asked the company to try and find me an alternative place, but I'll have to see what they come up with. Hopefully it won't be too far away and I don't end up commuting!'

Kit glanced at Coren and raised his eyebrows. 'What do you think, brother? Can Pencradoc take in another lodger for a little while?'

'I don't see why not,' Coren said. Then, it was the strangest thing. It was as if a shutter came down behind his eyes and he seemed to do that aloof, dictatorial thing again. 'So long as she stays in the east wing, of course.'

He didn't even sound like Coren.

1886

The weather held for a week or so, then, annoyingly, it was raining. Alys had disappeared with her notebooks to the Banqueting House, which overlooked the Pencradoc lake. It was on the opposite side of the estate to the folly, and she didn't want to risk anyone finding her at that tower again, quite so soon. The sound of the raindrops pattering on the wooden roof were, in an odd way, cheerful and comforting.

And anyway, the way Ellory virtually dismissed Zennor from any prolonged conversation with Mr Teague was bothering her. Even the atmosphere this morning over breakfast had pained her, and she just wanted to stay away from the poisonous air within Pencradoc's walls. There was a suppressed, crackling energy emanating from Jago, who had been overly polite with everyone for several days, and over-indulgent to Zennor – as if he was trying to make up for Ellory's treatment of her. Alys had caught Jago's eye once or twice, and their gazes had locked, then something quite indescribable had stirred within her before she had forced herself to look away. Jago's eyes were always haunted and stony, but she had noticed, with a little thrill, that they tended to soften momentarily as they settled on her.

Mr Teague had not joined them for breakfast this morning. Ellory had decreed, quite politely, that Mr Teague should perhaps take his breakfast in his room from now on. Nobody had argued with him, and Ruan Teague had simply shrugged, pushed his wayward hair out of his eyes, and smiled that ironic little smile again.

Poor Zennor. Alys would not wish to swap with her for the world, despite the fact she had this marvellous home and was just about to be painted by a rather famous artist.

A shadow fell across the door and she looked up, half-hoping to see Jago there. However, Alys jumped as

Zennor's familiar giggle broke the silence. Her cousin pushed the door open, Ruan Teague following her. 'In here,' she said, her voice light and playful; this was Zennor thoroughly enjoying herself. 'The Banqueting House is quite possibly one of the best places to hide out on the estate.'

Alys cleared her throat, quite loudly, and Zennor started. Alys was almost certain they had been holding hands, and they dropped one another's, quite quickly, when they spotted her.

'Alys!' Zennor stood, her expression surprised, her other hand still on the door. 'What are you doing here?'

'I could ask you the same thing.'

Zennor glanced at the notebook and suddenly laughed, brazening it out as always. 'Well, I see we all recognise the benefit of this place for the arts. Mr Teague, as I told you on the way here, I thought this would be a wonderful place for you to use as a background to a painting.' Her voice was too light, too innocent. Alys knew her too well to trust that tone. It had got her cousin out of too many scrapes before now. 'You see them sometimes, don't you?' Zennor continued blithely. 'The ladies holding their spaniels with lakes and country idylls behind them.' She pulled a face. 'Not that I like that style very much.'

Ruan caught Alys' eye and had the grace to smile, although his cheeks coloured a little, which was a startling contrast to his pale complexion. 'Me neither. I prefer work like Singer Sargent's. I know *Madame X* wasn't received particularly well, but *Lady with a Rose* was very popular.'

'They were beautiful models!' cried Zennor. 'I don't think one needs to fuss too much with backgrounds when one has such a stunning model. The whole idea is that the subject stands out.'

'You, I think, would suit that style very much.' Ruan's smile was transferred to Zennor. 'And I think Miss Trelawney has already commandeered this place, which makes my decision on the composition easier. Perhaps, therefore, we should leave her in peace.'

'If you need to use it, I can easily find somewhere else to work. I only need a chair and a desk.' Alys smiled at Ruan. She decided she liked Ruan Teague, and also decided she had imagined them holding hands. She was, after all, immersed in writing a romance. But it hadn't escaped Alys' notice that Ruan had looked at Zennor quite differently to the way Ellory looked at her – even after having only known her for a heartbeat. He was clearly entranced by her vivacious cousin and she didn't blame him.

'It was only an idea.' Zennor stood for a moment longer, her eyes meeting Ruan's, then dropping as her cheeks coloured. 'I don't really like that style myself. It was only because my husband ...' She bit her lip and looked at Alys. 'I don't believe Rose's portrait had a folly thing behind her. And to be fair, I did want mine to look completely different. But I really *don't* want a folly thing behind me.'

'Then don't have a folly thing. I think you'll have a wonderful portrait, whatever you decide.' Alys smiled at her. 'It's your picture. You need to decide the best way forward with Mr Teague.'

'Quite so.' Zennor gestured to the outside. 'Let us go, Mr Teague. I'll leave you in peace now, Alys, and I'll discuss a *different* style of art with Mr Teague. Mr Singer Sargent is *so* daring, but I think I'll adore it, whatever style he chooses, to be honest.'

She drifted out of the Banqueting House, Ruan Teague bowing a farewell to Alys, and closing the door behind him firmly.

Alys suddenly found the quiet unsettling and whatever she was going to write vanished from her mind as she stared at the door. Her romantic novel seemed quite silly now.

The door opened again, very slowly, and she caught the shadow of a woman in the gap: a dark-haired woman. Her hand, slim and white rested briefly on the doorframe, then she was gone.

A little tingle of disconcertment shivered up her spine. Then she looked back at her notebook and shook her head. It was just the shadows outside and a stray sunbeam, that was all. Really, she had too much imagination at times.

This was the more formal area of the gardens. It wasn't Jago's favourite part – it was too cultured, too ordered. But today, he had taken his horse for a wild gallop over the moor and returned that way.

The route took him by the Banqueting House, and as he rounded the corner, he saw two people leaving the building and walking, very closely together, towards the rose garden. He thought their hands may even have crept into one another's, but he couldn't swear to it.

He dug his heel into the horse gently, to get a better view of them – not that he had too much bother recognising them. The woman had dark hair, and as she threw back her head and laughed at something her companion said, his stomach clenched. She reminded him so much of Rose at that moment, it was unsettling.

But then he saw another dark-haired figure, a woman,

breaking away from the shadows behind the little building, then melting away into the trees behind it. His heart turned over. There were only two women on the estate that he knew of who would be here, dressed like that, in a long, fashionable gown; two living women, at least. One was dark, and one was fair.

He blinked and tried to see where the woman had gone, but the paths through the woods were empty. He kicked the horse again, and it trotted over to the building, where he dismounted it almost before it had drawn to a halt.

He pushed the door open and peered inside, wondering if she—

'Oh! Jago!

'Alys!' He stood in the doorway, momentarily thrown. 'I'm so sorry. I didn't know you were here. I thought ...' his voice trailed off and he frowned. 'I saw someone else here. I was ensuring whoever it is was entitled to be here and was safe.'

'I am here. As you can see.' She smiled at him, a little mischievously. 'Or am I not good enough to worry about?'

'You are most definitely good enough to worry about. And very much entitled to be here. Forgive me. I shall leave you in peace.'

He nodded and made to leave, when Alys spoke again. 'Might it have been Zennor? She and Mr Teague were here a few moments ago. I did think myself that she had come back for some reason, but it was not the case.' She shook her head. 'And as you can see, there is only me here. I think it was perhaps a shadow, something to do with the rain clearing outside?' It was her turn to frown. 'A shaft of light in the open door? I do not know.'

She shrugged. 'Anything else would be ... preposterous, would it not?'

'Very preposterous.'

They stared at each for a moment, refusing, perhaps to think of what it might have been, until Jago spoke again.

'May I ask, Alys, what the Duchess and Mr Teague were doing here? They seemed particularly ... engaged with one another as they walked away.' Inwardly, Jago cringed. That also sounded preposterous. He didn't want Alys to suspect there was anything to concern her about her cousin's burgeoning friendship with the artist.

Alys, though, held his gaze a little too long, and her voice was a little too calm and steady when she responded. 'They are searching for a background for her painting. I'm not entirely certain as to whether she wants a folly in the background or not. Zennor is, I suspect, taking Mr Teague on a tour of the estate. They do seem to be enjoying the chance to discuss the portrait away from the house. Ruan has begun some sketches, but there is more to a portrait than the subject, isn't there?'

'Sometimes, the subject doesn't need a background, though. It can hold the viewer's eye without that.' He stopped himself before he expanded on that, but Alys looked at him curiously. It was as if she knew.

'Indeed. And a subject such as Zennor is particularly striking, wouldn't you say?'

'I would.'

'And the first Duchess? Would you say the same about her?'

'Rose and Zennor are very similar in looks,' said Jago carefully. 'But they have, I hope, very different sensibilities.'

'And do you think that the Duke understands that?' Alys' voice was equally careful.

'Again, I hope he does.'

There was a beat.

'I see.' She nodded. 'I hope so too.'

'Alys—' He surprised them both by striding forward and leaning his hands on the desk, his face inches away from hers. The sunlight had sprinkled freckles onto her creamy skin, her fair hair was loose, as untidy as ever and her strange moss-green eyes regarded him steadily. 'Tell your cousin to be careful with Mr Teague. I am in no position to do that, but you have to tell her. I want her to be safe. That's all I want.' He held her gaze for a moment, unfamiliar feelings he thought he had buried long ago encompassing him – then he leaned down closer, fully intending to kiss her.

But something stopped him and he stood up again. How on earth could he do that to her? To someone as sweetly innocent as Alys?

Yes, she was beautiful and funny and had a smile that was infectious. But after Rose, he didn't know if he could inflict himself on another woman. That weight of guilt was still with him, and it wasn't fair to drag her into it.

He had to concentrate on Zennor – he had to make sure she was safe first.

Jago stood up and looked down at her, scanned her lovely, oval-shaped face, searching for the shadows of the dimples he knew were there when she smiled. 'Please, Alys, I take my duty seriously here. I would hate for anything to happen to you or your cousin. Promise me you will be careful?'

'I promise.' Her voice was a whisper, her lips slightly parted even now.

God, it would have been so easy; so easy to kiss her, properly, right there and then.

But he couldn't

Not yet.

And as he turned to leave, his emotions swirling within him in a maelstrom he didn't care to unravel, he saw a rose lying on the ground at the entrance to the summerhouse. He looked at it for a second, then dismissed it and didn't look back.

Chapter Twelve

'There's plenty of room in either wing.' Kit looked at Coren curiously. 'I'm not sure what your problem is.'

'What? Well, the only problem is that we are in the east wing, and Merryn might find it a little daunting to be on her own all the way over at the other side of the house.' Coren directed a smile at Merryn. 'But if you think differently ...'

'I don't think differently at all.' Merryn shook her head, aware of something going on between the men, but not sure what. 'It's very kind of you to offer for me to stay – but I will definitely have to go home first. I know it's a pain and I'll be spending all night driving, but if I go tonight and come back Sunday, will that be all right?'

'You're welcome to stay for the weekend, you know.' Kit smiled at her. 'I did promise you a trip to my studio. That's only an hour away. Surely it's better than going all the way home? I promise we won't make you work overtime.'

Merryn felt her cheeks grow hot. 'I'd love to stay – but I have a bit of an issue.'

'Do you? Oh God, I'm sorry. I never thought to ask.' Kit's cheeks flushed then. 'Have you got someone at home? A partner? Someone you need to get back to?'

'Oh no! Absolutely not!' Merryn didn't know whether to laugh or cry. Since she and her ex, Josh, had broken up six months ago, there had been nobody else. And to be fair, she couldn't wait to be rid of Josh, especially after she caught him texting his ex-wife and telling her he might have made a mistake, now he'd had time to reconsider it …

'Can I be honest with you?' She felt as if she was beetroot now. 'I really want a washing machine. I only packed enough clothing to last me a week. My friend Cordelia is looking after my flat for me, so it's not like it's standing empty. But yeah – I either need a decent shopping centre to restock or I need a washing machine!'

Kit stared at her for a moment then burst out laughing. 'I feel your pain. I packed pretty light myself. But don't worry – the washer is still plumbed in. I'll show you how to use it. And if you do need anything else, well, we can always go via Truro. They have decent shops there, I promise. And if it's that or a five-hour drive—'

'—four-and-a-half-hour drive!'

'Four-and-a-half-hour drive then, I'm damn sure I know what I'd want to do.'

Merryn laughed. 'I agree. When you put it like that, it does seem to make sense for me to stay. If that's absolutely okay with Coren, of course.'

She looked at Coren, hoping that the eagerness didn't show too much in her face. Staying at Pencradoc, *in* Pencradoc, sounded a damn sight better than sitting in a stuffy car for half the day or spending another night at The White Lady. Her eyes drifted over to the folly, as if it was whispering something to her and urging her to go and visit it by moonlight.

How fanciful.

But if she did stay here, she might actually get the chance to go there, which was delightful in itself.

'I don't foresee a problem,' Coren replied. 'As we said,

there's plenty of space. Do you want to go and get your things now? The library can wait another half hour or so, can't it? You might as well get settled in. Shall we ring Heptinstall for you and let them know what's happening while you go?'

'No thanks. I can do that myself.' Merryn got to her feet and brushed the grass off her skirt. The men weren't far behind her, as she went back through the French doors to find her mobile and call Jeremy back. She'd call Cordelia as well, just to make sure the arrangement was okay with her. She didn't think her friend would complain – she was renting a room in a house near Bethnal Green, but she loved decamping to Merryn's place whenever she could, thriving amongst the art galleries and creative spaces of Kentish Town.

Merryn was terribly excited to be leaving that pub which, being honest, had lost its charm the moment she realised that the inn-sign was supposed to be Rose. And she was even more excited at the prospect of clean, washed clothes.

She rang Jeremy first, and he was happy to agree the accommodation. 'Just make sure they bill us for any costs. We'd be paying for a hotel anyway, so we want to keep them sweet.'

'Is that a nice way of saying we don't want to upset the clients on a job on this scale?' She smiled into the phone, thinking that was exactly what it was.

'Absolutely!' Jeremy laughed. 'We don't want to upset any of our customers, but especially not the owners of the Pencradoc Collection.' She had already reported back on the de Amato, and she knew that Heptinstall were hoping that there would be more of the same – as she was. She didn't think they'd be that lucky twice, though.

Cordelia was next. As she suspected, her friend was delighted to stay on in the flat. 'Are you sure you don't want a flatmate on a more permanent basis?' Cordelia asked. 'I love it here – it's so much nicer not having people you can't stand in the lounge. Honestly, it's like being back at university at my place. I really think I've outgrown a room!'

'If I had more than one bedroom, you would be more than welcome to share! But as it is, it might be a bit snug.'

'Bijou is rather fashionable now. And seriously, I am desperate to get away from that lot.' She launched into a tirade that lasted a good few minutes about the shortcomings of her housemates. Merryn, having heard it all before made soothing noises, but there wasn't much else she could do to help her friend. Cordelia had wanted to be an actress and had found that temping jobs in various offices were a more reliable source of income than her dreams of treading the boards. 'So are there any nice chaps you've met down there, then?' Cordelia's butterfly mind had jumped to her next favourite topic: Merryn's love life.

'What? No – well, yes. I mean, Coren and Kit are both nice. They're the ones who own this place now.' She popped her head out of the library door, hoping that neither of those "nice" men were around to hear her conversation and misconstrue it all.

'But are they *nice*? Sexy nice. The sort of nice that means you'd fall headlong into it with them?'

'If by "it" you mean a bed or a relationship, I'm not quite sure. But that is not on anyone's agenda!' She crossed her fingers. It *might* be on her agenda. It was *likely* to be on her agenda if Kit demonstrated that he felt the same way as she did – and currently she felt that she was thinking about him a little too much for him being just a client. She'd even had a couple of weird dreams about him, but no way was she going to go into that with Cordy. 'So I'm not sure when I'll be back – but I'll let you know. I can imagine I'll be here for at least a week more, perhaps even longer.'

'Take your time, darling!' Cordelia sounded amused. 'Please. Be as long as you like. Me and your flat are very happy together.'

'I bet you are!' Merryn said goodbye to her friend, and placed the phone on the desk. She looked over at the books on the shelves and half-smiled. They were, at the end of the day, simply books, but perhaps there would be something hidden away somewhere. Perhaps there would be another hidden room – with that Dorian Gray picture in, after all. You just never knew. However, the library would have to be deferred again. The next real job on her agenda was moving out of the pub, and moving into Pencradoc.

She could hardly wait.

Kit just happened to be hanging around the gatehouse. Upon reflection, he couldn't have been more obvious if he'd tried. He'd overheard Merryn on that call to her friend: "*Kit and Coren are both nice.*"

He'd been carrying some cut-flowers past the still-open French window, intending to put them in a vase in Merryn's new room, in order to make it even more welcoming for her. He had dipped his head and grinned as he hurried past, not wanting to eavesdrop too much; but part of him was, he had to admit, intrigued to know what the whole conversation was about.

It was probably something as simple as "what are the Penhaligon brothers like?" But it would have been nice to know. He had thought about that phrase fleetingly as he came into the house and went up to the room Coren and he had designated for her, after a brief discussion to place the flowers in a vase.

However, the more time he spent in the house, with that phrase playing over in his mind, the more irritated he became with his brother. It was ridiculous – totally unreasonable. But he just kept wondering what he had to do to make her see that Coren was not so nice as she considered ...

He saw his brother's mouth twist into a cold smile he didn't mean at all. How could anyone be fooled by that? How could anyone think he was innocent ...?

'For God's sake!' He stood up, placing his hands roughly either side of the doorframe, glaring down at the floor, trying to keep his growing temper under control, for fear that he would punch the wall. 'What the *hell* are you going on about, Kit Penhaligon?' He pushed himself away from the frame and stormed out of the room, breaking into a run as he approached the stairs and headed down them.

Once he was outside, he looked up into the blue sky and felt his temper return to something pertaining to normal. He was usually fairly easy-going. It took a lot to push his buttons, but this last week or so had found him seething with anger at more regular intervals. The only thing he could point to was the fact that Merryn had come to Pencradoc – and he was jealous. Bloody jealous that she might fall for his brother the way the others had ...

That she might fall for Ellory, with no care or

consequence of what had gone before. He wanted to protect her, to keep her safe the way he had failed to do with Rose—

It was Alys he loved, and Alys he needed to protect now, though—

His eyes sought the tower, standing tall and looking down at him mockingly.

He had to keep her away from there. He had to.

So here he was at the gatehouse. Merryn had disappeared to The White Lady to pack up her things and bring them over to the house. He was hoping to catch her as she came back, with some really pathetic excuse that he was going to show her the best place to park her car. She'd walked every day, from the village to Pencradoc, and she'd parked here the first day – but it was the best excuse he could come up with.

It wasn't as if he could catch her on Bodmin Moor, by Dozmary Pool, was it, and be entranced by this rather fae creature that seemed to know him more than he knew her, and engage in a discussion about the ghosts of the area?

He brought himself up short. Ghosts. Yes, perhaps that was what was happening at Pencradoc. Because of the way they were working, the way they were planning a future and discovering hidden portraits was unearthing more than the place could cope with, perhaps? Overturning long-buried secrets which raised more questions than they answered.

He looked up and to his left as a woman in a white dress caught his attention, weaving her way through the gardens. He stood up straighter. She had dark hair – it certainly wasn't Merryn, and anyway how would Merryn have come through those gates without him knowing?

'Hey!' he shouted over at the woman, but she ignored him and disappeared behind a hedge. Without thinking, he left his position at the gatehouse and sprinted over to where she had vanished.

He shouldn't have been surprised really, to find that there was nobody there.

It was as he was poking through the undergrowth and trying to establish where she had gone, that he heard Merryn's car come through the gates and head straight on down the driveway. He swore as he saw the car pull up and Coren jog down the steps to welcome her and show her where she should park, and take her case in for her.

His sight blurred and his temper rose again as he thought the most irrational thought he'd had: *who the hell was trying to keep them apart? And why had the ghost or whatever it was appeared right then, at that moment? It was as if someone was making sure his brother was there to welcome her, and keeping him otherwise engaged.*

The White Lady herself perhaps?

Merryn sensed a shadow at the doorway of the bedroom. Someone had very kindly put a vase of flowers in her room, and she'd now found out who had done so.

'Oh, thanks Coren! They're lovely!' she'd said initially. She had gone over to sniff the collection of roses and lilies and lacey-leaved ferns from, she suspected, the rose garden and stumpery, pleased that he had been so thoughtful after the uncertainty of her future accommodation.

'Hmm. I'll accept your thanks, but they're nothing to do with me,' Coren had said, frowning. 'I can only assume my brother did it. It is a nice gesture though – he can still surprise me at times.'

They'd exchanged a few more words, and then he had left her, making his excuses and saying he had work to do in the other wing.

The wing, the little devil on her shoulder told her, *that she wasn't welcome in*. But she wasn't going to spoil the afternoon, and she had instead a glorious weekend to look forward to, instead of a tiring journey across the country and back. She noted with approval that not only was the bed in her room comfortable, but it was a king-size rather than a double, and really, she couldn't argue with that.

She looked at the doorway as she heard footsteps outside. There was a smile on her face as she prepared to thank Kit – who she assumed it would be; but the smile slid off as she caught the image of a long, white skirt swishing past the doorway.

Her stomach contracted, and her heart began to pound; but despite her fears, she forced herself to go to the door and look along the corridor.

There was nothing: no woman in a long dress, no ghosts floating along the passageways. There was, however, a window at the end of the hall, a few leafy branches waving beyond the glass. As one, particularly dense branch, bent forwards and blotted out the sun, it dappled a shadow along the corridor.

'Ah.' Merryn's heart began to beat normally. Shadows. It had, literally, been a shadow. That's what had darkened the corridor. The image of a skirt was a ray of sunlight, travelling along the carpet as the branches blew gently outside, and the swishing sound had to be the sound of the leaves brushing the window panes.

She walked along the corridor and peered out of the window. From here, the tower was visible, and she felt that odd pull towards it again. As the sun shone warmly through the glass and the waving branches mesmerised her, she found herself drifting off into a daydream where she sat by another window, in another time ...

It wouldn't have been a passionate kiss, she told herself as she sat on her window seat, flickering light from the candle casting shadows about her bedroom. It could, perhaps have been a kiss that was unplanned, a spark of spontaneity. Something that meant nothing more than a momentary lack of control. But it wouldn't have been passionate, not with her on the receiving end.

Of course, she had been attracted to Jago from the minute she had met him at Dozmary Pool, and his proximity in Pencradoc sometimes almost drove her to distraction. Who could fail to feel a spark of something with Jago Pencradoc; dark, handsome and just the right side of dangerous?

She flushed again at her thoughts and shifted position. She had never seriously considered that he felt like that about her. Rather, she thought, he was simply one of those men who all women took a liking to, and had his choice of who he dallied with.

His choice was clearly not her.

With that depressing thought, she sighed lustily and slid off the window seat. Padding over to her candle, she blew it out and slipped into bed, positive her dreams would be of a certain tall, dark-haired man with a smile to die for and a thousand demons she couldn't understand hidden somewhere deep inside of him ...

Merryn came back to reality with a start. The room she

had seen had very much looked like the one she had just recently unpacked her clothing into.

With a shiver, and without looking behind her, she turned and made straight for the staircase. She was leaving all thoughts of windows and bedrooms and going to the tower behind. She just had to.

1886

A few weeks after the kiss which didn't happen, Alys, annoyed with herself for building up a moment which clearly meant more to her than anyone else, peeked through the door of the library. That had been the room deemed most suitable for Ruan to use as studio – Ellory had told Ruan it was useful for him to be able to visit the library whenever he wanted to see the progress of the portrait.

Zennor, sitting on a chair, was illuminated by the natural light coming through the French doors, her face highlighted, her body more or less in shadow. She was, it had to be said, glowing with more than just that sunshine.

She looked different somehow. Alys would have found the thought difficult to put into words, despite the fact she was a writer. It was a sense of Zennor being content – as if she had some wonderful secret she wanted to share, but not yet – not quite yet. Her cousin looked happy and relaxed, and every now and then she would laugh at something Ruan said, or comment on little things that made him smile. He was facing her, and just his profile was visible through the gap, but the curve of his cheek and the crinkles at the side of his eyes told Alys that he was smiling right then.

Alys felt, deep within her, a little shiver of pleasurable anticipation. Might it be that Zennor had finally conceived? After all that heartache about the process. No wonder she looked content. She had good reason if she was carrying the heir to Pencradoc ...

But then she saw the way Zennor and Ruan Teague caught one another's eyes; the momentary stilling of the brush as they lost themselves to that moment.

Oh, Zennor – no. No, it wasn't possible that they had truly fallen for one another, was it? That the hand-holding she had imagined had been a reality? My goodness, what a dreadful situation to be in. Alys felt herself grow hot and cold, uncomfortable with the fact that she was, quite possibly, privy to that information. She was wrong, she had to be. It was her writer's mind, her imagination—

'What do you think the finished portrait will be like?' Jago's voice, quite close to her, made her heart race, but in a different way. And not as much as the warmth she could feel emanating from his body made her feel that way, or his breath tickling the tip of her ear.

'Oh! You startled me.' She hugged her notebook closer, trying, on some level to stop her heart hammering quite so loudly. She prayed he wouldn't hear it. Alys hadn't completely managed to abandon those thoughts she'd had of him since the Banqueting House incident, but he'd made no further advances to her, and she was starting to wonder whether she had dreamed it all. It was frustrating in the extreme, the way life just rolled on as usual, and they saw each other every day – but he had been as polite as he ever was to her, and even more courteous to Zennor. 'But in answer to your question,' she said, trying to quash the butterflies in her stomach, 'I have only one response. It will be beautiful. With Zennor as the subject, how could it be otherwise?' She was burbling, hoping that he hadn't witnessed what she had.

'Indeed.' He came closer to her, leaning in to the gap, opening the door slightly more so he could see better. The motion must have caught Zennor's eye as she looked across, her expression startled and wary.

Guilty.

The word was unwelcome in Alys' mind, and did nothing to calm her thoughts.

Zennor's countenance relaxed as she caught Alys' eye and cast a glance up at Jago, several inches above her, before bringing it back to Alys and smiling, relieved it seemed. 'Alys! Jago! Come in. Please – we were just about to stop for a moment.'

Ruan looked across and grinned. He, too, looked happy and relaxed: a man enjoying his work.

And in love with his sitter, that treacherous little voice in her head said.

Teague set the palette down and laid his brush next to it. 'Were we? I suppose if the Duchess says so, we must be accommodating. Yes – please enter my ... studio. If you'd be so kind.' He bowed, theatrically, and Zennor laughed delightedly.

'When do you start charging an entrance fee?' Jago pushed the door fully open, and took Alys' arm gently, guiding her into the room. 'I see an inordinate amount of artwork lying around. You could, potentially, open a real gallery here.'

'I could. But I'm afraid my subject matter is rather narrow and probably wouldn't interest many visitors.'

'Your subject matter being me, I take? So you indicate, Mr Teague, that I am utterly boring?'

'Not at all. Not you. Ever. My work, on the other hand ...' He shrugged and again bowed, this time to Zennor. 'Please, Your Grace, relax for a moment, regardless. You are correct. We do need a rest. Your beauty dazzles me and I can no longer concentrate.'

'Oh, Ruan!' Zennor was off-guard, teasing the artist. Alys felt her cheeks burn as she wondered if anyone else had picked that up. She glanced at Jago, worried that he might have misinterpreted it. Zennor had always been open and coquettish. Before her marriage, that was acceptable, attractive even. Now, well, she couldn't imagine Ellory condoning it.

And if her suspicions were true, and Zennor was indeed with child, then she would have to be utterly careful. It just wasn't seemly, was it? Again, Alys flushed. Being seemly was, absolutely the nature of being *enceinte*, but Zennor was, first and foremost a woman.

At least, on the positive side, the Duke was not at Pencradoc this morning. That was quite possibly why the atmosphere was so much lighter here today.

'So, Mr Teague – would you care to talk me through the process of creating such a wonderful piece of artwork? There are, quite clearly, several preliminary sketches involved.' Jago had a couple of the sheets of paper in his hand; loose charcoal sketches of Zennor, her head and face in different positions, the tilt of her cheek, the curl of her hair exactly as it was in reality.

'These are really quite splendid.' Alys was in awe. Jago shrugged and handed her one showing Zennor laughing at the artist. He had captured a look in her eyes that spoke of ... adoration? Truly?

A chill shivered up Alys' spine at that thought, and she placed the sheet, face down on the table.

'Splendid? Thank you. I sometimes find that sketches help me build up a picture of a subject's personality before I begin work on the picture properly. I've already made some inroads on the canvas, but I feel there is more to discover. So I am returning to the preparation. It has to be perfect and show Zennor exactly as I see her. Every artist is different, but that is the way I work best ...'

Ruan continued describing his methods of work to Jago, who sat on the edge of the table the sketches were scattered upon, nodding and commenting as appropriate.

Alys took the opportunity to walk over and see what Ruan Teague had already committed to canvas.

'What do you think?' Zennor came up next to her and together they looked at his work. 'Having said that, there's not a great deal to see yet, is there? As he says, he has started, but stopped again.' Zennor smiled and nodded at the canvas.

'There's a sort of ... blob ... appearing. I think.'

There was a space in the centre of the picture which had a vague structure, but it was certainly not clear as to who it was.

'A blob. Thank you. I am, therefore, a boring blob. I love you too, dear cousin.'

Alys laughed. 'Never boring and certainly not a blob. This will be a wonderful portrait. You are so fortunate to have the opportunity to sit for Mr Teague. You will be fêted in all the *salons* on the Continent.'

'Do you think so?' She laughed. 'And yes, you are, of course correct about being fortunate to sit for him. And I am certain he won't portray me as a boring blob in the end. Oh! Actually, I say – Ruan?' Zennor turned and smiled across at the artist. 'Would you be kind enough to perhaps sketch my cousin? I think she needs to see herself in a Teague portrait. It would be tragic if we didn't use you for our own nefarious purposes when we have you as a captive audience.'

'Zennor! You can't ask him to do that. He's commissioned to paint you, not me.'

'I don't mind who I sketch. I really don't.' Ruan picked up his sketchbook. 'It's nice to change one's perspective temporarily. It brings one's focus back more fully on the original subject, I think.'

Alys didn't miss the look that passed between Ruan and Zennor. They both looked so – happy – in that room. So comfortable with each other. So natural.

'With respect, I think I would like to see you as Mr Teague sees you.' Jago stood up and smiled. 'His sketches speak a thousand words; or at least the ones of the Duchess do.' He turned his smile towards Zennor. 'And I would be extremely interested to see how your cousin translates onto paper, wouldn't you?'

'I would!' Zennor laughed. 'Do you agree, Alys? If Mr Teague will oblige us, will you sit for him?'

It was Alys' turn to laugh. 'Only if *you* sit for him as well, Mr Pencradoc. I'd quite like to see the real Jago, as well I think.'

The you that's hiding something, she thought. Because he was. She was fairly certain about it. But whether it was something to do with his feelings for Zennor, or his feelings for Rose, she wasn't quite certain.

He was a man she was finding increasingly difficult to read.

Chapter Thirteen

Present Day

Coren had cornered Kit as he was coming back to the house, still trying to work out what – or whom – he had seen in the gardens.

'Merryn's settled into the room. Nice touch with the flowers.'

Kit wondered if Coren was being sarcastic, but his brother seemed to be simply passing a comment, disinterested and devoid of inflection, and it was too difficult to tell.

'I wanted her to feel welcome. Even though she's not allowed in the west wing.'

'Well of course she's not, and you know why. Anyway.' Coren blinked, and stepped further into the gardens and suddenly he seemed to be himself again. He grinned. 'We've got a whole weekend off, and I don't intend spending it digging around Aunt Loveday's attics. I'm heading down to Wheal Mount. I've got an appointment to see someone there about how they run the arts centre. You're welcome to come. I guess Merryn could as well, if she's at a loose end.'

'Cheers, but I promised to take her to Marazion. So she could see my studio.' He had mentioned it at least, but suddenly he saw a way of spending some time with Merryn away from Pencradoc and getting to know her a little better. It was an absolute gift.

'Fair enough.' Coren shrugged. 'The offer's there if you want it.'

'Maybe we'll call in and see you on the way back? I think Merryn would probably like to see Wheal Mount. I told her about it, you know...'

He didn't really know what he expected Coren to know, but Coren wasn't apparently bothered. 'Okay. I'll let you get on. You haven't found anything in those outhouses yet have you? Any rogue Teagues? Any de Amatos we might have forgotten about?'

'Nope. Not yet. I live in hope.'

'Excellent.' Coren nodded and headed off somewhere, the conversation done as far as he was concerned. It was pretty weird how they could act as they always had outside the walls of Pencradoc, but inside ... it was just strange. He watched Coren's retreating back and shook his head. He didn't even know if Coren felt the same.

However, he, Kit, was the creative one, the fanciful one. The one his parents had despaired of – and probably still did. They hadn't been one hundred percent happy that their boys had inherited Pencradoc, but had made the wise decision to stay out of it for their own sanity.

'Coren is sensible,' their mother had said with a worried frown as they all attended the will reading of Aunt Loveday. 'I'm sure they'll manage to sort something out for the place.'

Their father, however, had simply shook his head and said Loveday hadn't seemed to be going soft in the head, and he hoped she'd known what she was doing. That house was far too big, and she would *know* that it couldn't exist as it was. Working men nowadays just didn't have that sort of income.

Coren and Kit had, on the other hand, simply stared at each other, speechless.

It had been one hell of a weird day.

But that was all done and dusted now. They had this pile of a house, and Coren had plans for it; and somewhere around about the vast estate was a certain blonde-haired girl from a London art dealers and he desperately wanted to see her. He looked around him, hoping he'd catch a glimpse of her – because part of him was entirely sure that she wasn't in the house, and he was confident she would be wandering around the gardens somewhere.

The tower. That's where she'd be. He knew it.

And he couldn't let the taint of that place affect her.

He ran, and kept running, and pounded through the rose garden until he saw her – just outside that damn tower, with her hands on the door, ready to walk inside.

'Merryn!' She turned around, startled, her hand on the door, ready to push it open and walk in.

'Kit!' She dropped her hands by her side as if the old door was suddenly burning her. 'Hi. I was just … uhmmmm … yeah. Just looking around.' She shrugged, and folded her arms.

'It's not safe in there. I told you. We need to get it looked at.'

'Well if you're here, can't we just *both* go in? I'm just – curious. And it'll stop me coming back on my own in the middle of the night.' She smiled, trying to make light of it. Kit, however, didn't seem to find that amusing.

'It's really not a good idea to poke around here in the dark …' Then he threw his arms out to the side, helplessly. 'Okay, okay. If you want to go in, we'll go in. I used to go in all the time, like I said. I never came to any grief.'

'Thanks. I doubt we'll find a Teague in there, but hey, I'm open to trying.'

'No, you'll not find a Teague. Not if it's anything like it was when I was young. There was some interesting graffiti on the wall of the room upstairs as I recall – but it might creep you out. I guarantee it.'

Merryn was intrigued. 'Well now you've got me hooked.' She stepped back and let Kit open the old door. It resisted him at first, then opened stiffly.

Merryn stepped inside and wrinkled her nose as the smell of damp and dust assailed her. 'Ugh. I see what you mean.' She looked around, her eyes adjusting to the gloomy interior, and felt a sense of crushing disappointment as she realised it was nothing more than an empty shell, and a circular room with a staircase to the left.

'The staircase – that was the one Rose fell down, wasn't it?' She shivered and took a deep breath as a cool breeze wafted past her.

'She's not going to haunt here. Like I also said, she didn't die here.' Kit grinned. He was also, apparently, unaware of the breeze, and he walked further into the room. 'It would certainly make a pretty nice tea room, wouldn't it?'

'Ha! It would take a bit of TLC to get there, though!'

'Oh, that reminds me.' He turned to face her. 'Marazion. Forgive me for assuming, but now you're here for the weekend – well, the foreseeable future, if we're honest – then the offer is definitely on to take you down to the coast. If you want to go.' He shrugged. 'It's about an hour away, like I said. I'm happy to drive. I also told Coren that we might meet him at Wheal Mount on the way back. He's heading off down there to check out the arts centre. Well – I said we could meet him if you want to. In fact, if you want to go to Marazion, that is. You might not—'

'Shhh!' Merryn was amused and sweetly touched. She moved towards him. 'I'd love to go. I really would.'

'Really?' Kit looked down at her and something shifted. For a moment, they stood looking at one another, then he reached his hand out and touched the side of her face. He trailed his finger down her cheek and it came to rest under her chin. He tilted her face towards him and, very gently, he kissed her.

Shivers of a very different kind ran through her body and she leaned into him, responding hesitantly at first, then, finally, smiling against his lips and pulling away. 'How could I say no to Marazion after that? I'd love to come. Thank you.'

'Excellent.' He smiled back at her, his face inches from hers. Then he too pulled away. 'And now we're here, I'd best show you the upstairs of this place. Show you the graffiti. I don't even know if it'll be visible now, but we'll have a look. Let me go first – those stairs won't have improved since I used to come and hide out.' He started walking, tentatively, up the stairs. 'I used to pretend I was a highwayman or a smuggler and this was my den. I was highly imaginative.'

'I bet it was wonderful. Wow. I can see how you would enjoy coming in here!' They had emerged into a perfectly circular room, lined with bookshelves and with a window looking out over the moors, and another one looking towards the house. How splendid.

The plaster was, however, crumbling off the walls, and the shelves didn't look as if they could hold a magazine, never mind a book – but it was still splendid.

Merryn had sharp eyes, accustomed to searching out details on paintings, and she homed in on some scribbled words written on the wall.

'Is that the graffiti?' She walked over and read it.

Rose Morwenna Hammett.
Rose Morwenna Pencradoc.
Mrs Jago Pencradoc

'Rose used to come up here when she was young! Before all – that – happened to her.' She smiled, and touched the words, thinking of the beautiful girl in the de Amato. 'And this proves that she loved Jago.'

And that, a little voice whispered, *may have been what signed her death warrant …*

She pushed the thought aside, scolding herself for being silly. Even if Rose *had* loved Jago, she had married Ellory. And these words were so low on the wall, that Rose might not have been much more than a child when she wrote them.

'Yes, that's the graffiti.' Kit stood close to her, very close to her, and she was aware of his warmth. 'I remember some workman who had come to decorate bits of the house asked Aunt Loveday if she wanted this place repainted and re-plastered and she nearly took the poor guy's head off.' He smiled, seemingly remembering his feisty aunt. 'She said he had to leave the tower alone, as it had its own tales to tell and she wasn't going to be party to whitewashing the past.'

'I think I would have liked Aunt Loveday. If you did decide to revamp this place, and turn it into a gallery, you could put a piece of Perspex or glass over this bit – conserve it, rather than let it deteriorate any further; but still let people see it. It would be a talking point.'

'I can see where you're coming from.' Kit stepped away and looked around the room. 'I think you have a point. This place would be a fantastic space, if we did go ahead with the arts centre. You sure you don't want to leave Heptinstall and come down here to help us?'

Merryn laughed. 'To be fair, you've never asked me to do that officially. Either of you.'

'Haven't we?' Kit smiled, mischievously. 'Remind me to ask you then, when we're done with the Teague hunt. London is way too far away from us. You should consider it. Can't promise we can pay London wages though.'

'If I didn't live in London, I wouldn't need London wages.' The words were out before she had time to check herself; and despite the fact she laughed, turning it into a joke before she changed the subject onto less life-changing matters, the idea took root and she knew it would stay there for quite some time.

1886

His business in town had finished earlier than expected, and he was looking forward to relaxing with a brandy, avoiding everyone else in Pencradoc.

As he headed towards his study, though, he considered that there was too much laughter coming from the library. Surely, they understood the importance of the situation – how the portrait needed to be completed and hung with the minimum of fuss and disruption. How she needed to be fully engaged with it, and not distracted by his brother.

He threw the door open, ready to lambast the artist and his wife, or to perhaps politely suggest that they continued the work and reduced the levity. However, the sight of his brother and the Duchess's cousin dried the words up on his tongue.

The Duchess was hanging over the back of the artist's chair, and the artist had a sketchbook in front of him. Discarded sheets lay all over the room and Ellory scowled. He hated disorder and chaos, and this was what he was witnessing. His brother was talking to silly little Alys Trelawney and she was looking up at him and laughing. She had in her hands three sheets of paper.

Ellory also hated people meddling in other people's business.

'Alys? May I ask what you have in your hands?'

The girl looked over at him, her expression changing from laughter to surprise. 'Oh! Ellory. What a pleasant surprise to see you've come home early. I've been looking at some of the initial sketches for Zennor's portrait.' She held one up and he could see it was exactly that. 'Don't you think they are rather beautiful?'

'Rather – disordered, I would say. But—' he looked around and his eyes settled on Zennor '—it must be necessary. Is that correct, Mr Teague?'

'Very necessary. And I have just been showing the Duchess some of the studies I have already done of her, so we can select the perfect pose. Would you care to see them, Your Grace?' He lifted the book up, his eyes almost challenging Ellory to disagree with him. 'This one is, unfortunately, one which does not show her to her best advantage. She finds it amusing that I have added a small dog to it – she says you do not particularly like small dogs and asked if we could smuggle a Labrador in as a surprise element. I said I felt a Labrador would be rather large and would distract the viewer.'

'I want no dogs on the picture, large, small or

otherwise,' said Ellory. He glanced at the book and decided it wasn't worth pursuing the rather silly discussion any more. If his wife wanted to be ridiculous, she was only embarrassing herself. And at least there were four of them in the room. She wasn't in there, alone, with either Jago or Ruan Teague. 'I trust your eye, Mr Teague. Please, continue.'

'As you wish.' Teague nodded his head briefly, and turned his attention to Zennor. 'Your Grace? We must get back to work.'

Ellory waited a moment to ensure Zennor complied with the man's request, then, satisfied that she had sat back down in the window and composed herself, he nodded, and left the room.

'Well done,' Jago murmured the words to Alys, amused at the girl's quick-wittedness.

'Hmm. I didn't want him looking too closely at our pictures.' She looked up at him and smiled. 'There's only the one picture of Zennor. And the others are – ours!' She laid them out in front of her. One of her, one of him and one of Zennor. Ruan had signed them all, which had caused the laughter: 'Just in case they become rather valuable in the future!' he had said with a grin.

'I have no desire for your brother to tell me off again!' Alys shuddered. 'So this way, I think is best.' She smiled again and scooped the three sketches into one of her notebooks, then closed it up. 'I think it's almost lunchtime anyway. Perhaps we had best leave and get ready?'

'Perhaps. Are you taking those with you?' Jago nodded at the book. 'Because I'd quite like to study them further. I'd like to know the real Alys Trelawney after all.'

'And what else would I do with them?' She was teasing and he smiled. Then she picked the book off the table and tucked it into the shelves. 'Look. Just for you, I'll leave them here, yes? It's not as if I've written anything in this book yet beyond some notes. I'd quite like to see the real Jago Pencradoc as well. This way, we can both find the pictures when we want them.'

'We can.' And then he had a thought. 'Perhaps, though, a better way for us to discover one another is to spend some time together? Away from here. How would you feel about a trip to the coast? We could maybe travel to St Austell or Fowey. Tintagel, even. Somewhere away from the moors and away from Pencradoc.'

Alys studied him for a moment or two, then nodded. 'I think I'd quite like that. It's certainly true that I haven't really been further than Bodmin. That is, of course, if Zennor can spare me?'

Jago looked at Zennor. Again, she was laughing at something Ruan said, and the artist was watching her as if she was the only woman in the world.

'It seems to me,' he said quietly, 'that she can spare you well enough. But I think we need to at least extend the invitation to her in Ellory's company.'

Alys followed his gaze and nodded. 'Yes. I think we should. He won't want them left alone, will he?'

Jago shook his head. Sadly, he knew that to be the truth.

Chapter Fourteen

Present Day

Merryn woke up the next day and stretched out in the king-size bed. With her eyes still closed and a smile on her lips, she thrust her arms and legs out, starfish-like, just to see if she could touch the four corners of it. She couldn't. She turned over, still smiling and opened her eyes to look out of the window.

A hazy shadow of a fair-haired girl flickered into being amongst the sunbeams, and the girl pulled her legs up towards her and wrapped her arms around her knees as she stared out across the gardens. Then, just as quickly, the image was gone.

Merryn felt a chill from her toes up to the top of her head and stared at the space where the girl had been. It was the image she had daydreamed about yesterday, when she had been looking out of the passage window, across to the folly.

Okay. If that was the case, that was all right then. She relaxed, believing it to be nothing more than the result of her half-awake state, and the memories spinning around of what had been an incredible day. She smiled again at the memory of Kit's lips on hers, and felt a different shiver – a thrill of pleasurable anticipation, as she remembered what she was doing today.

She was going to Marazion. With Kit. And she could hardly wait.

She took her time getting dressed – thank God she had clean clothes today! Kit had been as good as his word and showed her where the washing machine was, and she took a nice long bath before slipping into a pair of denim shorts and a rose-pink vest top, that both smelled deliciously of fabric conditioner, rather than the inside of a pub.

She was heading down the stairs when she saw a fair-haired man studying the portrait of Ellory. Coren. She thought he was heading out earlier than they were, but she must have been mistaken.

'Merryn!' She turned, pausing on the staircase to acknowledge him. It was Kit, rushing along the landing looking sweetly dishevelled and tugging a shirt on over his white T-shirt. He too was in denim shorts, his nose sun-kissed as hers was and she felt her stomach *squidge* pleasurably at the sight. 'I was hoping that I'd be downstairs before you. So you could be welcomed properly to Pencradoc, with a good cup of coffee and a slice of toast for breakfast.'

'You remembered!' It was one of the things she'd mentioned about The White Lady. Every morning, there was a greasy fry-up ready for the guests at a buffet bar. It had been nice, the first couple of mornings; but as the week went on, she started to help herself to good old buttered toast and marmalade instead. Having such a large breakfast always made her want to fall asleep mid-morning, and that, she had told her employers, wasn't particularly good for business.

'Of course I did.' He grinned and caught her up, seemingly oblivious to Coren standing at the bottom of the stairs as he launched into a conversation about what she might expect at Marazion.

'Coren's still here.' She nodded towards the hallway, but when they turned to look, the space he'd been standing in was empty. 'Oh! Well, I thought he was. Perhaps he went into the kitchen when we were talking.' She frowned and stared at the spot where he'd been.

'I thought he'd left about half an hour ago,' said Kit. 'He popped his head into my room to say goodbye, and asked if we were still intending to visit Wheal Mount. Perhaps he didn't go straight away, after all. That's not like him, he normally doesn't linger once he's made his mind up to go out. Oh well.' He shrugged. 'Maybe he had a reason to linger today – who knows with Coren?'

He had continued chatting as they walked into the kitchen, and he made her the promised coffee.

There was no sign of Coren, but Merryn didn't have time to ponder his absence too much as Kit was making suggestions she quite liked the sound of. 'There's a nice sculpture garden not too far away from the town. Maybe another time we could go there? That's if a day in my company doesn't put you off spending any more time with me.' He cast a glance at her, one of those teasing glances that were becoming more familiar to her the longer she spent in his company.

'It sounds lovely. I'm sure it'll be great. I like the idea of a sculpture garden.'

'It's a very nice sculpture garden. Plenty of ideas to steal, come to think of it.'

'True. You could maybe do that for Pencradoc's future art centre? Perhaps update the stumpery? Maybe tame her old roses somehow?'

'Oh no – Rose's stumpery and secret garden stays.' Kit shook his head vehemently. 'I'd hate to wreck her Gothic fantasy.'

'But you know, there might be trails you could set out

around the Wilderness garden and in the walled gardens as well. It's a thought.'

'It's a very good thought. Not that I'd actually *thought* about it, until you mentioned it.'

'Happy to be of help.'

'You definitely were. See, it just proves that we make a good team.' He offered her a refill of coffee and she pushed her cup over to him. 'Seriously though, you've got some great ideas.'

'Hmm, I suspect I'm creative in a different way to you. I can't draw for toffee, which is why I appreciate looking at pretty things for my job.'

'I like pretty things myself.' He held her eyes just a little too long, a smile pulling at the side of his mouth. 'Some more than others. Some, I'm happy to look at for a long time. I especially look forward to spending time with pretty things.'

Merryn felt her cheeks heat up and she looked down at her mug, trying to hide her own smile. 'I suspect there are many pretty things in Marazion.'

'One or two.' He grinned, sitting back in the seat. 'We'll head off after you've finished your coffee, if that's okay with you? I'm really excited to be able to show you the gallery.'

Merryn drained the mug and set it down in front of her. 'Let's go.'

They went. As he had promised, it was an hour or so's drive, but the scenery flew past, and the journey didn't seem that long at all. Soon they were outside a two-storey, white painted building overlooking the beach and St Michael's Mount, with the car fitted into a neat little space in a sort of courtyard.

'This is it. Welcome to my real life.' He pointed at the building and smiled. 'It's my gallery, my workspace, my shop and my classroom. I run painting courses and they're pretty popular. But, as you can imagine, it'll never bring in enough cash to run Pencradoc.'

'I can imagine.' She peered out of the car window and took in the white building with its blue window frames and imagined how the light would stream in from the south-west coast and the crystal ocean. 'And there's St Michael's Mount.' She pointed out of the other window. 'You're very lucky to live here.'

'I am. I've got a cottage just along the road; it's a tiny thing, but it's big enough for me.' He nodded along the main road. There's no garden, it's straight onto the street and I've only got a yard out back – but if I want to sit outside in the summer, I just carry a deckchair over to the beach.'

'Very useful. My flat is one-bedroom, and I have no outside space at all. But on the plus side, I can walk to Camden Market and it's not far from the tube station.' She peered out of the car again. 'And I have no desire to be in London at this moment in time. Here, I can just take time to – breathe.'

It might have sounded silly, and somebody else might have laughed, or at least looked askance at her, but Kit didn't.

He simply nodded. 'I understand. Come on. Speaking of breathing, let's get out of the car and I'll show you around.'

He was happy to be here, in this seaside town, with Merryn Burton. And he'd missed the place, he really had. He doubted anything much would have happened in his absence, but he knew if it had, then—'Lowenna!' He stopped short as he pushed the door open and a figure dressed in scarves and beads and long, swirling skirts bore down on him.

Lowenna would have told him. He'd left her in charge, after all.

'Kit!' She rushed at him and embraced him. 'How's it going in that big old house of dear Aunt Loveday's?'

Kit frowned momentarily. She'd never met Aunt Loveday; yes, she'd come to the funeral to allegedly support him, but she'd spent most of her time trying to flirt with Coren, who hadn't been interested at all. That ship had sailed a long time ago.

Then, for a briefly horrifying time, she'd turned her amorous attentions to him. He had a feeling that it was more likely to be Pencradoc she was interested in, than either of the Penhaligon brothers. Lowenna, he thought, had an image of herself drifting around Pencradoc as mistress and chatelaine rolled into one.

'That big old house is fine. As is my brother. And as is me, thank you for asking.'

'Oh!' Lowenna at least had the grace to blush and fiddled with the edge of the silk scarf she had tied up to keep her long auburn ringlets out of her face. 'I'm glad you two are well. And who's this? A sister? A cousin? Someone else I should know about?' She smiled sweetly, and Kit took a couple of steps away from her. She was just a little too close for comfort.

'This is Merryn. Burton. She's staying at Pencradoc for a little while.'

'Oh! Merryn. Divine.' Her words didn't really match what her face was saying. 'So – *she* – has been at Pencradoc? *I* haven't even been and forgive me—' she turned her back on Merryn and lowered her voice. 'But I think I've a little more right to visit? I'm not sure you've ever mentioned anyone called Merryn before, darling?'

'I'm working on cataloguing the art collection.' Merryn's voice was equally sweet, but there was an edge to it Kit hadn't heard before. 'May I ask what determines one to have a "right" to visit a house? I'm there in a professional capacity, first and foremost, but I can't see that you have any more of a right to be there than I have. Unless there is something Kit isn't telling *me*?' She reached out and touched his hair, trailing her fingers down to his shoulder and squeezing it. 'I'm not sure you've ever mentioned anyone called Lowenna to *me*, before, darling?'

Kit bit hard on his lip, trying not to laugh. He wondered if the mischievous sparkle he saw in Merryn's eyes was visible to anyone except him.

'Lowenna is my good friend and assistant. She's been holding the fort for me down here. She was also in a relationship with Coren for a while.'

'Oh! How nice. Well, I'm sure you'll get a chance to visit Pencradoc at some point. Coren never mentioned you either. How strange.' And with that, she turned away and began to wander around the shop, as if the things Kit had for sale were far more interesting than Lowenna could ever be.

It was one of the first times Kit had ever seen Lowenna speechless. His old friend followed Merryn around the shop with her gaze, her mouth working as if she was going to say something but couldn't quite find the words.

Kit patted her on the arm companionably. 'We found a de Amato. That's interesting, isn't it?'

'De Amato? Well – he was slightly wild in his youth,

I believe.' Lowenna was still looking at Merryn. 'It depends from which of his periods it is, as to what value you'll get for it.'

'Yes. Merryn is going to take the information back to her company in London and we'll be taking advice from them. Have we been busy?'

'Oh – there was a flurry yesterday as I believe a coach trip were here to see the Mount, and they had some time in the town before they had to go back.' Lowenna shrugged. 'A few queries came in about the next course you're running. I told them they should email you. Of course, I *did* expect you to be back sooner – and not to be trailing somebody with you. You might have called ahead and warned me.'

'It's a big job. She lives in London. The local inn was crap, hence the fact her company are paying us to give her boarding for a little while. And I don't need to justify what I do or who I do it with to you.' He smiled to take the edge off his words. 'And I had booked a fortnight off, remember? This is technically still the middle of that holiday. I didn't have to come back at all.'

Lowenna looked away, pursing her lips as if she really wanted to show her disapproval but was making a point of *not* doing that. 'It's your time off. You do what you want with it,' she finally said with a distasteful sniff. 'I'll be around if you – or your *friend* – need anything.'

'Thanks, Lowenna. We're going to have a look around the shop, then we're going upstairs to the gallery. I want to show Merryn the workshops and teaching spaces. It's easier to understand what it's all about if you can see what a person is talking about, I think.'

Lowenna mumbled something which might have been agreement, then drifted back behind the counter with her nose in the air. Kit went to find Merryn, and discovered her lurking beside some seascapes.

'These are beautiful. They remind me of Laura Cooper's work – look at the clouds in that one!' She peered, right up close, at a watercolour.

'Do you think so? Look – I've got some signed books about her and her husband, Julian MacDonald Cooper. Miles Fareham was down here on holiday with his family, and actually Lowenna recognised him, so we were really lucky. She's a force to be reckoned with and I don't think he could refuse after she'd given him a thousand reasons as to why he should sign the copies we had. Laura was pretty active in Newlyn in the early 1900s. It's only about fifteen minutes away, down the coast. The time *after* we do the sculpture park, I'll take you to visit. I think they've turned her old studio into a museum now.'

Merryn laughed. 'I love your confidence. Okay – it's a date. The time after we do the sculpture park, we do Newlyn. That's if you can persuade your friend over there to allow me to go.' She nodded towards Lowenna. 'Was she serious with Coren? I feel a bit bad if she was and I said that about him not mentioning her.' She frowned at Lowenna, who was bustling around importantly behind the counter. Kit wasn't quite sure what she was bustling about with, but she was definitely giving the impression that it was awfully important.

'No. I think it lasted a couple of months. Coren charmed her, as he does, and she was smitten. Then they realised they were completely incompatible. He's so organised and loves detail. He's always got plans and ideas to do something. Lowenna is happy drifting around doing this and that. She hates planning anything.

But she obviously heard about us inheriting Pencradoc, and suddenly decided that she quite fancied a nice big house to live in. I don't think she actually thought beyond what would happen when she moved in. And, as you know, Coren is pretty much—' he lifted his arm up and pointed at the canvases hanging on the wall in front of him '—straight up – about what he wants to do. No wiggle room.'

'Oh dear.' Merryn looked over at Lowenna again. 'That was never going to work, was it?'

'No. It wasn't going to work with either of us. At one point, she told me I had a poet's soul and she could see it in the depths of my eyes, but I'm afraid I gave her a very strange look when she said that and made an excuse to go and do something else. But anyway – let's not talk about Lowenna. What do you think of this place? Come on – I'll take you upstairs and you see what you think about our view.'

'I'm loving the ground floor,' said Merryn, 'and I'm sure I'll love the view too.'

'Only one way to find out!' And he took her hand and guided her up the stairs.

Even when they were upstairs, even when they were standing by the window admiring the little village and the harbour over the sea, with the castle above it all on its wooded hill, Kit didn't let go of her hand.

'It's quite a nice walk across the causeway – not that you can see it now, with the tide covering it. I'll have to—' He stopped and looked away, trying not to smile.

'Take me across it another time?' Merryn squeezed his hand.

'Something like that.'

'Noted.'

'Do you want to see the classroom? It's just through here.'

He indicated a door and Merryn nodded. 'I'd love to. Let's see what your programme is like. I bet you couldn't make my painting any better. I suspect your pupils have to have a modicum of talent before they're even allowed to come through that door.'

'Not at all. They just have to have enthusiasm.'

'I've got that. Just no talent.'

They continued their conversation as Kit finished the guided tour and Merryn could tell he was a man who was absolutely passionate about his job and his life. She could see him working at Pencradoc as well, once it was the arts centre the brothers dreamed of opening. In fact, she could see, quite clearly, the circular room at the top of the tower displaying all sorts of artwork and Kit running some of his classes there ...

It was a nice thought.

'So how do you feel about getting some lunch? There's a nice pub along there, or we could grab a picnic – take it onto the beach? Have a walk past my cottage. But you can't come in. You know that, don't you?' He cast a sidelong glance at her as they stepped out into the little square and made to cross the road to the beach.

'Yes. That'll be another time.' Merryn nudged him. 'I get it. There's lots of things down here that you want me to visit and see. I'm happy to do all that, I really am. But I'm not sure how long cataloguing the artwork at Pencradoc will take. I want it to take ages – I absolutely do. But I don't want to outstay my welcome. I don't want to impose on you and Coren any longer than I have to – and let's be honest, I heard you tell Lowenna that you'd only booked a fortnight off work. I can see how much this place means to you – I think your heart is in Marazion. It would never be anywhere else, not even Pencradoc.'

'Of course you're not imposing! Don't think that. We're happy to have you and it'll take as long as it takes. If I need more time off, I'll take it. The place won't fall to pieces without me. Lowenna is *more* than capable.'

'Lowenna will completely hate me if she doesn't already. And part of me wants to get the Pencradoc work done, so I can start enjoying Cornwall more. Cordy is so happy in my flat, that I think I'll need a shoehorn to get her out. So in that respect, I think I might have to book myself a little holiday on the end of the Pencradoc job. I might see some of the sights then – some of the sights around Marazion. Perhaps. But at the moment, you're still, technically, my employer, and it's probably fine to do this sort of thing at the weekend, but I guess we have to be professional again on Monday.'

They were now on a little path, which led down to the beach, and she stared out at the sea and the wooded hill with the castle on top. 'And when I'm not being a professional any more, I wouldn't really have a place to stay. Unless I went back to The White Lady. Or found a handy hotel down here ... perhaps.'

Kit took hold of her shoulders, his hands heating up her sun-warmed skin even more. 'I know of a nice little cottage that might have space for you? If you wanted to try it for size?'

'Mmm? Really.' She smiled and tilted her face towards his. 'Next time, I might.'

'Do you mind ... not ... being very professional for a few minutes?' Kit's dark eyes were twinkling, flecks the colour of the sky and the sea, all mixed together in a glorious swirl.

'It's the weekend. I'm on my own time at the weekend.'

And lunch was, apparently, forgotten, as they kissed one another again; this time on the beach, in the midst of a Cornish summer.

1886

It was as Jago had suspected: 'Alys and I are taking a trip to the coast today,' he announced after breakfast, in a tone that he knew would not leave any room for argument. Indeed, he couldn't see why Ellory would argue with him – surely the idea of Jago leaving Pencradoc for a few hours was something he desired?

'And you are certain both yourself and Alys are going?' Ellory's eyes drilled into Jago's. 'So there will be nobody on the estate except my wife and the artist?'

'Certain. And you, of course.' Jago's tone was overly polite. He knew Ellory would never allow them to be alone at all.

Ellory dabbed the corners of his mouth with a linen napkin and laid it down beside his plate. 'No. As it happens, I need to go to Truro today, and I will not return until late this evening. I do not feel it is appropriate to leave the Duchess alone, or indeed have you and Miss Trelawney unchaperoned. Therefore, she shall travel with you, and Mr Teague will take the day as leave. I shall ensure the message is relayed to him, and he can resume his employment tomorrow.' He nodded and indicated the conversation was at an end.

Jago felt the temper rise within him and leaned

across to Ellory. 'And what,' he hissed, 'do you think I am likely to do with Miss Trelawney if we *were* to be unchaperoned? Not all of us have your morals. And I will not stand for your orders either. You have no authority over me. However, as the Duchess' company does delight me, as you well know, then I will be pleased to escort her to the coast as well.' He stood up and glared at his brother then looked at the women who were watching the spectacle unfold aghast. 'Alys, Zennor, would you be able to be ready for us to leave within the hour? I shall ensure the carriage is prepared for us.'

They both nodded and mumbled assent. He forced himself to smile at them both, hoping his humour was not too evident to them. He wouldn't allow Ellory to spoil today, he just wouldn't.

Alys and Zennor were waiting at the bottom of the stairs, each of them dressed for a day at the coast. Alys was practically fizzing with excitement. She loved the seaside, and hadn't spent nearly as much time there growing up as she had wished. It was simply perfect – the idea of spending the day at the coast with Jago ... she checked herself and looked guiltily at Zennor, who was primping and preening at the ribbons in her hat in a looking glass, turning this way and that, balanced on the last stair, trying to see what the fabric looked like draped from her bustle, smoothing the skirt down over her stomach as her brow creased ever so slightly.

Well – it would *almost* be perfect, if it were just she and Jago; but what could she do? She loved her cousin but had, if she was truthful, been looking forward to spending some time alone with Jago. The man intrigued her. Perhaps it was her writer's mind, but she was certain he was hiding more than she cared to guess at. She had hoped that today might draw it out of him.

But then she looked again at Zennor and felt her spirits plummet a little more. How could she ever hope to compete with Zennor? They were chalk and cheese, and Jago clearly held her cousin in very high regard.

She didn't want to say he "loved" her. She couldn't say that. But he was terribly over-protective of her. And she knew Ellory was cold and heartless at times, and deep down she also knew Jago's spark burned so much brighter. It almost seemed, though, that Jago had deliberately dampened his own spirit and it proved to her that there was definitely more to Jago and to the brothers' relationship than met the eye.

She felt herself flush as she caught herself wondering exactly how passionately Jago might burn in certain situations. Then she looked at the floor, lest anyone see her face was scarlet from imagining herself in those situations with him.

'I'm so sorry. Have I kept you waiting?' The main door opened, and a gust of warm air wafted in as Alys looked up quickly and found herself face to face with Jago. Her stomach somersaulted, and they stood there looking at one another for what seemed like hours. He was extraordinarily handsome, his grey coat, fastened just on the top button complemented with a grey waistcoat. His trousers were black and he had a black ascot tie around the starched collar of his shirt, which gave him just the right element of well-dressed finesse and something verging on darkly dangerous, especially as his hair was looking a little more unruly than it had done at breakfast.

'No – not at all,' Alys managed to say eventually. 'Indeed, I think we were a little early.'

Jago smiled. 'The carriage is ready, I made sure I brought it round for us. It was a ploy, perhaps, to ensure my brother had left for Truro and he has. His personal carriage is missing. As is one of the little landaus. I suspect Mr Teague has taken advantage of the day and gone somewhere. I don't blame him.'

'Ellory's *personal* carriage?' Alys couldn't help but feel amused and a little astonished at that.

'Oh yes.' That was Zennor. 'He has his best livery on that one – so everybody knows he is there. I prefer to travel with a little anonymity, personally. I— oh!' There was a *thump* as Zennor slipped off the step and landed in a heap at the bottom of the stairs. 'Oh! My goodness. I've turned my ankle. Ouch!' She leaned forward and rubbed at her foot. 'Oh how annoying!' She looked up at Alys. 'I'm so sorry. I'll be hobbling for a little while I think. Oh damn!'

'Zennor!' Alys suppressed a laugh as she helped her cousin to her feet. 'That's not appropriate language for a Duchess.'

Zennor pulled a face. 'Perhaps not. But it's the truth.' She leaned on Alys and together they made their way to the door, Zennor limping a little. 'It will not stop me though. I want some sea air.'

Then Alys was more serious. 'Are you sure you're all right?' she asked in a lowered voice.

Zennor cast a quick glance at her cousin and her cheeks flushed a little.'I'm perfectly well, Alys. Thank you for your concern.'

She set her mouth in a little line and Alys cast a glance up at Jago. 'I don't think we should let her come. She's a liability.' She tried to make a joke about it, simply to hide her concern. If Zennor was indeed pregnant, a fall wouldn't do the poor babe any good at all.

'Alys!' Zennor was indignant. 'I am coming with you, and that's it.' She peered out of the door. 'The weather will be fine, I can sit on the beach and wait for you while you wander around the town.'

'We will see.' Alys smiled at her and helped her down the steps to the waiting carriage. Jago helped Zennor onto the carriage and then Alys. His hand was warm in hers, even through her glove and she felt that flare of heat on her cheeks again as she positioned herself next to her cousin. Jago climbed aboard last. He sat opposite Alys and smiled at her. Then he looked out of the window, the smile still on his lips.

Alys dipped her head and stared at his feet. She hoped he wouldn't see *her* smile. She was conscious it would be on her face all the way to Fowey – and she knew it would have been there even if Zennor wasn't.

Chapter Fifteen

Present Day

The time they spent at Marazion went far too quickly, but they had to leave eventually. The car was warm inside, and Merryn felt that, had the journey to Wheal Mount been more than twenty minutes or so, there was a good chance that she might have fallen asleep.

However, she was pleased she'd stayed awake when they drove up to the long, low, grey two-storey building, with an orderly line of pillars seemingly holding up the first floor, which overhung the ground floor in the best tradition of Tudor buildings. Jago had obviously wanted to build something that looked old.

'What a great house!' Merryn was suddenly alert. 'So where are the studios? I'm guessing there are some.'

'Sure. They're at the back, overlooking the courtyard. These rooms at the front are the residential rooms, for the people choosing to do the retreats.'

'Residential. Nice. I hope the beds are a bit more comfy than the one I had at The White Lady.' She screwed up her face, remembering. Really, it hadn't been a particularly good experience. By the third day, she had started dreading going to bed as the mattress was so uncomfortable.

'I couldn't say. But the photos on the website look nice. I've never been into the bedrooms – I've taught the odd course here, but didn't say too much about the family connection in case the students had a tendency to start talking about Teague and Zennor. Teague is something of a local, romantic legend.'

'Yes. I can imagine. That's one legacy that will never die.'

'I agree. Look – there's Coren. Seems as if he's made a friend.' Kit grinned as he saw his brother leaning nonchalantly against one of the pillars and talking to a pretty brunette. The body language gave them both away and Kit raised his eyebrows, 'Interesting. And not surprising, He always likes the dark-haired ones.'

'So he would have liked Rose and Zennor then.'

'He definitely would have. I'll just let him know we're here, I think.' He tooted the horn as they drove past and solemnly waved as Coren jumped at the noise.

'Poor man,' said Merryn. 'That's spoiled the moment. That was mean of you.'

'It's no worse than he's done to me. Once, when we were sharing a flat in Looe, he turned up supposedly accidentally, when I was out for a romantic meal with one of my exes. Sat at our table, ordered himself a meal and called her the wrong name – then apologised as he said he thought I was still with this other girl, because he'd taken a message from her to say that she'd see me at seven p.m. in the restaurant. It was a load of tosh, of course.' He smiled, wryly. 'That relationship didn't last very long.'

'Why did he do that?' Merryn was horrified and amused in equal measure.

'Because he was jealous. He quite liked the girl I was with that night, and didn't want me to go out with her. It was clearly never meant to be, though. For either of us.' He parked the car and switched the engine off. 'So what about you? Do you have any evil brothers or exes in the habit of shouting at you in the middle of a crowded restaurant?'

'I only have the one sister, like I mentioned. That would be Tegan, and she's travelling in Europe at the minute. I think she was picking lemons in Italy or something, last I heard. She's not the best at keeping in touch. And just so you know, the last boyfriend I had decided he'd rather message his ex-wife than chat to me over a glass of wine in a cosy pub – although we were in that pub at the time.'

'But exes are exes for a reason,' said Kit. 'I'm sure I wouldn't be contacting any of mine. Especially not if I was with someone else. Anyway, let's see what my brother has to say for himself. And who his new friend is.'

Coren had by this time, walked over to the car and was standing beside it, looking as if he'd been caught out doing something nefarious. 'Hey guys. You might have let me know you were heading down. I could have been more prepared.'

'I like to catch you off guard,' said Kit with a grin as they got out and he locked the doors. 'Who's your friend?'

'Oh! That's Sybill. She's been really helpful. I've had a tour around the building, and we were just about to go and have a look at some of the business plans. Do you want to come along too? It might be something you'd be interested in. If we can make a go of it, then I expect you'd be involved somewhere along the line.'

'Oh – thanks for the offer. I'd love to, but Merryn might find it a bit dull if I went and left her,' began Kit; then Merryn shook her head.

'Honestly, you go and do what you want. I'm sure I can amuse myself for a while here. There's bound to be a tea room, isn't there?'

'Yes. Just over there.' Coren pointed to an orangery on the side of the building. 'The ground floor is open to the public as well for viewing. There are some rooms done out as the family would have perhaps had them. And there are portraits. I'm sure you'll enjoy looking at those. You'll know some of the names of the sitters by now, as well. And one of the artists is quite well-known.'

'Ruan Teague!' Merryn couldn't contain her excitement. 'There's really some of his work here?'

'Really. Just three paintings, but you'll like them. And one or two little surprises.'

'Great. I'll see you back in the tea room then – I'll have a look around, and head in for a cuppa. Just meet me there.' She cast a glance at Kit, wondering whether it would be acceptable to kiss him before they went their separate ways, and decided against it. Coren probably had a very good idea what was going on between them, but she didn't want to flaunt it: whatever 'it' was, because she was sure there was something more than just a flirtation going on ...

However, this was not the time or place to speculate. Instead, she nodded decisively and headed towards the main door. White-painted now, with a tasteful foyer behind it, Merryn could imagine it when it was newly built and newly decorated. She traced her hand across a beautifully carved dado rail and looked around her. It didn't seem right – she could tell that some work had been done on the interior; some doors had been blocked off and plastered over, and there had originally been a great big fireplace *there*—

'Stop being stupid,' she muttered to herself. She looked up and saw a huge, decorative skylight, pouring sunshine into the foyer and smiled up at it.

She had loved that – she had loved standing beneath it and listening to the rain pelting off the glass, or watching the snowflakes settle on it, or seeing blue sky above her or trying to count the stars in the night.

How on earth did she know *what* someone else had liked? And why had that someone's thoughts even entered into the equation? She was being silly. All she was thinking, was what she, Merryn, would have liked, had she been lucky enough to have this house.

Instead, she dragged her gaze away from the skylight and headed towards a young man sitting on a stool beside the door into what she assumed was the museum part of the house. He was, she guessed, an art student. He had a very individual look about him, several piercings and a bright smile.

'Is it okay to go and have a look at the rooms?' she asked.

'Oh yes – straight through and follow the route around. You'll come back out there.' He indicated a door at the opposite side of the foyer. 'It's just so people get an idea of what it would have been like to live here and follow in the footsteps of an artist. It inspires some of our guests.'

'But the artist, Ruan Teague. He didn't live here, did he?'

The boy grinned. 'He didn't. But they do say he was in love with Duchess Zennor even before her husband died.'

'I knew he had connections to the family, and he painted an incredible portrait of her, so that completely makes sense.' Her heart started to beat a little faster as she imagined the scandal that would have come to this house with the connection to Zennor and Teague.

'Yeah, they wouldn't be able to prove it, anyway, even if it is true.' He winked, amused. 'But then poor old Zennor wasn't a Duchess for long. Her brother-in-law, Jago, inherited the title. But you might be interested to know that we have a couple of family portraits in the drawing room by Teague. Here.' He gave Merryn an A4 laminated sheet of paper. 'There's a bit of information on there for you.'

A little thrill shivered up her spine. She was going to see some far more commercially acceptable Teagues and the thought was exciting. 'Thanks. If I have any more questions, I'll ask them afterwards.'

'And if I can't answer them, I'll try to find someone who can. Enjoy.'

'Thanks, I will.' Merryn smiled and walked past the boy into a reception room of sorts, all blue and white pastels, tasteful sofas and *chaise longues* scattered about, with a writing desk in the corner and a piano set with sheet music, as if someone had just finished a recital and walked away. She scanned the walls eagerly, wondering if this was the drawing room, but, when she checked the laminated sheet, it wasn't. Still, it was a beautiful room and if she half-closed her eyes, she could almost see a little girl sitting at the piano, a woman standing over her, showing her which keys to touch. A man was sitting on a sofa, a newspaper open beside him as another small girl scrambled across his knees, showing him a picture she'd drawn.

The man turned to acknowledge the child, and Merryn saw him glance across to the fair-haired woman at the piano, who turned to him and smiled back—

Merryn pulled herself up short. Imagination. That's all it was. It was the sun, potentially heatstroke from Marazion, and she was still groggy from that car journey.

Or at least, that was what she told herself as she put her head down and hurried into the next room, making a big show of looking at the information sheet she had, although she wasn't really reading it.

As she stepped into the next room, though, she froze. The atmosphere felt different in there; more homely than the lounge, if that was even possible, and she snapped her head up and found herself staring straight at a charcoal sketch of a long-ish haired man with an unfathomable expression and his brows slightly knitted together, the suggestion of a frown on his face, as if he was concentrating very hard on something just beyond the viewer's look.

A Sketch of the artist, Mr Ruan Teague. The words were written on the bottom on the picture, and there was a signature next to them: *Elsie Pencradoc, aged thirteen*.

'Good grief!' Merryn stared at the picture. This – this was Kit in a different time. If she had recognised some of him in the portrait of Zennor, she saw more of him in here. It was the expression he had worn when he had been staring out over the waterfall after they found the letter from Rose. It was a look she had seen in his eye so many times. Was this, then, one of the surprises he had promised her when they had parted at the doorway earlier? 'Seriously? Oh my *God*, Kit Penhaligon! Are you really, genuinely related to bloody Ruan Teague!' She laughed, suddenly amused at it all. It made sense. It so did!

Her spirits lifted enormously, she moved onto another picture. She smiled again, seeing the matching sketch of Zennor.

A Sketch of my Dear Mama and my Youngest Brother Arthur.

It was true! It had to be! Elsie, still aged thirteen, had drawn her mother and a small toddler brother in front of her. Zennor was clearly smiling right at her oldest daughter, even as she held one of Arthur's chubby fists in each of her hands and bounced him in front of her.

'Elsie Pencradoc, well I think I know where you got your talent from!' said Merryn smiling up at the picture. A little giggle seemed to tickle her consciousness, even as a soft breeze danced past her. Elsie, acknowledging that fact, perhaps? 'How wonderful.'

Merryn consulted her laminated sheet and nodded to nobody in particular as it gave some description of the pictures, and said how Elsie had been a frequent visitor to the house with her family, and had drawn the pictures on one of her sojourns there. She turned to face the fireplace and looked up at three more portraits.

These were, unmistakeably, Teagues.

The first one was of Elsie and a smattering of younger children, all with dark eyes and dark hair. It was obvious to anyone who had seen the marble bust at Pencradoc who she was. Amidst the abundance of children sat an older version of Zennor; still stunning, still beautiful. In this picture, Arthur was about six, and Elsie was, Merryn guessed, around about sixteen. She stood beside her mother, and Teague had lovingly painted her mischievous eyes and also, somehow, captured a sense of fun about her; as if she was ready to burst into Society and stun them all. There was no sign that Elsie's genetic make-up was any different to her apparent half-siblings and again Merryn smiled. The likeness was there for all to see. She was willing to bet that tongues had wagged quite a lot as far as Teague and Zennor were concerned.

That's why they had to keep Ellory's portrait up at

Pencradoc – so it looked as if they were honouring Elsie's father ...

Yes. Wherever that thought had come from, it made absolute sense.

Next to this delightful picture was a portrait of, so the laminate said, Jago Pencradoc, Duke of Trecarrow. Again, he was dark-haired and dark-eyed; half-smiling on the portrait, perhaps amused at something Teague had said while he was creating the picture – or perhaps thinking of something one of his own children had done. Merryn liked Jago. She looked at his portrait for a long time, her head tilted to one side, appreciating both the art, the artist and the model.

'Hello there,' she whispered. 'I think I would have fallen for you big time, Jago Pencradoc.'

At last, she tore her gaze away from Jago's laughing eyes, and focused on the final portrait in the drawing room that had any real links to the family she was so entranced with. Jago's Duchess, with her brood of beautiful, fair-haired little girls. They all looked a lot like their mother, all four of them. But they had Jago's eyes; the darkest brown, it seemed – and, in some of the girls' they were serious, but in some, especially the littlest one, they were impish: *Clara, Mabel, Lucy and Nancy.*

The litany of names burst into Merryn's head.

She had insisted on easy-to-spell Christian names for her daughters. Jago, however, had insisted on pure Cornish names for their middle names: Clara Bronnen, Mabel Gwenna, Lucy Ebrel and Nancy Verran ...

'Then,' he had said, teasingly, 'they can choose which part of their heritage they prefer to be associated with ...'

That information, Merryn realised, checking her laminate, was not written down anywhere for the casual

171

tourist to Wheal Mount. But she knew, as if she had been part of the original conversations, exactly what had been said.

She closed her eyes and could feel the soft, blanketed weight of a chubby, fair-haired baby in her arms as Jago's arm crept around her shoulders and he leaned in to kiss her:

'It matters not that we have daughters. Pencradoc will go to one of Elsie's sons, whether the bloodline rings true or not. Wheal Mount is ours, our family home. Pencradoc is on loan; it always has been. I have gifted it to Zennor and Teague, and they are the caretakers there. For whatever reason, they love it.'

'I prefer here to Pencradoc,' she had said, dropping a kiss on the baby's head. 'There are too many memories.'

'I agree.'

Then the memories faded and Merryn opened her eyes to find herself back in the drawing room, back in her own life. It was an odd feeling, but not uncomfortable. Rather, that she was back where she belonged.

She looked around, thankful that there were no other visitors there in the drawing room. Forcing herself to study the rest of the pictures in the room, which were far less interesting, she walked slowly out, into the next room, wondering who exactly she had left in there.

She found herself in a dining room, a roped off walkway around the perimeter. As if honouring the small girls in the portraits next door, the table had been set for what looked like a children's tea party, with tiny sandwiches and biscuits and cakes on pretty little floral plates. There was a teddy bear at the head of the table while several of his friends formed a centrepiece around a tiny china tea set and a small chequered tablecloth of their own.

There were more pictures in here of the little Pencradocs. They were angelic-looking despite the fact Merryn was sure they were nothing of the sort. They weren't Teagues though, although she was fairly confident Elsie had created a few of them, despite the fact they weren't signed. They just had the same look about them as the charcoal drawings Merryn had already seen.

Smiling, remembering, almost, the little girls tumbling out of the nursery, rampaging around the gardens, being kissed goodnight – every night – in their identically decorated bedrooms, Merryn stepped into the second to last room on the tour. This was the library, and it reminded her of the job she still had waiting for her at Pencradoc. She couldn't wait to get started on that particular library, but for now she took a cursory look at the books on the shelves here, imagined Jago sitting at the desk in the window, receiving visitors and scolding his children where necessary:

'Oh Papa, I am so terribly sorry. Please take the money from my allowance to buy Uncle Teague a new ink pen. But please, please don't make me tell him it was me who broke the nib. It was a beautiful pen!'

'It was. Which is why he is so sad you broke it.'

'But I didn't mean to. I simply wanted to draw as prettily as Elsie. Oh Papa, I only wanted to practice ...'

Then, as if following an invisible swirl of skirts as a small child – Mabel, that was right – rushed out of the room sobbing, Merryn hurried into the final room. A little boudoir of sorts, with a white-painted desk of its own, looking out into the gardens beyond.

Their mother's room. This was where she wrote stories for the girls, pasted mementoes into their scrapbooks. comforted the small whirlwinds as they fell into the room declaring how vastly unfair it was that Papa had scolded them.

Even these few rooms had the atmosphere and energy of a wonderfully happy, slightly chaotic home. Merryn walked around to the window and looked out at the gardens beyond, the sea in the far distance a ribbon of brighter blue against the skyline. It was as if she remembered it all. As if, once she left, the spell would be broken, and she would be back to her own world.

It wasn't a bad world. She loved her job, she loved her friends and family, even if Tegan annoyed her greatly at times. But she knew she would have loved this life as well.

She would have loved Jago beyond words.

She thought, somehow, standing in the spot she felt she had stood in a thousand times, she still did love him.

Alys.

The name came to her out of nowhere. It was *Alys* who had felt all these things for Jago … of course it was.

When Kit arrived in the tea room, leaving Coren and Sybill still chatting – much to his amusement – Merryn was sitting reading what looked like a slim guidebook.

'Interesting reading?' He sat down next to her.

She looked up at him, uncertainty in her eyes. 'Pretty interesting. So – Jago and his wife had four daughters?'

'Yes. Four in five years. I think I told you that's why Coren and I got Pencradoc, and nobody from Jago's direct line inherited it? Jago had no sons.'

'Yes, you did. Good. Do you know their names? Their full names? The little girls' names?'

'Oh – now you're testing me. Let me think. Clara. Maisie? Mavis? Lucy – and Nancy.'

'Almost. It was Mabel. But do you know their *full*

names? With the Cornish bits added? Think. Really *think* about it.'

'Okay.' Kit stared at her for a moment. He knew the girls had unusual middle names – beautiful names, but undeniably unusual, compared to their very classic Christian names. He wasn't sure that he'd ever been told, but sometimes, you just had to trust your instincts and let the names that were hurtling into your consciousness out … 'Clara Bronnen, Mabel Gwenna. Lucy Ebrel. Nancy Verran. Verran – it means little one. She was the youngest, they had no plans to have any more children, and Jago called her Verran because of that.' He blinked and looked at Merryn. 'Didn't he?'

'I think he did. Now. How did you know that? How did you know those names?'

'I guess I've seen a family tree. Or someone told me. And it's stuck in my mind.' He frowned. 'It's the only explanation. Oh! I think their mother wrote a little story book about the girls – you know, like *Alice in Wonderland*. Maybe that's what I'm thinking of.'

'An *Alice in Wonderland* book. By Alys Pencradoc. Jago's Duchess. Makes sense.' She smiled, briefly. 'It might be so. And those *are* explanations.' Merryn closed the little booklet and sat back, her cheeks flushed. 'But it doesn't explain how *I* knew that, does it?'

There was a beat. 'No. Unless you found some paperwork at Pencradoc? Or found a copy of her book in the library?'

'I didn't. I haven't started properly in there yet. But now I know of something else I can look for, as well as any rogue Teagues: Alys' story book.'

'If there's a copy there, that is.' There was a silence. 'I'd hope there was. It's very interesting.'

'Quite. And something to look forward to, perhaps. But the paintings are lovely, though, aren't they? The Teagues. And—' She grinned unexpectedly. '—the Elsie Pencradocs. She was one talented little girl.'

'Wasn't she just? Yet Ellory, by all accounts, had no artistic talent.'

'He had no soul, never mind any artistic talent.'

'Perhaps.' Kit smiled. 'I can't say for sure. But he certainly didn't seem that way inclined. Zennor, maybe? Was she talented?'

'Not at all.' Merryn shook her head emphatically. 'I think it's quite obvious Elsie took after a certain artist. Quite probably, her step-papa. And *your* relative!'

Kit grinned. 'I'm not denying that one. So – nature or nurture debate?'

'I don't think that sort of talent is entirely due to nurture. Do you?'

'No.' He laughed. 'I bet it made for some interesting dinner party conversation within Society, though.'

'I bet. Did you and Coren get everything sorted out?'

'We've got a good idea of which direction to take it. But I think he'll be relying on Sybill to help him out.'

'You're joking right? He likes her? He really *likes* her?'

'He seems to like her.' Kit leaned forward and let his fingers trail across the back of her hand. 'It's nice, don't you think?'

'Very nice. I'm glad he's made a connection.' She grinned. 'Do you want a cup of tea? I can get us another one.'

'I'm good, thanks. Sybill kept us well-watered.' He sat back and studied her. She seemed very at home here; almost as if she suited Wheal Mount, or Wheal Mount suited her. It felt right being here with her as well. As if they'd been there many times before.

'Would you like to have a look around at the studios and the workspaces? You might enjoy seeing the less public parts of the house – the ones the day visitors don't see. Sybill said we could roam freely for a little bit before we go home.'

'Home.' Merryn smiled gently. 'As in Pencradoc?'

There was a beat. 'I guess so. Pencradoc.'

'Wheal Mount seems more like home than Pencradoc does. Is that odd? I mean, Pencradoc is lovely, but ...' She left the sentence hanging and her cheeks coloured even more pink.

'But it's not like home.' He thought of the pictures in the drawing room; the desk in the study that seemed so familiar, even though he had only been here a handful of times. The image of a little girl rushing out of the library into the arms of her mama, after a scolding that she had completely taken to heart ... 'It's not like here, is it?'

'No. It's not.' She tucked the booklet into her handbag. 'And on that note, I would absolutely love to have a look at the rest of the place. I can't wait. Come on.'

'It would be my pleasure.' Kit stood up and held his hand out.

It was a great feeling when Merryn took hold of it, and smiled up at him.

1886

The carriage arrived at Fowey, and Jago helped Alys and Zennor climb out of it. Alys took a deep breath, appreciating the salty air and the tang of the ocean.

'It's beautiful,' she whispered. 'Look at it! Look at the little fishing boats. Oh –what are those big square buildings? They look like little castles.'

'How sweet!' Zennor was also entranced.

'They're blockhouses,' said Jago with a smile. 'See how one is on one side of the river and one is on the other? They had a huge metal chain between them, and they used to raise it to stop ships entering the harbour to protect the town. If my history is correct, then I believe we were under threat from the French and Spanish around five hundred years ago.'

'How marvellous.' Alys felt the excitement bubbling up inside her. 'What stories they could tell. What stories *I* could tell about them. Do you suppose there are shipwrecks, or smugglers?' She scanned the horizon eagerly, as if something of that ilk would suddenly oblige her by materialising.

'Most certainly.' His hand was warm on her waist as he guided her towards the coastline. 'There are some old fishermen who will still talk about Richard Kingcup. He was the landlord of the Crown and Anchor, and about fifty years ago there was a landing quite nearby, at Pencannon Point. Some of the coastguards got into a fight with the smugglers, and they captured almost five hundred gallons of brandy. They thought it was headed to old Richard's place, as he was well-known as a smuggler.'

Alys was spellbound. 'So what happened? Did they capture the smugglers?'

'Oh, you simply must tell us!' Zennor was equally rapt.

'No. Well, they did, but they were all acquitted.' Jago grinned. 'The jury said the clubs they had used as weapons against the coastguard were simply walking sticks, and the vicar was a character witness for one of the men. And the farmers defended the other chaps. So they weren't punished.'

'And I would imagine they all celebrated at the Crown and Anchor with that brandy!' said Alys, feeling quite certain of the outcome.

'Perhaps they did. Who knows?'

'It's a marvellous story, whatever the truth of it.' Zennor leaned on a stone wall overlooking the little harbour and smiled. 'It's absolutely delightful here. How wonderful to be at the coast today and to breathe this air. Pencradoc is wonderful but ... stifling. Do you understand?' She looked at Alys, almost apologetically. 'Or does that make me sound desperately ungrateful?'

'No. Not at all.' Alys cast a quick look at Jago. 'I think it's good to get away from Pencradoc. It's good to have a change of scenery.'

'Isn't it just?' Zennor turned, so her back was towards the wall. Her smile was brilliant. 'Would it be even more ungrateful of me if I were to ask you to leave me alone here? You two can go and explore. And I can just sit on the beach, have a little walk around. See the boats and discover the shops. Perhaps treat myself to a cup of tea.' She looked wistfully out to sea again. 'I miss the freedom to do this. I really do. I'm a little too old for a nursemaid. Even one as lovely as you, Alys.'

'I suppose that's up to Jago,' Alys replied. 'I don't think there's too much mischief you can get up to here, really.'

Jago shrugged, his face darkening for a moment. 'It may be against my better judgment, Zennor, but I am inclined to agree with Alys. What the eye doesn't see, the heart doesn't grieve over, as they say. My brother need never know about this. Shall we say we meet back here in three hours? The town may have enough to amuse you for that long, but please try not to get swept out to sea or to hitch a ride on a fishing vessel.'

Zennor laughed and threw her arms around him. 'Thank you. Thank you both. I promise I won't disappear on a fishing boat. I have too many other things to amuse myself with. But first, I'm going to walk down to the beach and rest my ankle a little.'

And with that, she turned and headed down some little steps, using her parasol as a walking cane.

Alys watched until she saw her cousin was settled and then turned to Jago, suddenly overcome with a mixture of emotions that ranged from excitement, desire and a heart-pounding anticipation and back again. Three hours! They had three hours to spend together – with nobody watching them.

That beautiful summer's day held such promise.

She rested her hand on his arm as they walked through the tiny, medieval streets. He pointed out St Finnbarr's Church and spun her tales of how French marauders destroyed it centuries ago, and how the Earl of Warwick had rebuilt it. He told her about Place House, the tower which stood behind the church; and how, not so long ago, the Reverend Treffry who owned it, had raced down to the beach with his congregation to take advantage of the spoils of a shipwreck: 'After,' Jago added mock-seriously, 'he had made them wait until he was in the porch so they could all start running at the same time.'

'Sensible Reverend!' Alys said with a delighted laugh.

They wandered along Fore Street, and saw the Old House of Foye, one of the oldest houses in the town, and stopped for a cup of tea at a little tea shop Alys thought was simply delightful.

At length, they headed along the Esplanade with all its grand houses, and soon they found themselves in a little cove. She'd heard someone in the town refer to Readymoney Cove and wondered if that was this place. It was, she thought delightedly, a smuggler's cove if ever there was one. And there was what looked like a stone-built castle perched on the rocks above them.

'Isn't that pretty!' Alys stared up at it, marvelling at how something so substantial could have been built on such a high, rocky place. 'What is it?'

'That?' Jago smiled at her. 'It's St Catherine's Castle.'

'Lucky St Catherine. Fancy having that built for you.'

'Lucky? Isn't she the one who ended up spinning on a burning wheel?'

'Oh, don't spoil it!' Alys shuddered theatrically and laughed. 'Can't we just agree it's a lovely castle?'

'Yes, we can agree that.' Jago laughed down at her, and drew her closer. 'So, would you like a castle built for you then?'

'Perhaps.' She smiled. 'Unless someone built me a palace instead. Much more comfortable and less draughty I think.'

'I'd build you a palace,' said Jago, teasing her. 'I'd make it look like that old folly you're so fond of. It would be a very small palace. But I'd call it Alys' Palace. It has a nice ring to it, don't you think?'

'A very nice ring. Wouldn't St Alys' Palace be so much better though?'

'I don't know. *Are* you a saint, Miss Trelawney?'

'Are *you* a saint, Mr Pencradoc?' Alys fired back, enjoying the to-ing and fro-ing of the conversation.

'That very much depends.' He smiled down at her. 'Most of the time, I do try.'

Alys looked up at him ready to respond in kind, and somehow sensed a darkness behind those words. She shivered a little, the smile slipping from her face slightly. She hoped she'd caught it in time, that he wouldn't realise she was trying to read what was behind those fathomless eyes and finding nothing but a barrier. It was disconcerting.

Her hopes, however, were unfounded. 'What is it, Alys? What have you seen that worries you so? What happened to ... this.' He touched the edge of her lips with his forefinger. 'There was a smile there before, and it's gone. Have I disappointed you in the fact I don't deserve a sainthood?'

'We are none of us entirely angels, Jago.' She summoned a smile again. 'But I do wonder what you might have to hide? There's something there.' She took her hand from his arm, and wrapped her arms around herself. 'I just don't quite know what it is.'

He looked at her for a moment, a haunted expression flickering across his face. 'There's nothing that can be changed. It's not something I'm free to share with anyone.' He shrugged and looked up at the castle on the rocks. It was quite possible his idea of ending the conversation, but Alys was not to be deterred.

'Is it Zennor?' she asked suddenly. Her stomach lurched as the thought popped into her head. 'Are you in love with her? Is that it? Is that why you hate Ellory so much?'

'Hate Ellory!' He snapped his head around and stared at her. 'What makes you think I hate Ellory?'

'It is quite obvious that you don't like him very much!'

'I detest him, but it's nothing to do with Zennor. I don't love Zennor. I never have done. What on earth gave you that impression?' He seemed genuinely stunned.

Alys was conscious that her face must have expressed the shock she herself felt. 'You always seem so – dismissive of Ellory, and you always seem to want to include Zennor in things that we – you – do.' She felt her cheeks flush. She didn't want to sound selfish, but it would have been so much better if they could have come here themselves today.

'Truly?' He turned to face her fully. 'I honestly love Zennor as a sister, nothing more.'

'Truly.' Her cheeks were burning even more fiercely now, but she might as well continue. There would never be a better opportunity. 'I think Ellory thinks you love her. I think he—' But the reason cut in and she bit her lip, stopping herself from continuing.

'You think he does what?' He stared at her, his eyes burning into hers. She realised his hands were on her shoulders and she felt faint. He was so *close* to her. So close!

'He distrusts you.' There, it was out, and she had to say it. 'I think he thinks the same as I do.'

'Good God!' His eyes were wide. 'Does *Zennor* think that?'

'No. No, she doesn't.'

'Good. I would never want to give that impression to another woman—' It was his turn to stop suddenly. Alys wondered what he was going to add to that, then all thoughts of what he was going to say, or who he was going to say it about fled as she realised that they were even closer than they had been. His lips were inches from hers and her face was tilted upwards, and his was looking down.

'Alys. I could never think that about Zennor. Not when you're here. Not when you're at Pencradoc.'

And then his lips were on hers and she didn't resist – couldn't resist – any longer.

But, even as his lips touched hers, she knew, without a doubt, that there was something stopping him; something holding him back from kissing her properly – from knowing that his heart and soul were completely in that kiss, as hers had very willingly been.

He pulled away, leaving her leaning forward, her lips still slightly parted.

'I'm sorry. I shouldn't have done that.' He was contrite, his eyes dark and troubled. 'I'm so sorry.'

'Please – don't be.' Alys looked up at him, her heart pounding in her chest. Tentatively, she reached out and touched his lips with her fingertips. 'Never be sorry. Just – let me in, Jago. Let me in. Please. There *is* something you're hiding, and I don't know what it is yet. I really don't.'

'Perhaps it's not something I want to share with you.' He half-smiled at her, his eyes sad. 'Perhaps I can't quite let you into that place just now. Come. We should go. Zennor will be waiting, and we don't want to be in trouble with the Duchess, do we?'

He leaned forward and kissed her again; chastely, almost – and, it also seemed, with some regret.

Alys was no closer to knowing the real Jago than she had been when she had stepped out of the carriage and into Fowey's cobbled streets.

Jago wished he could tell her. He wished he could tell

her everything, but it wasn't right to do so. How could he willingly put her in that position? How could he drag the past out into that harbour town and burden her, Alys, with it all?

The spectre of Rose would never go away, it seemed. She was still haunting his life even now.

Chapter Sixteen

Present Day

'So how's the weekend going? In that nice big country house?' There was a smirk, a definite smirk, in Cordy's voice, the day after that wonderful trip to Marazion.

Merryn raised her eyes heavenwards; pointless, of course, as Cordy would be unable to see her displeasure. But it made her feel better, anyway. 'Very well, thank you. Not that I've spent the entire weekend in the house. We went to Marazion yesterday, Saturday, and a gorgeous place called Wheal Mount. It was a house one of the owners had built and it's now an arts centre. It's kind of what Kit and Coren want to do with this place.'

'That's a shame – if I inherited a house that size, I'd live in it.' There was a lusty sigh. 'I'd close up loads of the rooms, so I didn't have to heat them all – and I'd have a room turned into a dance studio as well, I think.'

'But you can't dance.'

'And that's the *point*.' Cordy was indignant. 'If I had a dance studio, and heaps of money, I'd be able to *get* better at dancing, because I'd have a completely fabulous dance teacher and he would make me brilliant.'

'Dream on!' Merryn sat on the window seat and stared out over the garden; then she rapidly clambered off it again, the image of that girl she had seen there flitting into her mind once more. 'The point is, nobody has that sort of money to maintain the house. That's why they need to either sell the place or do something with it.' They could sell the de Amato, she thought. But she didn't think that was an option, somehow.

'Oh, I hope they can do the arts thing – at least people can use it and the house can feel loved and wanted again.'

'I don't think it necessarily feels unloved and unwanted. It's a very splendid house – for the right owner. And the right purpose.'

'Dance studio,' Cordy muttered. 'Absolutely a dance studio.'

Merryn laughed. 'With the Teague connection, it should definitely be arts!' And she had also filed the idea of Alys' story book away in her mind as well. How wonderful if she could find that! That would be very special indeed. 'Is everything okay with you, anyway? You're not starting to feel a bit lonely?'

'In a city like London?' Cordy snorted with laughter. 'Honestly, after a day at work and a zillion auditions every week I'm relishing coming back to some peace and quiet. But there's always something I can do, or somewhere I can go. Especially here, where you live. Honestly, if you ever want to sub-let, please let me know.'

'You'll be first in the queue. But I have no intention of leaving it any time soon, so don't get your hopes up.'

'Dammit. Okay. Well, keep in touch and let me know when you'll be back. So I can weep in the corner and pack my bags and go back to the horrid, over-priced shoebox-sized room I officially live in.'

'I will do. Anyway, thanks again for looking after the place for me.'

'Any time.'

They chatted for a little while longer, then said their farewells. Merryn hung up on her friend, smiling at her excited chatter about her latest horror of a blind date, and looked out of the window again. It had started to rain, now – that heavy, noisy, fat-dropped rain that suddenly gushes out of the sky in summer, and Merryn frowned. That put paid to her plans to have a wander around the Gothic rose garden for a little while, and she didn't want to impose herself on Kit and Coren, who had closeted themselves away in the library to discuss Sybill's business model.

What better excuse did she need, then, to go back and have another look at the de Amato? Her phone call to Cordy had made her think again about that painting – and to be honest, she wanted to feel a little closer to Rose. She had, she admitted in the quiet of her mind, quite a good sense of Alys, and also of Zennor. But she didn't know or – she felt her cheeks heat up with the silliness of it – sense – anything to do with Rose. That was part of the reason she had planned to visit the rose garden. Sitting quietly, she reasoned, might have brought Rose closer to her. But sitting quietly in that room might just do as well.

And at least she didn't have to pass that horrible, arrogant portrait of Ellory to get to the hidden room, did she?

She hurried along the upstairs corridor, into the west wing, part of her wondering why indeed she was hurrying. Was it so that she didn't risk the wrath of the Duke by invading spaces he had deemed private?

'It's probably easier to show you.' A soft hand taking hold of hers. 'Promise? A cross-your-heart promise that you won't tell him we know where it is?'

Merryn stumbled, even as she shook her hand, trying to get rid of the feeling that someone had touched it in those little-used corridors.

'Come with me!'

The memories were blurring at the edge of her consciousness, and she felt the years slip backwards. She was Alys, she was running along here with Zennor, the hem of her nightgown threatening to tangle her legs up in it as they sped along, hand in hand, giggling nervously, excitedly, knowing they shouldn't really be doing this. What would Ellory think? What if, God forbid, Jago saw her, dressed just in her nightgown? What impression would he have of her then?

But there was no more room to think or regret or to take notice of her better judgement, as she was here, outside the room, outside Rose's room, and she knew what she was searching for was inside.

Merryn tried the handle, half-expecting it to be locked; but it opened easily, as it had done the first time Zennor had brought her here. She caught her breath – the room was freezing, absolutely bitterly cold. She exhaled, a small puff of white vapour in the darkened room. Someone had closed the curtains against the summer day, but if Merryn hadn't known the season, she would have expected it to have been November at the very least.

Something rushed past her and she spun around, in time to see the indistinct figure of a woman in a white gown, her dark hair flowing past her shoulders vanish beside the bookcase with the shiny wooden owl decorating it.

'Oh God, oh God ...' Merryn couldn't breathe. She didn't think she'd ever been so terrified in her life. That vision, that moment, if anything, convinced her that this place was haunted; convinced her they were sharing Pencradoc with a selection of ghosts and memories of a time gone by. From approximately, the late nineteenth century if her instincts were correct. 'Dear God!' There was no way it could have been a shadow or a trick of the light – there was no light in there to play tricks on her. The curtains were still firmly closed, the grate empty. None of the lights were on, the lamp on the side table was switched off. 'Who is it? Who *are* you?' The words sounded trite and silly, and she was surprised she'd even managed to say something coherent. 'Zennor? Rose? I know you're not Alys. I *know* you're not her—'

A cold hand came down on her shoulder, long fingers squeezing it painfully, and she gave vent to the loudest scream she'd ever produced. She jerked away and spun around, ready to scream again. Nope – *this* moment, this moment *right here*, saw her at the most terrified she'd ever been in her life.

This moment, when she realised that there was nobody behind her, but she had definitely felt those fingers pressing into her flesh.

And the moment she turned and saw a faded rose lying in the grate of the cold, dead fireplace.

'What are you doing in here? This is forbidden. Nobody is to enter this room!'

He grabbed at the woman he saw in the shadows of the room – it had to be that Trelawney creature. His wife would not have dared to defy him, but this one, this fair-haired woman, with the queerly-coloured jade eyes that saw far too much, would defy him without a second thought. He had to watch her as well as his wife. His wife! Ha! His Duchess. He did not trust either of them.

But instead of touching warm skin and bony shoulders, his hand connected with nothing and fell straight through the image.

'What the hell?' He blinked and then he saw her –

*the dark-haired woman he had grown to hate, flit past
him and run towards the room where he kept her image
hidden away and where only he was allowed to go.*

*He stood rigidly in the room, his heart pounding as
his hand dropped to his side. He stared at where she had
disappeared, then turned, and slamming the door behind
him, left the place that was beginning to drive him mad.*

1886

For Alys, the remainder of their time in Fowey went far
too quickly.

'I think I know the real Alys a little more now.' Jago
smiled down at her. 'So for my part, the trip has been
successful. I don't necessarily need to study Ruan's
sketches very much.'

'I think I still need to look at the one of you.' Alys
glanced up at him. 'There's still something I'm not quite
sure about. And if you won't tell me, I have to find out
somehow.'

'Oh really? I can assure you – good God!' He drew
suddenly to a halt, his fingers tightening on her arm
where it was tucked into his side again. It had felt safe
and secure, and very *right*, despite the fact that she
wondered how and when she could reach inside of Jago
Pencradoc and draw his innermost secrets out. Now, it
felt as if he was holding onto her for support.

Alys looked over to where he was staring and clutched
him even more tightly. 'Mr Teague!'

'And your cousin. The Duchess.' Jago began hurrying
towards the couple, who were, it had to be said, sitting
very closely together on the beach.

Alys couldn't help herself. She broke away from Jago and, hitching up her skirts, ran as best she could over the soft, shifting sand. 'Zennor! Mr Teague! What a pleasant surprise.' The two seated figures sprang apart and turned to face her.

Zennor smiled, delightedly, and Alys halted uncertainly, wondering if she had perhaps been mistaken.

'Alys. What perfect timing. Have you seen what Ruan has been working on? He decided to come to Fowey for some sea air today, and we bumped into one another.'

Ruan Teague smiled at Alys and stood up. He bowed to her. 'When I discovered I had the good fortune to have the day to myself, I decided to come here and try my hand at some painting *en plein air*. I borrowed a landau from Pencradoc and came here. Imagine my surprise when I found the Duchess here as well. I wondered if we would find you in the town. Zennor said she was looking forward to having some time to herself as well – but I'm afraid I spoiled it for her by bothering her with my work. And perhaps taking her for a cup of tea, but that's our little secret, and I can neither confirm nor deny whether we went or not.'

Despite the circumstances, Ruan's smile was infectious, and Alys found herself laughing. 'It's certainly a surprise to see you here. Jago and I were in the town, as you can see. We abandoned Zennor to her own devices.'

Jago stepped in at that point. 'Good afternoon, Ruan. It is perhaps fortunate that you were here as well. I do wonder how circumstances conspired to bring you to Fowey today, but I'm sure Zennor appreciated your company.'

'Indeed. Fate is a wondrous thing, is it not?' Ruan smiled and nodded at Jago, then reached a hand across to Zennor. She took it and scrambled to her feet in a manner which did not particularly reflect her position in Society.

'It was pure chance, Jago,' she said quietly, but Alys saw that telltale flush again.

However, Jago didn't seem to want to argue. 'Whatever it was, I am sure it is nothing we need to take back to Pencradoc with us, is it?'

'Not at all.' Zennor seemed to visibly relax and let go of Ruan's hand. She smoothed her skirts down and looked at Alys. Her cheeks were still flushed prettily, but whether it was from the sun or Ruan Teague's company, Alys would not like to have guessed. 'Is it time to return then?'

'It is. The carriage is waiting just up by the inn over there,' replied Jago.

'Then I shall take my leave and find the landau. I drove it here myself, a skill of which I am rather proud.' Ruan bowed again. His eyes, Alys noticed, lingered on Zennor a little wistfully. 'And thus, I must also return alone. It is a shame, but there we have it.'

'A dreadful shame,' murmured Zennor, 'but one that we can do nothing about.'

'Exactly.' Ruan half-smiled and turned away to collect his painting things. Alys saw them now, neatly stacked by where the two of them had sat on the beach.

Inexplicably, and certainly on Zennor's behalf, Alys' heart felt a little heavy as she watched Ruan Teague walk away across the beach. She cast a glance at Zennor.

There was an odd little expression on her cousin's face, and Alys reached over and squeezed her hand. 'Don't worry, we'll all be back at Pencradoc in a little while and you can continue your conversation.'

'Yes.' A small sigh. 'But it won't be quite the same, will it?' Zennor looked over her shoulder, studying the waves as they softly lapped onto the shore, seeing the little boats out at sea and the harbour walls. 'Out here, it's all – different. Out here, it's not real life, is it?'

There was a beat and Alys felt herself flush. 'And it's better out here than it is in real life, is it?' She had to ask, she just had to.

'Yes.' Zennor's voice was firm, unequivocal. 'Yes, at this present moment in time, it is.'

Soon, the memory of that perfect day in Fowey became just that: a memory that Alys liked to keep close to her heart and think about. She had taken Ruan's sketches out of the book in the library on more than one occasion, and stared at the one of Jago for as long as she dared; but whatever secrets he was hiding, she couldn't read them through the loose, confident pencil lines.

Alys had also begun to spend more time in the tower, and to consider it as her own place; her own refuge. Zennor was still occupied with Ruan Teague and the portrait, and Alys had begun to feel like an extra limb – not necessary and quite an encumbrance.

Zennor was certainly more distracted, and even when they spent time together and talked, Alys knew her cousin's mind was elsewhere, somewhere she was unwilling to let anyone else discover. Occasionally, she saw her cousin gaze over the countryside, deep in thought and, once or twice, she had missed breakfast claiming a headache. Her headaches, however seemed only to last for the morning, then she was cheerful again by lunchtime.

Pencradoc, Alys was starting to think, was somewhere

which kept its secrets very close to its heart and she had ceased to love the place as she had once done. There was something dark there, and she wasn't willing to think too much as to what that might be.

And she very much wished Zennor would let her in again; she was definitely hiding something and Alys' suspicions remained. Yet, if that was the case and it was happy news, then why would she not share it with Alys? That had been, initially, the main purpose of coming here; to support her cousin in some future pregnancy. And if she wasn't allowed to even know a baby was a possibility, then why was she here? And why, more importantly, was Zennor hiding it from her? What was she reluctant to admit?

During these weeks, the tower, although a little dilapidated in places, became a haven for Alys. It was a good place to hide with her pens, her notebooks and her ideas. The Banqueting House had also lost its appeal somehow – the memory of what might or might not have been a hand creeping through the door had spoiled it; and even if the rumours were true about Rose, she hadn't *died* in the tower, had she?

Although, it had to be said, Alys wasn't doing a lot of work in the tower. Much of her time, against her better judgement, really, was spent daydreaming – about Jago Pencradoc no less, and trying to push Zennor's behaviour out of her mind. The day in Fowey had certainly reassured her that Jago wasn't in love with Zennor, but as she had told him at the time, there was still something he was hiding.

It was as she was considering yet again what this might be, that her eyes drifted over to some markings on the old white-painted wall. Alys was sitting on the floor, her books spread around her, when she found her gaze being drawn back to that same spot, time after time. In fact, as she looked at it and tilted her head to one side as if to see it better, she became more and more convinced that it was writing.

She scrambled to her feet and went over to the wall. The markings were, now she examined them more closely, in heavy pencil and about chest height. Almost, she thought bizarrely, as if a child had scrawled them there.

Rose Morwenna Hammett.
Rose Morwenna Pencradoc.
Mrs Jago Pencradoc

Alys' stomach lurched. There was no mistaking, really, whose childish hand had written those words. She touched the last line with her fingertips: *Mrs Jago Pencradoc*.

Jago. So many questions began to bubble up into Alys' mind ... had Rose been in love with Jago? Had Jago been in love with *her*? Then why had Rose married Ellory? Had she been forced into it – had she loved Jago all along? And, more importantly, did he still love Rose?

And that wasn't all. What unfinished business was there between them? Was that why he had disappeared abroad? And now he had come back to Pencradoc – was he here to punish Ellory by involving himself in his second marriage out of spite—

'My rebellious Alys. How did I know you would be in here?'

She turned guiltily at the sound of his voice.

'Jago! I was just ...' There was nothing she could

say really, her fingers were still resting on the pencil markings.

'What have you found? Do we need a coat of paint in here if you're commandeering it as your own little eyrie?' He was smiling, walking towards her, and her heart was pounding. She was frozen to the spot, and could feel the colour burning up her cheeks even as she watched him come closer. It was a warm day, and his coat was slung casually over his shoulder, his hair deliciously dishevelled as if he had just come in from a ride across the moors. 'Oh.' He stopped, staring at the words on the wall and she saw his eyes scanning them, reading and re-reading them. 'She loved *Wuthering Heights*. She thought it terribly romantic that Cathy had written so many iterations of her name on that window ledge Lockwood found. She only ever read the first half of the book though. Right up until Catherine died. Then she would always flick to the back and read how Heathcliff died and they met again. The rest of the book was incidental.'

Alys' heart was pounding now. He sounded strange, distant almost. Lost somewhere in the remote past with Rose. He dropped the coat onto the floor and reached out his own fingers to touch the words. Alys quickly withdrew her own. She didn't want to touch him, didn't want to be anywhere near him.

'I'd forgotten she did this. How could I have forgotten that?' Jago half-smiled and turned to face Alys. 'There's so much you forget when other things happen.'

'But you've never ... forgotten ... how Rose felt about you. How you felt about Rose.' Her voice was controlled; statements rather than questions.

Jago nodded slightly. 'I can never forget it for one

minute. I should have been here. I shouldn't have left her—'

A sob caught in Alys' throat. 'So that's it, then, Jago? That's what you're hiding? I knew there was something. I should have guessed. Excuse me.' She swept past him and ran over to the staircase. Heedless of the state of them, of what had allegedly happened to Rose there, she ran down them and out into the gardens. She needed to run as far away as she could from Jago Pencradoc and the ghost of Rose.

'Alys!'

But she wouldn't look back, even as she heard his footsteps behind her and the anguish in his voice.

Chapter Seventeen

Present Day

Merryn needed real people around her. Hell, she would even take the taciturn bartender at The White Lady for company if she was forced to.

But she would much prefer Kit. After their trip to Marazion and Wheal Mount she had definitely realised that she really *did* like him. A lot. In fact, she had spent much of the previous night replaying their trip. And because her mind was so much on Kit, she was totally ill-prepared for that incident in Rose's old room, and she had run out of the west wing and hurtled straight down the stairs, bursting out into the gardens and stood there, her face upturned, letting the rain soak through her clothing and dampen her skin.

'Merryn!' His voice startled her, and she jumped. Kit was heading towards her, his hair wet and sticking to his head, rain water dripping down into his collar. It can't have been pleasant, and his face was just losing a thunderous sort of expression as he approached her. 'Any reason why you're standing in the rain?' He shook his hair like a dog shakes its coat. 'You're not seeing our Cornish weather at its best here, I'm afraid.'

'I'm not, am I?' She pulled herself together and forced a smile onto her face, hoping he didn't hear her heart going nuts in her chest and the flapping of a million butterfly wings somewhere in her stomach as he smiled back at her. No need to tell him about what had just happened. He'd think she was bonkers, especially after

Wheal Mount, when she'd confessed that she'd known all those facts about Alys and Jago. 'Still, at least I had a sort of beach day yesterday. Why didn't we have candy floss? I'm pretty sure that would have gone down a treat.'

'Because you had a clotted cream scone instead?'

'Quite possibly. It was a very good scone.'

'You can have candy floss …' He raised his eyebrows comically and they disappeared into his soggy fringe.

'… next time.'

'That's right. But you still haven't told me what you're doing out in the rain. Shall I stand next to you? Is it fun?' He walked over and stood, quite deliberately, beside her, matching his stance exactly to hers and lifting his face to the rain.

Merryn couldn't help but laugh. 'Not really, but at least it's warm rain. I just got a bit spooked inside, that's all.' *Dammit!*

'Spooked? How come?' He looked at her now, his face was concerned then it hardened. 'Is it my brother? Is he throwing his weight around again?'

'No! No, not at all!' The expression that flitted across Kit's face was disconcerting, then it was gone, and he was himself again. Merryn shivered. She was pretty sure she wasn't imagining this; these changes that were coming over the men more and more frequently over the time they were together here. Was it just because they were siblings who had outgrown living in the same house as one another long ago? Or was it Pencradoc itself and the memories that seemed to be lurking around every corner? She was pretty sure that, had Loveday known about the effect it would have on the brothers' relationship, she would never have left it to them. Yet, they were fine, absolutely fine together at Wheal Mount; and when, last night, they'd all decided to go to an Italian restaurant in the town for dinner, they'd had a marvellous night, and kept her laughing with their reminiscences about growing up and the spats they'd had as boys.

There hadn't been one inkling of bad blood or jealousy between them, and she even found herself warming to Coren again – she'd almost begun keeping her distance from him, she had realised; although if anyone had asked her why, she would have found it impossible to answer, and the idea of that horrid portrait of Ellory was the kind of image she'd mentally assigned to the poor guy whenever he crossed her mind.

After all, despite his questionable lineage, Coren had the same colouring as Ellory, even though that was where the similarities ended.

In fact, in Merryn's mind, the answer to her see-saw of emotions was simple: it was Pencradoc. The idea of Pencradoc; the atmosphere of Pencradoc; the shadows around every corner of Pencradoc. She was definitely less in love with the place now, than she had been twenty minutes ago after that incident in Rose's room – although part of her adored the old place fiercely.

Yes – it was impossible to give herself any answers, never mind if anyone else had been inclined to ask what the problem was.

'Because if it's my brother—'

'No! No it's not him at all.' Merryn put her hand on his forearm and looked up at him. He was warm, if a little damp, and the feeling of touching him grounded her. 'I can tell you, but you'll think I'm certifiable this time. Not just bonkers.'

'Try me.'

'I really do think I saw a ghost in there. And I think

one touched me as well.' There. It was out. She shuddered and moved her hand away but, surprisingly, he caught her hand and raised it to his lips.

He kissed it gently and returned it to her. 'You're not certifiable. I think I've seen things in there as well. A woman. I saw her the first day you were here. She was up in the window of one of the rooms in the west wing and I thought Coren had decided to start the inventory in there. I thought it was weird.' He shivered and frowned, staring off into the distance. 'And I'll tell you where the oddest place is. The top of the waterfall. I often think there's someone up there, but when I look she's gone. Whether it's just the water spray and the way the light hits it, though, I'm not sure.'

'She? It's a woman? The same woman you saw in the west wing?'

'She. The same woman. I can't describe it, as I don't think I've seen her properly, but I've more got an impression of her, you know? White dress, dark hair ...'

He left the sentence hanging and Merryn's stomach turned over. 'I was in the west wing too, when I saw her before. I was at a loose end and wanted to see the de Amato again. I hope you don't mind.'

'Why would I mind? You're an art expert, you're here to price things up for us. It's natural you'd want to go back there.'

She felt a flood of relief. 'You're happy for me to do that?'

'Of course. I doubt we'd sell it, but I understand the pull of her.' His face shadowed again and Merryn suddenly understood.

She touched his arm again. 'You've been there too? You've been back to look at her?'

'Is it that obvious?' His face twisted into a strange sort of smile. 'She's got some hold over everybody here – and I hate that she's hidden away. Like he was ashamed of her or something. I mean, I don't think she was exactly what Ellory wanted in a Duchess, for whatever reason.'

Merryn looked at the ground, embarrassed. It was exactly what she'd been thinking, but didn't feel it was appropriate to voice that right now. She'd already called her mad in front of him and look how that had ended up. Poor Rose!

'I hope Zennor had a happier time with him than Rose,' said Merryn. 'And at least she seemed to be very happy afterwards, despite losing her husband.'

'It was fortunate that good artist was there to pick up the pieces.' Kit laughed.

'Well they seemed to have lots of children and enjoyed visiting Jago and Alys. Let's maybe just leave it at that, yes? And he was obviously happy to take on Elsie as his own.' She knew there was amusement in her voice.

'Yes. We shouldn't pry too deeply. Anyway. I'm feeling pretty drenched and the desire to stand outside in the rain, despite the company, is rapidly losing its appeal. I'm going to head back inside. Are you coming?'

'No, I don't think so. Not yet, anyway. I'm wet already and I had planned to look at the old rose garden. I might just head over there anyway. I'll catch up with you later. I was thinking about looking in the library – for the story book Alys wrote, if that's okay with you? It might be on the shelves, you never know.'

'It might be. And I'm happy for you to rummage, but are you sure you want to work on your day off? It's Sunday, after all.'

'Believe me, this isn't at all like work. I'll get back to

valuing artwork and things tomorrow – today, I want to see if I can find Alys' story book and get to know Rose a little better – outside. I don't want to bump into any more ghosts in there.' She shivered, still thinking about the hand on her shoulder and the image of the woman flitting past her in the sitting room. Yet out here, it didn't seem possible. She looked back at the house, and it looked perfectly friendly and happy.

Then she glanced over at the path to the stumpery, entangled with roses. The rain had begun to form an eerie, grey mist which hung hazily over the gardens. In the distance, if she listened very carefully, she could hear the waterfall and remembered Kit's words about the woman he sometimes saw.

What could have been a white figure, half-hidden by the mist, or simply an illusion in the currently indistinct landscape appeared behind a tree, and drifted off towards the waterfall.

Her stomach lurched again. 'Do you know what, Kit? I think I'll give Rose's Gothic garden a miss. The library sounds a better option right now.'

Kit seemed unaware of the figure she had just seen. Instead, she realised, he was looking at her. There was a half-smile on his face, and her eyes met his. A droplet of water was just about to fall from his hair, and she reached up, catching it on her fingertip. He caught her hand again and this time, he didn't let it go.

He drew her closer and leaned towards her. 'Yes. The rose garden isn't a great option right now, is it?' he murmured. 'I can think of something much nicer to do in the rain. I don't think I've ever kissed a girl in the rain before.'

'I can categorically say I've never been kissed in the rain before.'

'So it'll be a first for both of us then?'

'I think so.'

'Shall we try it?'

'I think we should.'

It had been amazing, kissing Merryn in the rain. He had tangled his fingers in her wet hair, and she had held the back of his neck, drawing his face down towards her. She was damp, and warm, and her lips were warmer, and the combination was strangely alluring.

'Was it as nice as kissing yesterday? At Marazion? In the sunshine?' Merryn's eyes were full of mischief, as the pair of them finally parted and came up for air.

'Strangely, it was nicer.' He grinned. 'I think I would need to do it again though, in both sorts of weather, just to check.'

Merryn nodded seriously. 'Yes. I agree. I don't know – this one might have had the edge.'

'We're just getting better at it.' Kit was equally serious. He still had hold of her hand and squeezed it. He was just about to say something else, when Coren's voice interrupted them, shouting across the grounds.

'Kit! There you are. I worked out those figures.'

'Figures?' Merryn raised her eyebrows. 'That doesn't sound as much fun as what we were doing.'

'Sadly not. But necessary. Once Coren gets an idea in his head, he won't let it drop. And he was determined to work some stats out – based on the very wonderful Sybill's discussions. That's why I buggered off. I've learned the hard way you can't help him and you can't influence him, and we were just going to end up shouting at each other. Which isn't fun for anyone.'

'I'm sorry.'

'No need to be. I think it's just the stress of this place; you know, trying to work out what'll be best long term, but it seems we can't be in Pencradoc for more than five minutes at the moment without yelling at each other.'

'It's true then? I thought it was just me making it up in my head, blowing the discussions out of proportion.'

'Discussions? Nope. Arguments. And you thought we were like this all the time?' Kit laughed. 'No. Usually we get on okay. I can't imagine Aunt Loveday would have left Pencradoc to us if she thought it would cause a family rift.'

Coren was striding over, holding a piece of paper. 'It's doable, but I think we need to capitalise on the Teague connection. Pencradoc has more right to exploiting that than Wheal Mount; but if we had a plan for renting the studios, and then a reasonable commission on anything sold through the website or the exhibitions it would help. We'd really need to push the residencies and the retreats though, and we'd need a fair run of courses. Can you deliver say two a month without it impacting on Marazion too much?'

'Two a month? It depends on how long they'd be. My intensive courses are usually a week long. It would be a struggle to come here and do that, as well as keep Marazion going. That would be almost halving my income at the studio.'

'We'd need to look into it. You could reduce the ones you do there to, say three days, then—'

'Woah, Coren. Why should I have to stop my own workshops to come up here? Lowenna relies on me, as well as the other staff, to pay their wages.'

'Then go heavy on your café or whatever it is you're planning. That reminds me, I need to scope one out for here as well.'

'Coren! Are you even listening to me? I want to help, I really do. I want to get involved, and I will, but not at the expense of my livelihood in Marazion.'

'Kit, it's the only way—'

'It's not the only way. We've covered some more options, but you aren't open to any of them! Jeez, Coren, what is it about Pencradoc that's got you like this?' Kit stared at his brother, half-wondering who he was even looking at. Coren had, as he had told Merryn, been ridiculously focused on work and plans forever, it seemed, but this was just crazy.

'I'll just leave you to it,' said Merryn, clearly taking advantage of a lull in the latest spat. 'I'll catch you in the library.'

'I'm coming with you.' Kit wasn't going to stand by and have it out with Coren a moment longer.

1886

'Alys!' He shouted her name again, but even as he did so he felt a chill, and something like a cold hand clutch at his arm; so cold, he felt it through the fabric of his shirt.

Jago ...

He didn't stop to find out if it was his imagination, or if Rose herself was standing there, calling him back. Instead, he shook whatever it was off him and ran after Alys. He had to explain, he had to go after her.

'Alys, listen to me!'

Jago, don't leave me!

The voice was insistent, and he shook his head, spitting out the words. 'No, Rose. No. This isn't our place or time any more.'

But I love you. You love me …

'Used to love you,' he wanted to shout. 'I used to love you. When we were children!' But he ignored her and kept running.

He caught up with Alys by the waterfall. The girl was scrambling across the rocks, determined it seemed to get back to Pencradoc the quickest way possible, and not via the meandering paths that threaded through the formal grounds.

'Alys! Listen to me. It's not what you think. I used to love Rose, but—'

She stopped scrambling and steadied herself, glaring at him. 'There's no used to about it. You're preoccupied with the idea of Rose the entire time. That's what your secret is, that's what you've been hiding.' Alys' face was tear-stained and angry. 'You can't let her go, her spirit is all over this place. She's not at rest, and neither are *you*.'

'It's not a case of not letting her go. It should never have happened the way it happened.'

'I agree.' She was on the highest rock, looking down at him. Out of nowhere, a breeze whipped up and her skirts billowed out behind her, her hair flying free even as her hands curled into fists and she shook her head. 'I can see why you think it shouldn't have happened. Because if she'd survived, I wouldn't be here, and Zennor wouldn't be here, and I wouldn't be saying this to you now. She'd be here, and you'd be here, and who knows where Ellory might be.'

Jago felt the anger boil up inside him. 'No. The three of us would *not* be co-existing happily here. That would never have happened.'

'You're right. Again.' She laughed, mirthlessly, and shook her head once more. 'Because you couldn't stand

208

to see her with another man; especially Ellory – someone so cold and heartless couldn't possibly make her happy. Make the woman you loved happy. Could he?'

'*Nobody* could have made her happy!' he was exasperated. It was on the tip of his tongue to say that within Rose was something that would never have allowed her to be happy with anyone who wasn't him, Jago. Rose was obsessed with him. Unhealthily so, and that, perhaps was one of the reasons he felt so responsible and so helpless in the situation. There was also, of course, the fact that he had let her down so badly, hadn't protected her as he had promised; and if he had read that damn letter when he should have done—

'Exactly. And I can't make you happy. Like I said, she's here. She's still *here*.' She flung her arm out behind her, and despite himself, Jago looked over Alys' shoulder.

And that was when he saw her – saw Rose. She was standing on the top of the waterfall, watching them. No – watching *him*. She stretched her hands out, glimmered once or twice, then faded.

'Rose!' His voice was a whisper. He hadn't meant to speak her name, but he had and Alys sobbed, then clambered down from the rock.

'You can't love a ghost – no matter how beautiful she was. And yes. Yes, I've seen Rose. I know what she looked like, and I know I'm nothing like her.' Her voice caught. 'But I can't stay here any longer and have – you – so close to me, knowing how you feel. Knowing how I feel. So, this is goodbye, Jago. I mean it. I'm leaving, just as soon as I can. Zennor doesn't need me, and you most certainly don't *want* me.' She put her head down and ran off, away from the waterfall, away from him.

'Alys!' But she either didn't hear or didn't respond. He

watched her go, watched her retreating back, knowing it was useless to go after her, knowing he hadn't told her what he meant to say.

Her name was drowned out by the rush of the water splashing over the rocks far below him. He had never felt so conflicted in his entire life. There was a misplaced loyalty, he knew, to Rose; more so to Rose's memory. After she had died, he had left Pencradoc, distraught, mourning for a lost love and the loss of innocence. He knew, realistically, the love he had for Rose had died long before he had returned from Madrid – even before he had gone to Madrid.

With Alys, it was different. But if he had failed to protect Rose so spectacularly, how could he trust himself to care for another woman? To promise to love and protect her; to carry out his duty as a man, and God willing, a future husband and lover? He had to work out his own feelings, wrestle his own demons and face his own guilt before he could let someone else in so completely again.

But for Alys, he realised, he was prepared to do that. He wanted to do that. And he had to do it, before it was too late.

He looked down and saw a faded rose at his feet. He stared at it for a moment, then picked it up and threw it as hard as he could into the waterfall. It was taken by the current and swept away, dancing and swirling downstream until it disappeared from sight.

Then he turned away from the waterfall and began to walk. He didn't care where he was going, but he had to walk and he had to find those demons and kill them, right now.

Chapter Eighteen

Present Day

Merryn felt vastly uncomfortable. She wanted no part of this argument. The library, at the moment, felt like a refuge, and that was where she was heading right now.

Kit was keeping pace with her, his presence a furious storm cloud, even as Coren followed several steps behind, still going on about profit margins and the future of Pencradoc.

'Look, Coren, let's discuss this another time. I really don't want to get into it with you. Have you *heard* yourself, man? It's like this place is the most important thing to you! It's like you've lost a sense of reality for anything else!' Kit had stopped and turned, his brother's voice raising as he shouted a bit more about Kit giving up his life in Marazion, to get the arts centre established.

Merryn didn't wait to hear the outcome of it, but she suddenly started running towards the house. She was going, she decided, to pack her things up and leave this place just as soon as she could. She'd start work again today, despite it being Sunday, and that would give her a few more hours. Then by the end of the week she might be free. By the end of the week, she could leave here and let them fight it out. She had Kit's number, she knew where he was based. If she wanted to, she could contact him – but not while he was here; not while he and Coren were at each other's throats. It was like she was trapped in some hideous circle of Hell rather than the lovely place she had been so excited to come to, just a week or so ago.

Pencradoc, you have a lot to answer for.

She ran even faster, racing into the library and slamming the door behind her. Leaning against it, she stared at the rows and rows of books lining the walls. How on earth could she ever hope to find Alys' story book in here? She didn't even know if a copy existed on these shelves; it was just a hunch. The whole idea was so ridiculous and a sob caught in her throat. It was a mess, a complete mess. The whole situation with the brothers, and whatever was going on between them. It seemed so much worse between these walls, and there were too many things lurking in the shadows of Pencradoc to make sense of.

Suddenly, she yearned for her uncomplicated flat in Kentish Town and a dull and boring commission from Heptinstall. But if she was away from here, how could she bear being so far from Kit and the things they had promised to do together at some unspecified time in the future? Would it be better if she had never met him?

But part of her knew, just knew that they hadn't "just" met, and whatever Fates were guiding her life were drawing her inexorably closer to Pencradoc and this angry younger brother. It was like he was everything her life had been leading up to until this point, and despite the fact she had only been here a week, she couldn't imagine not knowing him.

And there was something about this library that had pulled her from the very first moment she had stepped inside. At this moment in time, she wasn't entirely convinced it was Alys' sweet little story book about her girls, either. There seemed to be something much darker all together drawing her in.

'Pencradoc, I don't know if I hate you or if I love you!' she spoke out to the empty room, daring any of the ghosts to answer her. They didn't, of course, and she pushed herself away from the door angrily.

The only place to start looking for this book, if that was what she had to find, was the beginning of the shelves – but the thought of looking through all the spines would only take time she didn't have any more. No – crazy as it sounded, she would trust her instincts on this one.

'Alys – or whoever you are – show me whatever I need to find in here. Please. It's the only way I – we – can help you.' She stared around the library again, trying to calm herself down and listen with her whole body to whatever the place needed to tell her. 'Please.' Her voice was a whisper now. She walked over to the shelves, trailing her fingers along the spines.

As she did it, the room seemed to change around her, but she concentrated on the books and what she might find hidden away ...

The fingers she saw on the books weren't her own: they were slimmer than hers, paler, with an inky stain on the middle finger, where perhaps a pen had rested as she thought about the next line to write. Her nails were quite short, with none of the colourful nail polishes Merryn herself favoured. There was the edge of a lacy sleeve at her wrist, and the scent of pipe smoke and furniture wax surrounding her.

Merryn's heart began to beat faster – she knew, without a doubt, that Alys was here now to guide her. She held her breath, trying to go with the moment; trying not to let herself be so damn scared, that she ran out of the room and never came back.

But she wasn't to be disappointed: her hands hovered over a collection of dull-looking, leather-bound books on geography and, pushed slightly back, was a slim, red volume that had nothing written on the spine.

Merryn blinked and her fingers, her own fingers now, closed over the book and pulled it out.

As if someone else was encouraging her to do so, she very carefully opened it, and her heart missed a beat at what she found within the pages.

'Merryn!' Kit struggled a little with the door, wondering if she'd locked it. He wouldn't be surprised, after the debacle outside. For now he'd stormed off and lost Coren, and wanted to find Merryn and apologise. Maybe, he thought wryly, pick up the conversation where they'd left off. But to be honest, he wouldn't be surprised if she'd run upstairs and resigned from the job in hand immediately. The arguments he and Coren were having weren't something she would want to hang around and listen to. The door suddenly opened and he half fell into the room.

And there she was, in the library, holding an open book in her hands. Her head was bowed, and for a minute she seemed to have a different image overlaying her own – someone who had much longer, fair hair, and a long, pale green dress on. The second image dissipated like the mists outside and it was suddenly just Merryn, in the same position, holding the book.

She looked up, a confused and faraway expression in her eyes, which disappeared as she focused on him.

'Alys showed me it,' she said, by way of an explanation. 'Look. Look what she showed me.' She held the book out to him and three sheets of paper were on the open pages. 'Look. Tell me, are they what I think they are?'

His heart jumping around in his chest, and not exactly sure what he had just seen, he walked over to her. 'What do you *think* they are?' It was a poor attempt at a joke and he knew it. He met her gaze, and her eyes must have matched how he assumed his looked at this very moment in time – shocked, scared and full of disbelief.

'You tell me,' she replied softly.

He held out his hands for the papers, trying to stop them trembling. The atmosphere was charged, and he wasn't sure what with.

The first picture was what appeared to be a head-study for the Teague portrait of Zennor which took pride of place in the room upstairs. It was rough and free-flowing, but confident and full of passion. Zennor was laughing on this portrait, and Ruan Teague had concentrated on her eyes and, despite the fact the sketch was much smaller than the portrait, it was definitely her – and there was desire, not just simple love, shining out of those eyes, directed straight at the artist.

The second picture was of a woman – it was obvious that it was Alys Trelawney, long before she was the poised, picture-perfect, confident Duchess at Wheal Mount, surrounded by her dimpling, angelic children. This was Alys as she really was; full of mischief and dreams. There was humour in her eyes, a slightly dishevelled look to her as if she enjoyed roaming around the moors, calling up spirits by Dozmary Pool and racing ponies against Jago Pencradoc just as fast as she could. This was the Alys that was visible, in miniature, in four perfectly imperfect little girls who laughed and loved just as much as *they* possibly could.

How the hell did he know all that, just by looking at this sketch? But he did. Either Ruan Teague was even more of a genius than they had originally thought, or Kit knew Alys, *this* Alys, better than he plausibly should.

The third picture, however, was the most startling. It was of a man – quite clearly Jago Pencradoc. His hair was dark, thickly drawn in an almost black pencil. His eyes, however, were haunted by something Kit couldn't identify. Guilt? Despair? Hopelessness? He didn't know. He knew, somehow, it was linked to Rose, and he shuddered, not wanting to let those thoughts loose in his mind. If he let them in, they would take him over and the demons he had fought off so many lifetimes ago would come back.

He dropped the picture of Jago onto the desk as if it burned him.

'He's signed them all.' Merryn's voice was quiet, shaky. 'Ruan Teague has signed them all. We've found some Teagues. Some uncatalogued, hidden Teagues. Pencradoc has *showed* us them. They could be a way of raising money for your arts centre, if you could bear to part with them. They're probably worth a lot of money. I'd say upwards of £200,000 each. You're looking at maybe half a million there. Kit, this is amazing.'

'The only one I would want to keep,' he said, eventually, 'is the one of Alys. The others can go. But it's not up to me. And that one – the one of Jago. I'd burn it before I gave it wallspace anywhere near me.'

'Kit! How can you say that? It's Jago. He's – Jago.' She looked at it, her voice a whisper on the last word.

'He is – but can't you see? There's something in there that he's hiding – he would *never* want that exposed! *Ever*!'

*

'Want what exposed?' Coren looked at the pair of them and the anger started to fizz up inside him, taking him back ever so many years ...

The door to the library had been partially open. There were voices coming from beyond, and he threw the door open, ready to lambast the artist and his wife, or to perhaps politely suggest that they continued the work and reduced the levity ...

His brother was talking to Alys Trelawney and she was looking up at him. She had in her hands three sheets of paper.

He hated people meddling in other peoples' business.

'And,' he continued as he took in the scene, 'may I ask what you have in your hands?'

'Coren!' It was the girl. But who was this Coren she spoke of? 'Look what we've found. Three Teagues – three sketches.' She was brazen, he would give her that. Defiant, almost, speaking to him in such a direct way, even though there was a flicker of unease in her eyes. And what did he care for Teague's sketches anyway?

'And I should be interested in this because?' He glared at her, expecting she would quail under his glance as they all did.

'Because it's a way of finding funds for Pencradoc. Look – one is of Jago, one is of Alys and one is of Zennor.' She held one of the pictures out and he stared at it with distaste. It was the one of her, the witless little blonde creature that was so consumed with following in her cousin's wake and trailing around after his brother staring at him with those big doe eyes. The anger stirred again, as he recalled the way *she* had looked at Jago once upon a time. He refused to be cuckolded again.

'They are worthless,' he said, dismissing the picture with a wave of his hand.

'They are absolutely not worthless!' The girl pulled herself to her full height, and still he looked down on her. 'This one of Zennor in particular. Look – just look at her! It's actually quite priceless when you think of the provenance.' She thrust the picture at him and he forced himself to take it, trying to control the shaking of his hand as his fingers closed around it.

He stared at it, saw the lust in her eyes, the sensual tilt of her chin.

'You can see exactly what Teague saw in her.' Her voice was excited.

And it was the wrong thing to say, because that was exactly what he could see in it ...

1886

Much later, after more soul-searching and more time replaying the scene by the waterfall in her own private hell, Alys was in the drawing room, collecting some of her books and notes. They would go in her packing case and, just as soon as she could, she would leave Pencradoc and go home—

'Alys.'

'Jago!' She turned at his voice, even as her heart bounced around in her chest. She clutched her books and raised them, meaninglessly, it felt. 'I'm finished in here. I need to find Zennor. I need to say goodbye to her. As I said, she doesn't need me anymore, I'm quite certain. And even if she does need me, she certainly doesn't seem to *want* me here. Excuse me.'

'No. No I won't excuse you.' He stood in the doorway of the drawing room, and there was no way past him. 'I should have found you sooner. I've searched all over for you – I should have guessed you'd be here. But now I *have* found you. And I won't let you say goodbye: to me or Zennor or anyone else. Please – listen to me. I need to let you know why things are the way they are. Why things can't continue like this.'

'I *know* why they can't continue. I told you. You still love Rose.' Alys looked at Jago, tracing the sharp edges of his cheekbones, her eyes drawn to his dark, troubled ones, and her heart shattered into a million pieces. As she watched his eyebrows draw together, his face darken as he clearly prepared to deny it, she suddenly felt emboldened to express something.

'Forgive me for saying so, but before I came to stay here, I was envious of Zennor. My cousin had married a Duke, and suddenly she was a Duchess, in possession of all … this.' She waved her hand around the room. 'I thought she was in love. I thought he would cherish her and look after her and do everything that real love suggested. And then I *came* here. And I realised it wasn't like that at all … for her, anyway.' She flushed and looked away. 'It's not, is it? She doesn't have real love with Ellory. Real love is much, much deeper. Real love is that sudden, overpowering feeling; the feeling that you have to be with a certain person and your life depends on being with them. It's what you must have had for Rose, and I can understand that. I can respect that. She was beautiful, she was yours. Never his. Never Ellory's. And that's why you can never have that feeling for anyone else.

'I think ghosts can appear in many forms. They can

be the spirits of the people we've lost and loved. Or they can be the spirits of lost love itself. Sometimes, you have to choose if you want to continue to love a ghost, or you want to set it free ...' She pressed her lips together and turned away, her face scarlet. 'I've said too much. I apologise.'

But Jago grabbed her arm and pulled her back towards him. 'I know exactly what you mean, love, *real* love, and not the ghost of a love is that overpowering feeling that takes your breath away. That instant you look into their eyes and you're lost in them. The moment you realise you never want to be without that person. I don't see that with your cousin and my brother.' He drew her closer, put his hands either side of her face and looked into her eyes. 'I have a confession. I never had that with Rose. I loved her, but we were young and idealistic. It was never meant to be and it *couldn't* have been. I feel guilty for what happened to her, and sometimes the past confuses us and memories crowd in and things change. But one thing I have realised since you came into my life, Alys, is that I think I know a little of that feeling that you've just described. You see, I'm lost. I'm lost in *you*, Alys Trelawney. I never *ever* had that with Rose.'

Alys met his eyes and for a moment, stared up into them in shock. 'But she was beautiful. You were going to marry her.'

'We decided we would marry when she was ten, and I was thirteen. I decided also that I would be a highwayman. The things we decide when we are children don't always translate well into adulthood.'

'Oh!'

'Oh indeed.' He gently removed his hand from her arm and held it out for her books. 'Now. If this is truly

220

what you want, then neither me nor anyone else can or will stop you. But Alys. Is it truly what you want? Is it?'

Alys shook her head slowly, still looking at him. 'No. No, I don't want to leave. But I knew I had to, because of how I felt about you. It was wrong, and it wasn't going to change and I couldn't – can't – compete with her. With Rose.'

'You have no cause for concern. There is no competition. Now – I think there is somewhere else which is a better place to talk about this than here. Anybody could disturb us.' Jago cast a glance over his shoulder, as if her was checking that nobody was about to come through it. 'And I would not want them to disturb *this*, let alone anything else.'

And he smiled, and he took her books from her and laid them down. Then he drew her towards him and she closed the gap and raised her face. He dropped his head and touched her lips with his, and this time he kissed her properly. She felt him share his heart and soul and more with her, and she was happy to respond. His hands were either side of her face, her fingers tangling in his hair. The world beyond was forgotten as they poured out that urgency to one another, pressed close together and wishing that kiss would never end.

Jago's hand somehow found hers as they walked out of the house together. By mutual agreement, they were going to the folly; Jago needed to lay his ghosts to rest and to do that, he had to face his demons.

They wound their way through the pathways, through the rose garden and the Wilderness garden Zennor had laughed about: 'How can there possibly be a Wilderness garden here? It's perfectly tended!' she had said, as they surveyed the trunks of several carefully placed felled trees and the meticulous planting of hundreds of roses at the edge of the woods beyond. Then she had climbed up to the highest tree trunk in the stumpery, oblivious to Alys ushering her down in case the gardener caught her and told her off.

When they reached the tower, however, the door was half-open, and there was a very faint sound coming from inside. Sobbing. Alys looked at Jago and the expression on his face mirrored the surprise she felt inside. Whoever had come here, had come after she had left earlier, and goodness knows how long they had been here. For a chilling moment, Alys wondered if it was someone who was living – or the tears of someone who was dead.

Then sense took over. Of course it did.

'Zennor!' Dropping Jago's hand, and picking up her skirts, she raced forwards and burst into the building.

Chapter Nineteen

Present Day

'Coren?' A sense of unease prickled between Merryn's shoulder blades. This hadn't been the reaction she was expecting. Trying to cheer the brothers up with her discovery had quite clearly backfired. Kit had dropped Jago's picture like it was poisoned, and Coren had just – frozen.

He was staring at the picture, gripping the paper tightly, as if he wanted to kill someone. Either the person in the picture, or the person who had drawn it. And his voice – he was speaking in a horrible, autocratic, stilted voice. Almost as if it was – her heart skipped a beat and a memory of another voice from long, long ago came back to her – almost as if it was Ellory speaking.

'What is it?' Merryn approached him, intending to take the picture from him, hoping she was wrong and just being very silly and over-imaginative. 'This discovery could help you in so many ways. Neither of you like these sketches very much, and I could get straight onto work tomorrow to get a decent value for you. I'm sure someone would snap them up at auction—'

'I'll burn them before they get to auction.' Coren turned on his heel and began to head out of the library, clutching the sketch of Zennor. He grabbed an old-fashioned letter-opener from the desk on his way out. The opener was shaped like a dagger, and clearly dated from before the days of health and safety.

'Kit!' She turned to Kit, helpless. 'Please, don't let him burn it! We have to stop him. I don't think he understands.'

'He's gone bloody mad!' Kit stared after his brother. 'For God's sake, where the hell is he going?' He didn't wait for an answer, but instead hurried out of the room after Coren – and beyond telling him that she thought Ellory was the one responsible for this outrageous turn of events, Merryn couldn't give him an answer anyway.

But even beyond that…'Kit! Be careful!' The sight of the letter-opener in Coren's hand had terrified her, and she didn't like to think what he was capable of.

'Coren! Just stop. I don't know where you're heading, but just bloody stop right there!' Kit strode after his brother, his long strides soon catching him up. 'Coren!' He reached out and put his hand on his shoulder meaning to spin him around and make him face him, make him explain himself.

But instead, Coren spun around and yelled at Kit, right up in his face. 'Do you think I didn't suspect any of this was going on?' There was rage in his brother's eyes, and Kit was momentarily taken aback. He had never seen him look like this before. For God's sake, he didn't even *look* like Coren, let alone sound like him. It was as if another person's face and features were overlaying his. Coren raised his fist and shook the sketch at Kit. 'This – this proves it. I need to go and speak to her. I need to confront her immediately.'

'Coren! You're crazy, man! Who the hell are you going to confront?'

'My wife. The Duchess.' He brandished the letter-opener. 'Good *God*, where the hell is my pistol? No matter. I can do the job with *this*.'

'Woah.' Kit took a step backwards, the glint of the letter-opener in Coren's hand instinctively making him want to stay well clear. Coren pushed him roughly away, and took the opportunity to run up the stairs, towards the west wing. Kit knew exactly where he was headed and this was terrifying. This was uncharted territory, and his stomach twisted with nausea, and yes, fear. 'You aren't married. Never mind to a Duchess. Coren!' He ran a few more steps up so he was on the landing next to his brother. 'Look – let's go outside, and calm down? You don't know what you're doing.'

'I know enough.' Coren's eyes – or whoever's eyes were staring out of what should have been Coren's face – were burning with hatred now. 'I need to speak with Zennor and I *shall* get answers.'

A flash of memory seared across Kit's mind, and it was as if someone else forced the next words out of his mouth. 'The same way you got answers out of Rose? The same way you made her speak to you? In the folly?'

'How dare you! She deserved everything, She deserved it all!'

And then it all descended into chaos.

1886

It was dim inside, but then Jago saw her.

'Zennor! *Zennor*!' Alys flew to the back of the building. Zennor was sitting on the floor, her wrists roughly tied together with some rope. The girl had obviously been struggling, as there were red welts on her wrists which had started to bleed.

'Alys! Jago ... oh thank God. Help me, help me please!'

'Who did this to you? Who *did* this?' Alys dropped to her knees and untied the girl with shaking hands.

Zennor fell into her arms, sobbing. 'Ellory. It was Ellory.' Zennor's face was white, and there was more blood was coming from a gash on her cheek. 'He thought ... he thought ...'

'Is he still here?' Jago dropped down beside them, and moved Zennor's hair away from her face.

'No. He's gone. I think he's gone after Ruan.' Her voice caught and she looked at Jago, almost pleadingly. 'We have to stop him.'

'But what's *Ruan* ever done?' Alys looked from one of them to the other, clearly hoping someone would enlighten her.

Zennor dropped her gaze and flushed. 'I'm pregnant. I didn't want to tell you like this, I really didn't. I was going to, I was, honestly. I just wanted to be sure myself – that it wasn't wishful thinking on my behalf. Oh Alys, forgive me, please. But Ellory thinks it's Ruan's. He thinks I'm in love with Ruan.'

Alys stared at her. 'I knew it. I *knew* it. But you've got it wrong, He *can't* think that.'

'I can and I do. I'm no fool, although my *wife* appears to think I am.'

'Ellory!' Jago scrambled to his feet as he saw the man in the doorway. He looked so different from the icily polite, aloof man he usually was. He looked colder than ever, but instead of his rather pale, soulless eyes, there seemed to be a different person staring out at them. This one was calculating, and, Jago realised, murderous.

Ellory spoke again, his voice quiet and deadly, ignoring Jago and staring at Zennor. 'You're the same as she was. The same as Rose. Trying to cuckold me. I've had it with you all.'

'Ellory! I don't know why you're accusing me of this.

It's awful! We've been as man and wife, we have shared a bed. We have—' Zennor sounded desperate, as if she was trying to convince herself as well as Ellory.

'Do *not* lie!' Something glinted and Jago realised Ellory had produced a pistol and was pointing it, shakily, at Zennor. He was also slurring his words.

His brother might be murderous, but clearly he was also drunk; and there was no way on earth that pistol was going to fire straight at his intended target.

'I'm not lying—'

'Listen! Listen to yourself. You *are* lying. Yes, we've shared a bed, but you've shared one with *him* too.' He laughed, and the pistol wavered. 'And here you are. Pregnant! I guarantee you fell around about the time Teague graced us with his presence.' He gestured to Zennor's stomach with his pistol. 'I know that you are lying. The same way *she* lied. And I am not prepared to raise the bastard child of an artist and a whore. I suspected as much and now I know for sure. I suspected when Rose—'

'Ellory! Please – can't you see how distressed she is!' Alys, brave little Alys, stood up, shielding Zennor from Ellory. Her face was white and terrified, but she spoke strongly and firmly. 'My cousin is pregnant. With *your* child. With the heir to Pencradoc.'

'So she has *you* lying for her as well? I'm not surprised, you're nothing but a little whore yourself. I've seen you looking at my brother – the same way *she* used to look at him. My first Duchess, God rest her soul.' He was sneering, and Jago was willing to bet that none of them thought that he actually meant that comment. 'What *is* it?' Ellory continued, drunkenly waving the pistol around. 'What is it with the women who come to this cursed place? They are, none of them, faithful to their husbands. And you – *you* are no better.' The pistol came to settle on Alys, and Ellory closed one eye and took aim, cocking the pistol.

That was more than enough for Jago – he wasn't going to stand there and allow that to happen. Seeing Alys there, so vulnerable yet so brave made his heart contract. It was, perhaps, that moment more than any other that had come before that made him realise that his life, his future, *was* Alys; that Rose had been a charming, childhood love, and he had grown apart from her even sooner than he had admitted to himself.

After she died, he had thought, he acknowledged now, that he had made a mistake, and he would never feel love – or indeed – affection – for any woman ever again. If he couldn't protect Rose, how much of a man did it make him? He had, he felt, led her to disaster. But here, now, was Alys – and he could and *would* protect her – with his life, if necessary.

It was Alys he loved.

'Ellory!' Jago took a few steps towards his brother, thinking quickly, trying to mitigate any impending disaster. 'Have you heard yourself, man? There's no need for this.'

'What the hell do you know?' Ellory spun around to face his brother. 'You just want Pencradoc. And *my* father's title. Well, you're not going to get it. Neither you, nor my *wife*'s lover.'

And then several things happened at once: Jago saw the pistol change direction, so it was facing him; he crouched down and leapt towards his brother, then there was an almighty *bang* as a gunshot rang out above his head, then a cry of pain and a female scream. A red-hot pain grazed his skin and everything went black.

Chapter Twenty

Present Day

'Deserved it? Deserved *what*, exactly?' Kit found himself yelling at his brother, who was still glaring at him full of hate.

'She deserved to die,' Coren hissed. 'She played me for a fool – she thought that she could live with me and still bed you and any other man who took her fancy. She was a whore. I knew that child she carried wasn't mine. It was a bastard, and had I allowed you to stay at Pencradoc it would have been *your* bastard. As it was, I knew it was de Amato's. And I would not assume the child my present Duchess carries is mine either. It could be yours or it could be *his*. *That* damn artists's. Teague's! Either way, she will not live to carry it. She must pay, the way Rose paid. I shall not be cuckolded a second time.'

'You know nothing!' Kit was answering without even thinking, facing the man down on the staircase. 'It is *not* mine! I don't know where you get these wild fancies from, brother – but you are wrong! And now! Now, I have proof that you did intend to kill her. You *did* kill Rose. She told me your intentions, she knew what was in your mind. And yes, it may have been the ramblings of a half-mad woman, but it wasn't, was it? It was the truth. Well – now I know as well – and now—' he flung his hand out behind him, to where a fair-haired girl stood trembling at the bottom of the staircase, one hand on the handrail, '—she knows as well. And if you kill me, she will still know and she will see justice done.'

'She will be next.' Coren turned to face Alys. *Alys? Was it not Merryn?* He laughed. 'She will not be difficult to silence. She's just as bad. She knew all about it. But first you ... *brother*.' He spat the last word out, undoubtedly hating the meaning of it, making it clear that he had always hated the relationship that he had been thrust upon him.

'No – I won't let you hurt her.' Kit launched himself at Coren, all reason deserting him, all thoughts that it was deadly dangerous to attack a man empty-handed when your opponent had a weapon was truly ridiculous, but the men fought each other as if they hated the very air each other breathed.

There was a scream from somewhere below him, probably from the girl on the staircase. Coren flung the sketch of Zennor away, and out of the corner of his eye, Kit was aware of it floating through the handrails and drifting down to the ground floor, twisting and turning in the air, Zennor's face turning this way and that as it disappeared out of sight.

Half of him, the half that was still undoubtedly Kit Penhaligon hoped it would land safely because that was a hell of a lot of money which could be ploughed into the arts centre and nobody really liked it anyway – and the half that was apparently Jago Pencradoc was more concerned about stopping Ellory racing upstairs and confronting his pregnant wife with a blade.

But that wasn't how it had happened at all, was it? It hadn't happened in the house. It had happened elsewhere – in that folly, in that damn folly. And it hadn't been a blade at all. It had been a pistol, hadn't it?

Kit paused, hesitating, images and sounds of that fateful day crowding into his mind. He cried out clutching his head as the story played out, battering his memory in relentless waves of shouting and pictures he didn't want to see again. He had tried to hide them, tried to pretend none of it happened the way it had. They had all pretended, and it had worked. Damn, though, it had worked well, and they'd all gone on to live with it for the rest of their lives, the way they had wanted to believe it had happened and the way they had sworn it had happened. They were all guilty in some way, but none so guilty as—

He cried out again as more images flashed into his mind, as if the worst sort of migraine he had ever experienced was exploding throughout his memory. It had been no good, no good at all, because look what had happened anyway. Just look at what was happening today!

He gathered enough presence of mind to force himself back to reality, back to the twenty-first century where he could confront the danger he was in right now, not right then. Not in 1886.

1886. The year Ellory, Duke of Trecarrow had died.

He looked up, just in time to see the man throw himself at him again, the blade glinting, and this time, he was too slow to avoid it.

All Merryn could do was watch. She was clutching the handrail, two steps from the bottom of the grand staircase, screaming as the brothers punched and kicked each other at the top. One of them was going to fall, she just knew it, and they would tumble down the stairs, just like Rose had, and die.

'Stop it! Stop it! It's just a sketch!' The words were silly, inadequate, but she didn't know what else to do.

She didn't even know what they were fighting over any more. She ran up a couple more stairs, sobbing, moving out of the way as the precious Teague sketch floated past her and landed on the floor. There were more important things to worry about.

She turned quickly, feeling sick, noticing she was right next to the portrait of Ellory. That horrible picture seemed to be oozing an evil sort of energy, filling the stairwell and the foyer, feeding off the anger of the brothers as they shouted and battered each other. Kit was dodging about, trying to avoid the sharp point of the letter-opener which Coren was expertly wielding like some sort of duelling weapon.

A duelling weapon?

And yes. That would explain it. Ellory had to be responsible. For as much as she had sensed the kindred spirits of Jago and Alys around, she had never felt threatened by any of them as much as she had this one – because surely, this had to be Ellory wielding that blade and trying, for whatever reason best known to himself, to kill his brother. It was he who had been poisoning the brothers' relationship from the moment they had stepped into Pencradoc. Ellory and Jago had some unfinished business and whatever it was had carried forward to this time and this place and was playing out in this macabre scene in front of her.

It might be pointless, but she had to try: 'Ellory!' If she called his name and appealed to him, it might throw him off balance a bit and give Kit time to retaliate and defend himself.

Ellory, if that was indeed who this was, looked her way, furious as he raised the letter-opener above Kit's chest. Thankfully, the distraction gave Kit enough time to duck out of the way and the man with the letter-opener swore and lunged at him again.

Merryn put her hands to her face in horror as the fight continued and tried shouting Ellory's name again – but this time when he looked at her, his face was thunderous, twisted in a way she couldn't describe any other way than "evil".

The last time he had looked at her like that had been in the folly, and they had all been there; all of them – Alys and Jago and Zennor and Ellory ... and Alys had thought she was about to die. The man was pointing a pistol at her, and saying all sorts of cruel things. She was trying to defend herself, and defend Zennor, and Zennor was crying and he was there – Jago was there, trying to help, and then there was a gunshot. And there had been blood, and screaming, and she thought that her life had indeed ended in that moment.

And then – then – what had happened after that? She closed her eyes and balled her hands into fists, feeling Pencradoc slipping away, feeling the cold stone floor of the folly rough beneath her feet, feeling the fabric of her dress brushing her legs, the tight bodice as her heart fought to escape her chest in terror. The sound of crying and shouting, then the gunshot, then silence. The sound of a heavy weight hitting the ground: a body. But whose body? Who *was* it? And the flash of sunlight glinting off another blade, another knife blade, dripping with blood.

'*I had to do it. He was going to kill Zennor.*'

Fear. All she was aware of after that was pure, unadulterated fear, for what was to become of them all afterwards?

Coren was back in the tower, back with Ellory's thoughts

spinning around his mind, blotting out everything that was Coren Penhaligon, his mind filling with the poison that was the Duke of Trecarrow ...

He stood over his brother, both of them bruised and bloodied, knowing that one of them was going to die that day. There could be no other way.

There were excuses, of course; accusations that he knew were founded in truth. He pointed the pistol at her, at his wife, determined to get the truth out of her one way or another. And they were all aware of it, they had all stood by and watched it happen: his wife, her silly little cousin who saw more than people gave her credit for, what with her nose stuck in books and her head stuck in the clouds. And his brother. His very own brother, although the term galled him; his half-brother, who had led them all to this. Jago. He was the one who was to blame. He was the one whose head it all came down upon.

He had led him to Rose. He had done nothing to stop Zennor's flirtations with that artist and had encouraged the liaison. As if he didn't know about Fowey! He had associates all over the county, and he had been told enough to understand what had happened. And Jago had consorted with that little blonde idiot, turning her head the way he turned every other woman's, so even she was thrown off the scent. Deliberately so, it seemed, just to bring him, Ellory down, yet again. Ellory hated Jago with a passion and had done all of his life.

So – which one of them today would die first? That was a decision he had to make, and he had to make it rationally.

He pointed the weapon at his wife. Then at her cousin. Then at his brother.

Then he pulled the trigger.

But it was wrong; this was *wrong*, thought Coren, surfacing for just a brief second from the swirling, black mess in his mind. There seemed to be no sense to these thoughts. Didn't he have a blade in his hand, right now? It should have been a pistol. But very well – if he must use a blade, then he must use a blade.

He raised it up and brought it down, burying it deep in his brother's flesh.

Ah! Now *it was clear. So Jago would be the one to die first, then …*

1886

For a moment, it was as if the world stopped turning. Everything stopped: no birds sounded outside, no wind breezed through the cold building. Alys' vision began to blur at the edges and then everything came sharply back into focus. Zennor grasped her hand, and together they struggled into a sitting position. The girls had grabbed each other when the shot rang out, and thrown themselves to the ground.

'Are you hurt? Is the baby all right?' Alys wasn't sure if Zennor would even know the answer, but Zennor was shaking her head. 'I'm all right, I'm all right. Are you?'

'I am. Yes.' But then she looked across the room, and saw Jago in a crumpled heap, Ellory on the ground beside him. A dark red stain was spreading across the floor and Alys wasn't sure who it came from. Behind the men, Ruan Teague stood, the blade of a knife dripping with blood.

'I had to do it. He was going to kill Zennor.' The

artist's face was pale and set, his jaw clenched. 'That child is mine. And Zennor and I both know it.'

Alys, she acknowledged to herself, had long suspected as much, but she had no time to process the information any further. She would have burned in hell before telling Ellory that he was correct.

'Ruan!' Zennor scrambled to her feet and ran to Ruan, at the same time Alys dismissed those dark thoughts and rushed towards Jago.

'Jago? Jago!' Alys shook his shoulders and leaned in to listen to his chest. She was sure his heart was beating, she was sure ...

'Alys?' His voice was possibly the sweetest thing she'd ever heard.

'Jago!' She searched his face and touched her fingers just above his ear. His hair was damp and matted, and when she took her fingers away, they were sticky with blood.

'It's nothing.' He struggled to sit upright, and took her hand in his, looking at the blood. 'The bullet must have ricocheted and caught me ... Ellory!' His expression cleared and he suddenly seemed to register the fact that his brother was on the ground next to him.

'I suppose this is the point where you accuse me of murder and alert the authorities.' Ruan's voice was surprisingly steady.

Zennor clamped her hand over her mouth, a shocked gasp escaping. 'No! You were *saving* us, Ruan. He was going to kill us all. Jago? Could he hang for this?' Zennor was pale and Alys herself felt sick. The ball was very much in Jago's court. It was his brother after all. His *brother*. The Duke of Trecarrow.

Alys flashed a glance at Jago, praying that he would

make the right decision. Ruan's face was chalk-white, his jaw set, and she knew he was simply holding it together for Zennor's sake. But, oh God, Ruan Teague was a murderer, was he not? The father of Zennor's child was a murderer.

Jago got to his feet. Alys found herself reaching for his hand and was gratified to feel his fingers curl into hers.

'No,' he said, not looking at Ruan, never taking his eyes from Alys. 'I'm not going to tell anyone what has happened today. There are four of us here living, and that will be all who ever know. Once we are all gone, then the truth may find a way of revealing itself. But it will not be told in our lifetime.' He looked at the group, his eyes like flint. 'Do I have your oath? Every single one of us here today, must swear that they will never come to tell what happened. We say ... I don't know. That it was a highwayman? A footpad? A smuggler? God!' He raked his fingers through his hair and shook his head. 'I can't think straight. But I will not see Mr Teague charged for this. If he had not been here, the outcome ... this ...' he waved his hand around the room '... may have been quite different.'

Jago couldn't quite believe he had said that and wasn't quite certain he had made that decision rationally. But as he looked at the faces around him, one of them dearer to him than anyone had ever been before, then he knew, right or wrong, that he couldn't tell anyone what had passed here this day.

There was a long moment of silence that stretched into an eon.

Then one voice spoke, clearly and firmly. Alys. 'I swear that this will go to my grave with me.'

'I agree.' That was Zennor; then she laughed, quite bitterly. 'I suspect I have the most to lose if this tale comes to people's attention. I should *never* have stayed with him.' Her hand crept into Ruan's. He tossed the knife away from him once her hand was safely enclosed, almost as if he wanted nothing more to remind him of what he had been responsible for. 'I should have left.' She looked up at Ruan. 'I should have disappeared with the man I love. The man I'd die for.'

Ruan met her eyes and leaned down to kiss her. 'I should never have put you in this position. But I am the one who killed him. None of you should have to protect me like this. I can take my chance in the courts.'

Jago closed his eyes and raised his face skywards, hoping for strength from somewhere. They all blamed themselves.

He opened his eyes and looked at the group again, shaking his head. 'None of you are to blame. And anyway, I already have Rose's death on my conscience.' He tried to laugh. 'What's one more murder at Pencradoc?'

He shook his hand loose from Alys', hating not touching her, but hating his thoughts more: they were as dark as they had ever been.

'What are you trying to say?' Alys was by his side, looking confused and scared.

'Perhaps what I'm trying to say is that if Ruan hadn't done it—' His face was, he knew, thunderous. 'That *I* would have done it. In fact, I *should* have done it, and well before now.'

'But that wouldn't have been right.' Ruan's voice was low and steadier than Jago expected. 'And you couldn't have done it, despite your own suspicions. Do what you have to do now, and leave this with me.' He held his hand out. 'Go. To the other side of the estate. Then if anyone ever does ask you what happened to your brother's body, you can at least tell the truth about that.'

Jago hesitated only for a moment. 'No. As much as I would love the man to disappear, there is too much else to explain. Look at Zennor. Look at *me*. None of us are entirely unscathed.' He was right. Each one of them had blood on their clothing; either their own or someone else's.

'Then it was a villain in the woods. A struggle.' Alys suddenly spoke up, her voice cutting through their dreadful conversation. Jago stared at her, half in awe, half in horror.

'Alys! What are you trying to imply?'

'I'm a writer.' She stared right back at him. 'Let me do this for you. It will be my greatest work, I promise. Please.'

Jago nodded, stunned once more at this beautiful creature who seemed to have her mind clear on one thing at least.

'I propose,' she said calmly, 'that the story is as follows. We found the Duke here, in the tower, the Duchess tied up. We managed to rescue the Duchess, but sadly, we were unable to rescue the Duke, who, it seemed, had bravely tried to protect his wife and paid with his life. The three of us appeared and scared the villain off.' She looked around at the group, a challenge in her eyes. 'Are we all in agreement? Does that not make us into heroes of a sort?'

Ruan smiled briefly. 'I am a creative-minded individual. I have the soul of a poet. And, also, I am bent on saving that soul. Yes. I adore that story, dearest Alys. But please.' The smile flickered and died, and he turned to Jago and bowed. 'It is your decision. I am a murderer, as you have all seen. Let this not be the way you remember me. Let me try to make things right. The Devil knows I have no regrets that the man is dead, or how, indeed, he met his end.'

Jago shook his head. 'We do as Alys suggests, Mr Teague. If we are all in agreement?' He looked at Zennor and she nodded, her face pale and drawn. He didn't miss her moving closer to the artist, or the brief gesture as she held her hand protectively over her stomach. 'Good. Let us work our story out, and let Alys work her creative magic.'

Chapter Twenty-One

Present Day

As the world came back to life, and the terrifying images of long ago disappeared, Merryn forced her eyes open, realising that there was something going on here beyond any earthly understanding. And what she saw made her stomach turn and everything else fade into insignificance.

Coren was standing over Kit, the letter-opener in his hand. Kit was clutching his shoulder, blood dripping through his fingers, his face white as he swayed on the top of the stairs.

'Kit!' Merryn screamed his name, trying to hang onto the handrail as the staircase seemed to shift beneath her. 'Kit – it's not Coren. It's Ellory!' And there was more. She understood why. She knew that whatever secrets they had all been hiding were suddenly somehow exposed in all their ghastly detail. 'He knows that we know what happened. He blames you. He thinks you're Jago!'

'Oh Alys.' Coren – or Ellory, as the man sounded nothing at all like Coren – must have heard her. His voice dripped sarcasm. 'I know it was him. I blame him for it. I blame him for it all. If he hadn't encouraged my wife, none of this would have happened.'

'He didn't encourage her – he tried to stop her from doing it. It was you. You forced her into it. You—'

It was the wrong thing to say. The fair-haired man spun around and suddenly he was above her, wielding that blade, the blade he had buried in Kit's shoulder.

'Alys. Your turn. Then I'm going to hunt down

Zennor. And Teague. I know what they did – they should have let me finish you off the first time.'

'No! I'm not Alys – I'm Merryn. Alys and Jago, and Rose and Teague and Zennor – they're all dead. All gone. Coren, I know you're in there. I know you're stronger than he is.'

'No! No – I refuse to listen to you, you sly bitch. Little Alys Trelawney. Little Miss Deceitful. You're in on it too. You led Zennor straight to that pathetic artist. You helped hide the truth from me. And they aren't dead. They won't be dead until I've finished with them—'

Then it all seemed to happen at once. Coren raced down the stairs, the letter-opener aloft, ready to plunge it into her, and she tried to turn and run away, screaming. But then out of nowhere, it seemed, Kit pounced, hurtling down the staircase, tumbling them all towards the floor. Merryn tripped on the last step and landed on her hands and knees, skinning them all in the process. Kit was yelling and, with Coren off-balance, managed to wrestle the weapon out of his brother's hands. It bounced across the floor and settled far too near Merryn for comfort. It was still dripping with Kit's blood and she wanted to throw up.

'Drop it – just fucking drop it, Ellory, you bastard!' Kit was still shouting at his brother, or at least at the man who was inhabiting his brother's physical form at the minute.

Coren turned and lashed out at Kit, but he ducked and somehow found the strength to bend Coren's arm up behind his back, forcing him to double up, still spitting abuse at his brother.

The painting. My husband's painting. The blade...

The voice was urgent, right in Merryn's ear.

Now! Do it! That's what keeps him here ...

It wasn't the time or place for quibbling over the voice – *my husband*? It could have been Zennor, it could have been Rose – the dark-haired woman Merryn had caught sight of around Pencradoc could have been either of them.

All she knew, was that she had to try – she had to do something, and the main thing was to get the letter-opener away from Coren. He had thrown Kit off now, and they were both battered and covered in blood.

'Give that to me!' Coren lunged at her again, his fingers inches from the blade. There was no more time to think.

Merryn grabbed the letter-opener the handle of which was slippery and sticky with blood. Coren's fingers came too close to her and she acted instinctively, shouting out and crying as she stuck the tip of it into his hand. It went so against her principles to harm anyone, let alone someone who was paying her to look at his family's art collection, that she felt even more sick; but the soft voice was there again, urging her and encouraging her.

You have to do it, darling Alys. He'll kill us all if we don't stop him ...

'Alys!' Whoever this woman was, she was caught in the past as well. But she was right, Merryn had to do it.

As Coren was screaming and clutching his hand, still trying to grab at her despite the obvious pain he was in, Kit rugby tackled him to the floor, and Merryn scrambled to her feet, her knees smarting horribly, and dashed up the stairs to face the portrait of Ellory again.

Stabbing the heart of the Duke of Trecarrow on the painting felt better than it probably should have done – normally, destroying a valuable portrait was frowned upon. But what Heptinstall Studios didn't know would never hurt them.

And just for good measure, she cried out, and dragged the blade down the painting, slashing it right down the middle.

There was a yell from behind her, and she spun around, the letter-opener held out ready to protect herself again if need be – but what she saw made her freeze.

A black shadow was breaking away from Coren, swirling around the two men then heading towards her. She realised it was speeding towards the painting and she threw herself to the ground, covering her head as it pelted against the frame.

'Give me that!' Kit was on the floor next to her, his hands on her shoulders. 'The blade. He needs to be destroyed properly.'

'Kit—'

'Don't ask me how I know,' he growled, his eyes steel. 'Don't ask me, I just know I need to do it!'

'Take it! With my blessing!' She thrust it at him, and, standing up, with all his weight behind him, Kit threw himself at the portrait, and for a few seconds he was swallowed up in the black, swirling mass.

There was a howl, an unearthly scream, and the shadow imploded, leaving Kit leaning against the tattered remains of the canvas. He dropped the letter-opener with a clatter and slid down the wall, his eyes closed and his face white.

'Kit! Oh God, Kit!' Merryn crawled across to him and took his head in her hands.

His eyes flickered open. 'Hey. Hey you. How are you doing? Did we get him?' Then they closed again and he slumped to the side.

It was only then that Merryn realised he was holding a sheaf of yellowed papers in his hand. She looked up at the painting and saw a torn corner of paper sticking out of one of slashes he'd made.

Then her attention was taken by Coren. Who sounded a lot like himself again: 'What the fuck was that? What the absolute *fuck* was that all about?'

She turned to see him, and he was staring at her and Kit, a dawning horror in his face. 'Did I do that? Did I do any of that?'

'Do you really need me to tell you?' Merryn asked. '*Seriously?*'

'Well yes. I mean – ouch!' He looked at his hand and swore again. 'What happened there?'

Merryn wondered if she should tell him that Merryn had happened, but she thought better of it. 'It was an accident. Things got messy. Your old friend Ellory paid us a visit, and he's gone now. But we've got to get Kit some help. Look at him!'

Kit looked even paler than he had done before, and his shirt was saturated with blood. His eyes were closed and his fingers had slackened on the papers.

'Good God. I'll call an ambulance. You stay with him. Tell me later – tell me everything. I insist.' Coren managed to get to his feet and he limped to the telephone in the hallway. He must have taken a hell of a beating himself. But he was back to being Coren, and Ellory had gone and Merryn felt sorry for him. Poor guy. He didn't have a clue as to the extent of what had really happened, did he? She would definitely tell him later. Kit was the priority now.

But even as she settled herself closer to Kit and put her arms around him, she managed to slide the papers into her pocket. They could look at them later as well. Together.

1886

Much, much later, after the authorities had been informed and the necessary arrangements had been made to remove Ellory's body, Alys found Jago by the waterfall in the rock garden. He was sitting on a large, flat stone staring at the water and she crept up behind him.

'Jago?'

He half-turned and there was the suggestion of a smile on his lips, but not in his eyes.

He picked up a stone and tossed it into the water. 'This is where she told me,' he said, looking at the water, his eyes seeming to search for the stone that had settled in amongst all the other stones on the river bed. 'Rose. This is where she told me she was pregnant.'

Alys suddenly felt faint. She sat down heavily next to him and drew her legs up, wrapping her arms around her knees. She hoped, oh she so desperately hoped she was wrong …

Jago cast a glance at her, then his smile widened and for a moment there was that glint of amusement in his eyes. 'I've shocked you. I'm sorry.' The light died and he looked back at the water. 'It wasn't mine, if that's what you're thinking. Rose was a beautiful girl and, given half a chance, many men would have sold their souls to the devil to make love to her. One of them did.' He leaned back, resting his hands on the sun-warmed rock behind him. 'It was de Amato.' His face hardened. 'Rose wanted to pass it off as Ellory's, and live happily ever after. I wanted to help her do that. Ellory, however, had a different plan.'

'That's terrible! Did he – hurt her? Was her death not an accident?'

Jago turned to her, his eyebrow raised wryly. 'What do you think?'

Alys flushed. 'I think I know the answer to that, actually. Just this afternoon, we were all shot at by the man. I will have nightmares forever, I'm sure. I don't even know who his proper target was, and if Ruan hadn't appeared.' She clamped her lips together as if afraid someone would hear her. 'Regardless.' She lowered her voice. 'I'm finding it quite difficult to have any sympathy for him. In fact, I can understand why Rose did as she did. And Zennor, as well.'

'I feel the same, may God forgive me.' He dropped his head, then looked back at her. 'We're half-brothers, you know. Not full ones. Our mother had a lover, and I am the result. Ellory swore that he would never be cuckolded by a woman as his father was, yet here we are.' He shook his head. 'And seemingly it happened to him twice.'

'Oh, Jago. I'm so sorry.'

'What for?' He looked genuinely baffled.

'Because you've clearly suffered all these years from Ellory's resentment.'

'Perhaps. After Rose died, there was nothing to keep me at Pencradoc. I'd tried to protect her and I failed, tried to talk my brother into believing the child was his. He would never appear convinced. And Rose made the mistake of writing it all down.'

Alys stared at Jago in horror. 'And he read it all?'

'Rose thought he had. He sent me away on some pretext abroad before de Amato came. I never met the man, and to be fair it shouldn't have been de Amato who came here. Another artist was commissioned; Russo, his name was, but de Amato came in his place. Rose told me everything in her letters, and when I came home, I brought them with me. They disappeared from my room, and I can only assume Ellory took them. I've scoured this damn place for them – more to protect her than anything. There was no reason for anyone to know the secrets of her heart. But, to cut a long story short, she told me that she thought she was carrying de Amato's baby; and once he discovered that, my brother would quite probably kill her. It was almost as if she knew she would die by his hand. Her last act was to write the facts down as she saw them – and she entrusted that letter with those facts in it to me. But I was too late. I didn't read it, and when I did, I still thought she was simply unbalanced. Then a few hours later, I discovered her at the foot of that staircase. But it was true, wasn't it? It happened as she predicted. And I can still see it all. I still have the images in my mind from when I found her. I know he's responsible, I just know it.'

'Oh my goodness.' Alys didn't quite know what to say. 'So he was watching Zennor, perhaps, and suspected?'

'I think so. But for some reason, he deliberately put temptation into her way by inviting Teague here – it's like he had the need to test her, and to justify his actions. And when she announced she was pregnant, it must have pushed him over the edge. I took Rose's final letter to India with me.' He laughed, shortly. 'Then I brought it back ...'

His voice trailed off, and Alys understood.

'You kept this one to try and prove murder. If the situation ever arose.'

'Call it an insurance policy. In my heart, I hoped it was enough; despite poor Rose's mind breaking up towards the end. But maybe it wouldn't have been, and that was part of my worry as well. But I still have it and it's well-hidden. And when my brother married Zennor, I knew I had to come back and be her guardian as well. As much as I could be, anyway. However, I don't think Rose's letter would help our friend's case today. There were, as you probably know by now, too many rumours of her being in an odd frame of mind. And she was. Near the end, especially. And perhaps even longer than that. I don't know.' He looked at her. 'But I do know you've seen the portrait. I knew before you told me. I saw you and Zennor in the room.'

'You followed us! I thought there was someone there ... in the corridor. In the shadows. It was you!'

'Quite. But I wasn't following you. More, I think, that we all had the same destination in mind. I had a knife. I was going to her portrait. That letter I had? It's now safely hidden behind the canvas. I doubt we will ever need it, but if we ever do, it's there. Under the top left-hand corner.' He smiled. 'It's the least exciting part of the picture – just shadows. As you know, Rose is looking to her left. The viewer's eye is drawn that way – in the direction of her bare shoulder.' A half-smile flashed across his face. 'Nobody is interested in where she's been. There's nothing in that corner that would encourage anyone except the greatest art lover to appreciate and linger over. Rose's face is far more arresting.'

Alys had to agree but then a thought struck her. 'Do

we need it to prove Ellory's intent – so Ruan can plead self-defence? If the situation ever demanded it.'

'Unfortunately, a stab wound through a person's back doesn't usually lend itself to that theory. And Ruan was never really threatened anyway. Ellory was in the room with us. He threatened *us*. You. And Zennor.' He reached out and touched her cheek briefly, tracing the curve of her chin. 'The story of the footpad is, I think, strong enough to hold water. Who is going to doubt the word of a pregnant Duchess, her delightfully innocent cousin and the Duke's heir, the Earl of Pencradoc?'

'Very true.' Alys tossed a stone into the water. 'Zennor always was a good actress. Me, not so much.'

'It was a rather handsome swoon you enacted, though, when you were moaning in terror in Teague's arms. But we had to deflect suspicion somehow.'

Alys grinned. 'Yes.' She risked a glance up at Jago. 'Were you jealous?'

'Terribly.'

'Good.' She flushed and dropped her gaze again. 'I can't believe I actually thought you were in love with Zennor. But then I saw her with Ruan and I knew, I think especially at Fowey, what the truth was. I suspect that meeting was planned, you know, having considered it, but I couldn't confess that to anyone except you, Jago. They had enough time to arrange it. Zennor was fortunate she hurt her ankle though; it gave her a better excuse to separate herself from us.'

'Yes. I would be inclined to agree. But their relationship will be a scandal they have to deal with when their affair becomes public – which it won't do, for a good long while I am sure. Well, they are both welcome to stay here.' He looked sideways at her as she risked another glance. 'As you are. She will want you near her as her pregnancy progresses, I am sure.'

'I'll be happy to stay. But not just for her.'

'No. For me. Selfishly, I want you here. And I want you here as my wife.' He turned suddenly, and took her face in his hands. 'You, my darling Alys, are the only woman I will ever love and ever want. I've told you I felt love for Rose, when we were very young – and I did hate my brother for marrying her, but I was never destined to be with her at all.'

Alys' heart pounded as she stared into his eyes. 'Do you mean that?'

'I do. From the bottom of my heart. Will you marry me, Alys? Will you be my wife?' Suddenly, a light danced in his eyes and made them mischievous. 'I can't however, promise to make you a Duchess. If the child Zennor is carrying is a boy, that will of course, be *his* title. His parenthood will not be in question, I'll see to that. Pencradoc will be their home for as long as they want it. You and I, my love, can go somewhere else entirely. Perhaps I can build you your palace after all. How does that sound?'

'It sounds wonderful. And absolutely perfect. Of course I'll marry you. But do you know something?' She reached up and covered his hands with hers. 'I don't care. I don't care if I'm never a Duchess. That's not what I would marry you for. I would marry you for you – because I love you as well. And I can't imagine ever not being with you.'

Jago leaned in towards her, his mouth an inch from hers. She could feel his warm breath as he spoke. 'You never have to worry about that. I will protect you with my life and will love you always. You will be a queen in my heart, and I hold your heart in my hand. In fact, do you know what I thought, the very first time I saw you – that first time at Dozmary Pool?'

'No?' She smiled, her skin tingling with anticipation as he imperceptibly closed the gap, then whispered against her lips:

'I thought, wherever you go, Alys Trelawney, I will follow. And do you know something else?'

Alys giggled. 'No. But Please tell me.'

'I mean it. I absolutely do. I always have, and I always will.'

And when their lips met again and he kissed her properly, she knew every word he said was true.

Chapter Twenty-Two

The ambulance had carted Kit to A&E, but he'd insisted on coming back to Pencradoc after he'd been patched up. He'd been lucky – the wound was nowhere near as bad as they had originally suspected. Yes, he'd lost a bit of blood, but he was stitched up and rattling with painkillers. Things could have been much, much worse.

Coren had also collected a couple of stitches in his hand, and Merryn had sticking plasters on her knees and the base of her thumbs; the likes of which, she said wryly, she hadn't sported since she was seven. Between the three of them, they'd managed to evade the awkward questions as to what had happened. And no, they said firmly, they wouldn't be pressing charges against anyone.

And now they were back at Pencradoc, and Kit was sitting with Merryn on the flat rock by the waterfall. The whole atmosphere had shifted though; the energy was settled, happy. There was no negativity hanging around, no dark shadows. He shuddered slightly as he recalled the moment at the painting where he was sure he had come face to face with Ellory, the Duke of Trecarrow, swirling around him in a shadowy mass.

'Are you all right? Do you need another painkiller?' Merryn was concerned, her beautiful moss-green eyes filled with worry. He smiled into them, and leaned towards her, briefly resting his forehead on hers. His fingers found hers, and they entwined loosely.

'I'm fine. Now Ellory has disappeared.'

'Do you think Alys has gone? And Jago?'

'Not really. No.'

Merryn looked at him, surprised. 'You don't think they've moved on somewhere nicer? Somewhere happier?'

'I think they'd always been somewhere else. I think what we saw were just memories – just thoughts and emotions they left behind. And besides.' He nudged her gently with his good shoulder. 'I think they came back anyway. In a different way. They were back together again the moment you drove through those gates.'

Merryn grinned. 'That's your poet's soul talking again, isn't it?' She nudged him back.

'It is. I suppose. Can you see it deep inside?'

He opened his eyes wide and Merryn giggled. 'I can, actually. All the way down to the core, like you're a big stick of candy rock.'

'Sure you can. But look – I know you've got something to show me. I can tell. I've known you – oh ...' he sucked his breath in, pretending to work it out '... a century or so.'

'God, that's scary!' She laughed and shook her head. 'Scary that you know me so well. You're right. I've got some more letters for us to read. You found them, in Ellory's painting, in case you don't remember. Hidden away. It seems as if Jago wasn't the only one who thought a canvas made a nice receptacle.'

'Runs in the family? Okay – come on. Let's see them. Have you read them yet?'

'No. I was waiting for you. It's almost killed me.'

'Hmm – less said about killing people the better.' Kit frowned, then his face cleared. 'All right. Are there dates on them? Let's sort them out.'

Together, the excitement almost crackling visibly between them, they shuffled the letters around; and, once they were in order, they began to read them ...

1884

Dearest Jago.

I hope this letter finds you well. I am missing you terribly! Pencradoc is so large and comfortless without your smile greeting me in the morning over breakfast, or spying you in the stables amongst the horses we both love! The corridors simply echo with my own footsteps and I shouldn't be lonely, Ellory tells me I can't possibly be lonely, but I am.

The artist is engaged to begin next week, however. A gentleman from Italy. A Mr Russo. Does that not sound exotic? Perhaps he will be a lively old gentleman and talk with me of the salons in Europe! I do hear he is of a great age?

I say – perhaps you have met him already on your travels? Now wouldn't that be marvellous?

If you do perhaps meet him before next week, then please tell him I am sincerely looking forward to seeing him. But actually, how silly – by the time this letter reaches you, he will be here, and that will be another week of your travels over with. Another week since we parted. How depressing! But! Another week closer to you coming home. I must think of the positives.

God knows there isn't much to be positive about here at the minute.

I miss you, dear brother – for, sadly, that is how I must view you now, is it not?

Rose, Duchess of Trecarrow.

Dearest Jago,
My word! I simply must write to you and tell you this. Mr Russo did not come in the end. The poor man was ill, and sent one of his students instead.

I say student – the man was *a student, but is also a renowned artist in his own right so I am probably doing him a disservice. He is a gentleman by the name of Giovanni de Amato. Have you heard of him? He is much younger than Mr Russo. Perhaps just a little older than you? Definitely no more than thirty, I would say. He has garnered such success for such a young age, I applaud him.*

He is a very interesting man. We have had great discussions over the Gothic movement and we find the same sort of literature and art appealing. I must say, it is nice to be able to converse with someone other than the Duke, and it does help to make the hours of sitting for his sketches exciting.

Am I being disloyal again? Perhaps.
With love, my dearest brother.
Rose, Duchess of Trecarrow.

Dearest Jago,
The portrait is still in its infancy, but Giovanni has begun to put paint to canvas! It is so very exciting to see myself come to life at his hands.

I look at the canvas and I can't quite think that I look exactly as I do in the rough image that is appearing. But he says I do.

I must believe him then. Mustn't I?

I took Giovanni for a walk around the estate, as it was a beautiful day today, and I felt quite confined in the house. He said he could not concentrate on painting me when my heart was elsewhere and not with him. How dramatic! So I capitulated and I introduced him to some of my favourite places at Pencradoc.

I took him to our tower. He liked it. But not, he said, for painting. He said it seemed a very romantic place, and as he spoke to me about it, I saw it with fresh eyes and fancied I had seen memories of us there; little ghost children, perhaps, playing, and I remembered how we always loved each other and how you always told me we would marry. I felt quite sad, for a little while afterwards.

I also took Giovanni to the Wilderness garden. He said that there was so much else we could do with that area. He is going to sketch a few ideas for me, and perhaps help me to create it. Whilst the paint dries he said!

When will you be home? I do think you would enjoy meeting him. You would have a lot in common.

Yours, dearest brother,

Rose, Duchess of Trecarrow.

Dearest Jago,

It is to be a rose garden amongst the old stumpery! Yes, I can now reveal what I am creating – what we are creating, Giovanni and I, in the Wilderness garden. I know it is an area we both love – you and I, that is – and where you told me of the good fortune that I was to be painted by an artist. Don't you

*think it will be a wonderful addition to it? I think
the greatest feature will be the waterfall 'our' stone
overlooks, and we will build around that. Giovanni
says it will be a lasting testament to the beauty of the
rose – which made me laugh, especially as he bowed
and pointed quite theatrically to me when he said it.*

*Unless you would prefer we didn't spoil the area?
I know you love it so. But imagine how wonderful
it will look! Please – do write soon and tell me what
you want to happen!*

As always,
Rose, Duchess of Trecarrow.

Dearest Jago,
*Please – it is NOT Ellory's decision. Yes, I know he
owns Pencradoc, but I am the Duchess! Surely, I can
exert a little authority now and then? In some things,
anyway.*

*I'm still not with child. I'm sorry – you probably
didn't want to be party to that, but you are the only
one I can confide in, dearest Jago. It's been so long
now, I don't know what I'm doing wrong.*

I think he is starting to hate me because of it.

*The rose garden will be a great distraction, and if
you have no strong feelings either way, as you say,
Giovanni and I will begin to work on it.*

Much love
Rose.

Dearest Jago,
*Our rose garden is in its infancy, but already it is
looking remarkable! The whole area is like a fairy
grotto. In fact, we have created a little place that is*

so hidden away and so pretty that one could really believe one was in fairyland. We have spent some happy times in there, Giovanni with his paints and sketchbooks, and myself with my books on topiary and botany, as we plan the visual, Gothic delight I anticipate. Imagine all those roses and thorns creeping through the stumps of the old trees, and winding their way through the fallen masonry we already placed there! I must show you when you come home!

When *will* you be home?

I asked Ellory when you would be home, and he dismissed my questions quite viciously. He said it was no concern of mine … you *were* no concern of mine.

My greatest concern was, he told me, when I would eventually breed and carry the heir to Pencradoc. Then he … well. I won't tell you what he did, in the privacy of his study. But I am sure you can well imagine.

He said that if the velvet glove approach wasn't working and I wasn't conceiving that way, then he would have to try some other means. And he did. Brutally so.

Giovanni understands, I know he does. I have broken down in front of him, and he held me so closely, I simply sobbed until I felt better.

Then he kissed me. He kissed my tears away.

Jago – what is happening? I wish you were here with me. I need to talk to you properly.

With love,
Rose.

Dearest Jago,
This is so difficult to write – but I find my feelings
for Giovanni are terrifying me. Passion is a foreign
concept to Ellory. He is cold and harsh and grows
more bitter and more distant every day. If you were
here I would maybe feel more settled – who knows?
You've always been a grounding influence to me,
dearest Jago. But instead, I find myself seeking
Giovanni out, and sometimes he looks at me as if he
doesn't quite believe what I am doing. Perhaps I am
misreading the situation? I also catch Ellory looking
at me strangely, calculatingly, almost, and I feel
my cheeks redden, and I dip my head and hope he
doesn't see it. Because, you see, I am thinking about
Giovanni more than I think I should be.
Your Rose.

Dearest Jago,
I have a confession – I have loved him, Jago, I loved
him properly with my whole body and my soul
and everything in between. It happened in the fairy
grotto, but Giovanni has suddenly distanced himself
from me as if it never happened. He refuses to be
alone with me, and tells me the portrait is almost
finished and he will be leaving soon.
What am I to do, Jago? What can I do? I cannot
but help feel I have cheapened myself, and to what
ends? I hope and pray my husband never finds out.
Rose.

Jago.
Giovanni has gone – he left without a word of
goodbye, very early one morning. The portrait was

left in the hallway, propped up against the stairwell, with a note "thanking the Duchess for her interest in the humble artist and his work". Honestly Jago, I could have cried when I read it!

I can't help thinking that if you were here, none of this would have happened. I missed you, Jago, and I think I confused my feelings for you with the fact that Mr de Amato was here and real and physical and you are so many miles away from me and I miss you more than I have words to explain ...

But as for Mr de Amato. I feel so silly. I feel so terribly used. I also feel that he was subtly telling my husband and anyone who cared to read it what I had done. Or perhaps I am reading too much into it because of a guilty conscience? Only he, myself – and you, of course – know what actually happened. I could die just thinking about it, I really could.

On a day to day basis, I simply plod on as I always have. Ellory barely speaks to me, although he did tell me that he thinks the portrait "was money well spent". It seems to be quite a coup to have a de Amato. Little does he know how much that possession cost me.

And do you know something else? I look so ... compromised in that painting. It's full of secrets, Jago, and I hate it. I actually do! And he's tormenting me by having it on display so I look like a harlot to anyone who comes into Pencradoc.

Rose.

Jago.
I need you. Come back. Please.
I can't tell you the reason in a letter.

But I need you.

Come back.

Please.

You are the only one who can help me. We need to leave Pencradoc. Will you take me away from here, darling Jago? Will you? Please.

I love you. I've always loved you.

It's you.

Your Rose.

Chapter Twenty-Three

That was the last, desperate little letter in the pile.

Merryn stared at it as if she couldn't quite believe the words that were written on the paper.

'She had a secret. She had something to tell him.' She looked at Kit, hoping he had picked up the same information. 'And she's lost the plot. Hasn't she?'

'The date. What's the date on the letter again?' Kit's eyes were as round as hers must have been when she looked at him.

Merryn read it out. 'May 1884. When did she die again?'

'July 1884.'

There was silence as they both did the maths.

'So – that baby was de Amato's. It was never Ellory's child.' Merryn was quiet for a moment. 'I think Ellory discovered her secret, then lost his temper with her, and that's how she died. And he blamed Jago as well. He could never forgive him for the way Rose felt. She's laid her heart and soul bare in these letters, and in that one she left before she died. Ellory must have messed her up more than anyone thought.'

'But Jago never felt the same about her – not once they had grown up. Much as he hated Ellory, he would never compromise his brother by overtly loving the Duchess. He wanted to protect her. That's what he wanted to do. We know he found her at the bottom of the stairs in the tower. He was with her at the end. He must have come back from wherever Ellory had sent him when she wrote to him. It's anyone's guess what happened then.'

'My guess,' said Merryn slowly, 'is that Jago brought the letters home with him, and Ellory found them. These were *his* insurance policy – his reason for doing what he did. He carried all that anger around with him even afterwards. Then Zennor did the same thing to him. With another artist. God. In one way, I'm not surprised he flipped – although it was terribly, terribly wrong to do what he did.'

'And try to do it twice.'

'Three times. Technically.' Merryn's voice was wry. 'How do we tell Coren this one? And actually, what a horror Ellory was! He deliberately put Teague in Zennor's way to test her, didn't he?' The thought had struck her out of nowhere. She was no psychologist, but that seemed to be a pretty screwed up thing for a person to do. Although, murdering one's wife wasn't exactly the sanest thing a man could do either.

'I don't know. We tell Coren the truth, perhaps? Then he's got a bit of closure. He's still determined to keep the place, despite everything. But at least the ghosts have hopefully gone ...' Kit's voice died away as he apparently saw something on the other side of the waterfall.

Merryn followed his gaze, wondering if it was that image of the woman she now suspected was Rose; but instead she saw Coren, wielding a pile of broken pieces of wood and slashed canvas, walking determinedly to a spot in the middle of the clearing.

He tossed the pieces of, she could only assume, Ellory's portrait, into a big pile, and doused it with some sort of fuel out of a squeezy bottle. Then he lit a match, and tossed it into the pile. It was only a moment before there was a huge whoosh, and the pile went up in flames, destroying the picture once and for all.

'Well. Remind me to delete *that* one from my laptop inventory,' said Merryn, staring at the spectacle.

'Quite.' Kit watched for a moment with her. 'It's the only way, I guess. And she wanted her letters burned, didn't she? Rose said she wished Jago had burned them.' They looked at each other for a moment. 'We owe it to her to carry out her wishes.'

'*You* owe it to her,' said Merryn softly. 'Jago needs to do it. He's the one who would have carried that guilt around with him for the rest of his life.'

'And he'll do it. Come on – let's go and make amends.' Awkwardly, hampered by the sling on his arm, he got to his feet and held his other hand out to help her up. 'I hate family feuds,' he said with a grin.

'Me too.'

'Let's break the cycle, shall we? Let's make sure everyone lives happily ever after this time.' Kit drew her closer and leaned down towards her. When their lips met, and she pulled him closer to her still, it was as if it had always been meant to end this way – here, at the waterfall, at Pencradoc.

Thank you. Thank you for doing this for me. And I know you'll be happy with him dearest Alys, I know it. I couldn't hold him – but you can. You always could ... you always had his heart. Always. Even before he met you ...

The voice whispered in her ear for the very last time, making her break away from Kit, who looked at her curiously, a smile tugging at the corners of his mouth.

'What? What is it?'

'Our ghost was definitely Rose. But she's fine now, I

think. She's happy. She's happy for Jago and Alys and – oh! Look!' Lying on the edge of the rock, just beside the drop to the waterfall, was a perfect red rose. 'It's truly her, isn't it? She's here. She's given us her blessing.'

Kit simply nodded, understanding. And casting, she noticed, a quick glance across her shoulder in case the girl should appear there and hover before them for a moment or two.

It had been Rose who had spoken to her. Rose who had told her what to do with the blade, Rose who told her how to destroy that picture of Ellory – and why it had to be done.

'Ellory was kept here by his anger and his hatred and he wanted revenge on them all. Rose told us how to save everyone this time.' Merryn knew it just needed to be said out loud.

'Wonderful Rose. We should thank her.'

'We can thank her by destroying those letters.'

'We can. But first – I want to kiss you again. I want to see if it's like I remembered – from all that time ago.'

'We've kissed before!' Merryn giggled.

'We have. But I think in the 1800s it would have been extra special. Don't you? They probably wouldn't have done much else before they were married. Shall we see if we can recreate it? Recreate that moment when they knew it was meant to be, when everything was still innocent.'

'Hmm. I don't know if any of them were entirely innocent at the end.'

'Maybe not.' He rubbed his nose against hers, making her giggle again. 'But it was what they thought they had to do. And nobody needs to know *anything* about that, outside of us three. But there is something that I do know, quite definitely. Wherever you go, Merryn Burton, I will follow you. I always have done and I always will.'

'I'd expect nothing less of you, Kit Penhaligon.'

'Good.'

And then they did kiss again; and Merryn knew that this time the ghosts of Pencradoc had been laid to rest properly. The past had gone, and the future was hers and Kit's; now, and forever more.

Epilogue

Pencradoc – the Passion of the Penhaligons

Today saw the official opening of Pencradoc Arts Centre, near Bodmin.

Pencradoc, the former seat of the Dukes of Trecarrow, was recently converted into an art gallery and exhibition centre, and will also host artists' retreats, house several studios and run workshops throughout the year. The links forged with the successful Wheal Mount Centre – another former Trecarrow family home – and Heptinstall Studios in London have ensured this project, the vision of brothers Coren and Kit Penhaligon, will more than live up to the reputation of Ruan Teague, the nineteenth-century artist who fell in love with Zennor Pencradoc, a former Duchess of Trecarrow.

'We were incredibly excited when Merryn Burton from Heptinstall Studios discovered some original Teague sketches in the Library,' says Coren, 'The sale of two of these at auction helped us to raise funds to create the centre, and we have plenty of plans for the future. It's a really brilliant time to be here, and to be right in the heart of Teague's world. I hope he appreciates it, wherever he is! We're also delighted to report that Merryn has now joined the team at Pencradoc, and we look forward to harnessing her expertise. She'll be based mainly in Marazion, where Kit's own studio is, but she'll be a regular visitor here and I'm sure Kit would agree that we couldn't have made this work without her. The design of the Tower Tea Room, for example, is all Merryn's idea, and I'm sure it'll prove to be a great area for people to relax in and kick back a little.'

Pencradoc also has links to the portrait artist Giovanni de Amato, and there is a stunning life-size depiction of Rose, Duchess of Trecarrow, in the entrance hall. Rose sadly passed away in 1884 at the age of twenty-two, and was the first wife of Ellory, the Duke who was subsequently married to Zennor. Ellory also tragically died young, but the gorgeous image of Lady Elsie Pencradoc – Ellory and Zennor's daughter – is captured in a beautiful marble bust, also in the grand entrance hall, and it is from Elsie that the Penhaligon brothers are descended.

However, when questioned as to his thoughts on the discovery of the de Amato, Coren Penhaligon simply grins and shakes his head. 'Rose was never really lost, but she deserves to be in a special place now. We love having her back where she belongs.'

We must say we agree with Coren, and we wish the Penhaligon brothers, and indeed Pencradoc Arts Centre itself, much success.

Thank You

Thank you so much for reading, and hopefully enjoying, *A Secret Rose* – like I say, it's been a long time coming and I hope that it's the first of several *Pencradoc* novels; and that it doesn't take twenty years to write each one, or else we will all grow quite old waiting for them!

However, authors need to know they are doing the right thing, and keeping our readers happy is a huge part of the job. So it would be wonderful if you could find a moment just to write a quick review on Amazon or one of the other websites to let me know that you enjoyed the book. Thank you once again, and do feel free to contact me at any time on Facebook, Twitter, through my website or through my lovely publishers Choc Lit.

Thanks again, and much love to you all,

Kirsty
xx

About the Author

Kirsty Ferry is from the North East of England and lives there with her husband and son. She won the English Heritage/Belsay Hall National Creative Writing competition in 2009 and has had articles and short stories published in various magazines. Her work also appears in several anthologies, incorporating such diverse themes as vampires, crime, angels and more.

Kirsty loves writing ghostly mysteries and interweaving fact and fiction. The research is almost as much fun as writing the book itself, and if she can add a wonderful setting and a dollop of history, that's even better.

Her day job involves sharing a building with an eclectic collection of ghosts, which can often prove rather interesting.

For more information on Kirsty visit:
www.twitter.com/kirsty_ferry
https://www.facebook.com/kirsty.ferry.author/

More Choc Lit

From Kirsty Ferry

Some Veil Did Fall

Rossetti Mysteries series

What if you recalled memories from a life that wasn't yours, from a life before …?
When Becky steps into Jonathon Nelson's atmospheric photography studio in Whitby, she is simply a freelance journalist in search of a story. But as soon as she puts on the beautiful Victorian dress and poses for a photograph, she becomes somebody quite different …

As she and Jon begin to unravel the tragic mystery behind her strange experiences, the natural affinity they have for each other continues to grow and leads them to question … have they met somewhere before?

The Girl in the Painting

Rossetti Mysteries series

What if you thought you knew a secret that could change history?
Whilst standing engrossed in her favourite Pre-Raphaelite painting – Millais's Ophelia – Cori catches the eye of Tate gallery worker, Simon, who is immediately struck by her resemblance to the red-haired beauty in the famous artwork.

The attraction is mutual, but Cori has other things on her mind. She has recently acquired the diary of Daisy, a Victorian woman with a shocking secret. As Cori reads, it soon becomes apparent that Daisy will stop at nothing to be heard, even outside of the pages of her diary …

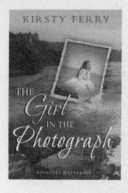

The Girl in the Photograph

Rossetti Mysteries series

What if the past was trying to teach you a lesson?
Staying alone in the shadow of an abandoned manor house in Yorkshire would be madness to some, but art enthusiast Lissy de Luca can't wait. Lissy has her reasons for seeking isolation, and she wants to study the Staithes Group – an artists' commune active at the turn of the twentieth century.

Lissy is fascinated by the imposing Sea Scarr Hall – but the deeper she delves, the stranger things get. A lonely figure patrols the cove at night, whilst a hidden painting leads to a chilling realisation. And then there's the photograph of the girl; so beautiful she could be a mermaid ... and so familiar.

A Little Bit of Christmas Magic

Rossetti Mysteries series

Any wish can be granted with a little bit of Christmas magic ...
As a wedding planner at Carrick Park Hotel Ailsa McCormack has devoted herself to making sure couples get their perfect day, but just occasionally that comes at a price – in this case, organising a Christmas Day wedding at the expense of her own Christmas.

Not that Ailsa minds. There's something very special about Carrick Park during the festive season and she's always been fascinated by the past occupants of the place; particularly the beautiful and tragic Ella Carrick, whose striking portrait still hangs at the top of the stairs.

Watch For Me By Moonlight

Hartsford Mysteries series

"It was the first full moon since that night.
She waited and watched by moonlight, as
she had promised ..."
When her life in London falls apart,
Elodie Bright returns to Suffolk and to
Hartsford Hall, the home of her childhood
friend Alexander Aldrich, now the Earl of
Hartsford. There, she throws herself into
helping Alex bring a new lease of life to the
old house and its grounds.

After a freak storm damages the Hall
chapel and destroys the tomb of Georgiana
Kerridge, one of Alex's eighteenth-century
relatives, Elodie and Alex find a connection
in the shocking discovery brought to light
by the damaged tomb.

Watch For Me By Candlelight

Hartsford Mysteries series

"The stars are aligning and it's time
again ..."
Working at the Folk Museum in Hartsford
village means that Kate Howard is
surrounded by all sorts of unusual vintage
items. Of course she has her favourites;
particularly the Victorian ice skates with
a name – 'CAT' – mysteriously painted on
the sides.

But what Kate doesn't realise is how
much she has in common with Catriona
Aphrodite Tredegar, the original owner of
the skates, or how their lives will become
strangely entwined. All Kate knows is that
as soon as she bumps into farrier Theo
Kent, things start getting weird: there's the
vivid, disconcerting visions and then of
course the overwhelming sense that she's
met Theo before ...

Watch For Me By Twilight

Hartsford Mysteries series

The past is never really the past at Hartsford Hall …
Aidan Edwards has always been fascinated by the life of his great-great uncle Robert. A trip to Hartsford Hall and an encounter with Cassie Aldrich leads him closer to the truth about Robert Edwards, as he unravels the scandalous story of a bright young poet and a beautiful spirited aristocrat in the carefree twilight of the 1930s before the Second World War.

But can Aidan find out what happened to Robert after the war – or will he have to accept that certain parts of his uncle's life will remain forever shrouded in mystery?

Watch For Me at Christmas

Hartsford Mysteries series

When midwinter magic brings you home for Christmas …
When Emmy Berry arrives at Hartsford Hall to work at the Frost Fayre she immediately feels at home. Which is odd because she's never set foot in the place in her life. Then a freak blizzard leaves her stranded and things get even weirder when she bumps into Tom Howard. Tom and Emmy have never met before but neither can ignore the sense that they know each other. With Christmas fast approaching and the weather showing no sign of improving it soon becomes apparent that Hartsford Hall has a little bit of midwinter magic in store for them both …

Spring at Taigh Fallon

Tempest Sisters series

From old secrets come new beginnings ...
When Angel Tempest finds out that her best friend Zac has inherited a Scottish mansion, Taigh Fallon, from his great aunt, she immediately offers to go and visit it with him. It will mean closing up her jet jewellery shop in Whitby for a few days but the prospect of a spring trip to the Scottish Highlands is too tempting.

Then Kyle, Zac's estranged and slightly grumpy Canadian cousin, unexpectedly turns up at Taigh Fallon, and events take a strange turn as the long-kept secrets of the old house begin to reveal themselves ...

Jessie's Little Bookshop by the Sea

Tempest Sisters series

Take a trip to the little bookshop by the sea ...
Jessie Tempest has two main interests: reading books and selling books. Her little bookshop in the seaside town of Staithes is a cosy hideaway from the chilly Yorkshire wind, but it's also Jessie's sanctuary from the outside world.

When writer Miles Fareham and his son Elijah arrive to stay in the holiday apartment above the shop, it's a test for Jessie who has always felt clueless when it comes to kids. But as she learns the story of the single father and the inquisitive eight-year-old, Jessie realises that first impressions aren't always the right ones – and, of course, you can never judge a book by its cover!

Summer at Carrick Park

Tempest Sisters series

A summer wedding, fifty cupcakes and a man she thought she would never see again ...
When Joel Leicester walks into the hotel where Rosa Tempest works, she can't believe her bad luck. Out of all the hotels in all of North Yorkshire, the man who broke her heart would have to walk into Carrick Park!

The last time Rosa saw Joel it was after a whirlwind holiday when they'd been greeted at his flat by a woman claiming to be his fiancée. Rosa never stuck around to hear Joel's side of the story but now, six years later on, Fate has another trick up its sleeve as a potentially disastrous summer wedding at Carrick Park can only be saved by Joel and Rosa working together ...

Christmas on the Isle of Skye

Tempest Sisters series

How far would you go to be with the one you love at Christmas?
The Isle of Skye is a magical place, especially at Christmas, and there's no place Zac Fallon would rather be. But whilst Zac has everything he needs on Skye, there's still something missing – and that something is a somebody called Ivy McFarlane.

Every Witch Way

Schubert series

Time for a Halloween road trip ...
Nessa hates her full name – Agnes –
which she inherited from her great-great
grandmother – but is that all she inherited?
Because rumour had it that Great-Great
Granny Agnes was a witch, and a few
unusual things have been happening to
Nessa recently ...

First, there's the strange book she finds
in her local coffee shop, and then the
invite from her next-door neighbour Ewan
Grainger to accompany him on a rather
supernatural research trip. What ensues is
a Halloween journey through Scotland in
a yellow camper van (accompanied by a
big black cat called Schubert), a mystical
encounter in an ancient forest and maybe
just a touch of magic!

A Christmas Secret

Schubert series

**What if a secret from Christmas past was
stopping you from moving on to Christmas
future?**
When Hugo McCreadie steps into Isla
Brodie's pet portrait studio to get a 'Festive
Furball Photo Shoot' for his sister's cat
Schubert, he does question his sanity. But he
knows the photographs will be the perfect
Christmas present for his eccentric sister,
Nessa – and he finds himself quite taken
with ditzy, animal-loving Isla Brodie, too.

Will a Christmas secret from long ago
prevent Hugo and Isla's new friendship
from going any further? Or will a certain
big, black cat taking matters into his own
paws lead them into each other's arms for
Christmas?